DYING FOR MONEY

Warmest wishes

Vicky

DYING FOR MONEY

A MEG SHEPPARD MYSTERY

BOOK FIVE

VICKY EARLE

ISBN: 978-1-78324-273-3

This book is a work of fiction. Any resemblance to actual persons, living or dead, events or locales is entirely coincidental.

www.vickyearle.com

Published by Wordzworth
www.wordzworth.com

This book is dedicated to
Nicholas, Jonathan, and Leah

1

Murder

My carry-on bag bounces from one wheel to the other as if a reluctant follower. It's past my bedtime and the seven-hour flight has made my feet swell, my head ache, and my stomach grumble. It's as if I've woken up from a bad dream, but I haven't had any sleep.

My mobile tells me there's a message. I hope it's William to say he's here to meet me. It's hard to read as I walk—made more difficult because my eyes are scratchy and don't want to focus. It's not him. It's someone I don't know. Another text pops up. This time it's Melissa. She's here to drive me home.

The opaque glass doors open as I yank my wheeled bag behind me. Rays of bright light bounce off creamy walls and shiny floors and almost dazzle me. A slim arm, wrapped in a purple jacket sleeve, waves frantically. Melissa strides from behind the barrier through the opening.

"I'm glad to be home," I say, as I give her a quick hug with one arm, not wishing to part with my bag for even a second.

"Kelly will be ecstatic to see you and I'm so relieved you're back. It's not been fun."

"What do you mean?"

"I suppose I should ask you how your cross-Atlantic flight was." Melissa snatches the handle of my bag away from me, and we set off at a brisk pace despite my stiff legs.

"No worse than usual. What's been happening?"

"William and Jake aren't at the farm."

"Where are they?"

"William wouldn't say."

"That's odd".

The damp darkness of the multistorey car park is scented with vehicle exhaust. Kelly's silky black and white head noses out of the partly open pickup window and follows our progress. Her excited whines can be heard above all the comings and goings. I've missed her. My legs are energized, our steps more rapid as we near the truck.

"Kelly looks okay." I can't wait to rub her ears and look into her deep brown eyes.

"And there's some strange man who keeps on asking when you'll be back. He's not nice. He's even come to the farm. Kelly growled. She doesn't like him."

"I've only been away four days."

"How is she? I suppose I should ask."

"Our mother's okay." Kelly licks my face as I get into the truck but scoots behind the front seats—which is a sure signal to me that she wants us to get going. "She's not very happy in the retirement home, but she's managing."

"Thanks for deterring her from visiting right now. I couldn't cope."

"You're back at university soon, right?"

2

"Very soon."

Melissa steers the truck ably around the tight corners and sharp spirals of the car park, and we emerge onto the wet road heading home.

"Tell me about William. Fancy him taking Jake. Doesn't Kelly miss her buddy?"

"I'm sure she misses both of them. I know I do. He said something had come up and he'd have to be away for a few days."

"Did he look anxious?"

"You know he doesn't wear his emotions, but I thought he was sort of uptight. It's not like him to be secretive, is it?" She gives me a quick glance. "Part of it is I feel hurt he didn't tell me what's going on."

"Family is all about being there for one another, whatever happens."

"Yeah, well. Seems like he doesn't think we're here for him, only the other way around."

"Tell me more about the unpleasant character who's been asking when I'll be back."

Melissa sighs and clutches the steering wheel as if to brace herself.

"You seem tense, Melissa. What's wrong?"

She turns to face me for a split second. Tears have pooled in her eyes—they reflect the sporadic lighting around us and sparkle.

"Let's talk when we get home," I say, as I reach behind to pat Kelly. I get a lick on my fingers as a reward. "Meanwhile, I'll tell you what little there is to report on my visit to see our mother." What I won't tell Melissa is that I told our mother she could come and visit sometime while Melissa is at university. Melissa says she'll never be able to forgive our mother for abandoning her as a baby. I understand. And I can't excuse our mother's lack of protection of me from the unconscionable abuse by my stepfather.

But Melissa and I have found each other, and my life is better for our sisterly relationship. Despite having different fathers and difficult childhoods and not meeting until we were adults, we've developed a strong bond.

There's no exciting news to impart about my visit to England. Melissa wants to know what the weather was like and isn't surprised to hear there was persistent drizzle augmented with sea mist rolling inland most of the time. I was in a perpetual fog when I walked along the gritty beach, and a salty taste lingered in my mouth. Those strolls were when I missed Kelly the most.

Someone's lurking by the gate to our farm—not more than a silhouette in the semi-darkness. Kelly grumbles. She's not sure what to make of this figure and nor are we. His vehicle is parked on the road, almost in the ditch. Melissa pulls into the entrance, and I get out to unlock the gate.

"Are you Meg Sheppard?" asks the man.

"What do you want? I'm tired after a long journey and would like to get into the house." Melissa drives through the gateway, stops, and springs down from the truck to let Kelly out, but they stay by the vehicle. Kelly barks and snarls, showing her white teeth. She's convinced this man has no right to be here.

"I texted you to say I'd be here. William Porter gave me your number."

"William did?"

He nods.

"I didn't get your text." Just as I say this, I remember receiving a message when I was still in the airport terminal, but I paid no attention. I was on the watch for one from William. "Who are you? And why did William give you my number?"

"I'm Noah Pestel. You don't know me. Can I talk to you? It's sort of urgent."

We're standing at the edge of the road. Melissa tells Kelly to stay by the truck and walks over.

"What's this about?" she asks.

Noah ignores her. "William said you're a private investigator and you'd be able to help me." He pushes back his hood.

"Did William mention Noah to you?" I ask Melissa. Noah is shuffling from one foot to another.

"No." Kelly emits a low, grumbly growl and creeps closer to us. Her judgement of people is almost infallible. She's made very few mistakes. But Melissa's told me she's been edgy since William and Jake took off. I look into Noah's eyes in the fading light, and it's as if he's in pain. They're half shut under a deep frown and above unshaven fuzz.

"You can come in," I say. "I'll give you ten minutes to tell me the problem. If I ask you to leave and you don't, I'll call 911."

"Got it," he says.

"Drive your car up and park at the side of the house. We'll go in the backdoor." He's in his car with the engine running almost before I finish speaking. Melissa gets into the truck. Kelly and I cut across the grass to the house and go around to the back.

"We're having hot chocolate," Melissa says as if there's no question of anyone asking for anything else. Kelly has given up on growling and accepts that we've allowed an unknown, suspicious character into our house. She laps up some water and Cooper rubs against her as if she's been away for a week rather than for a couple of hours.

"Okay. You have our attention," I say, as Noah sits down. He runs his trembling hands through his lustrous ginger hair.

"I'll start at the end, and then go back to the beginning if you're willing to hear me out," he says. Beads of sweat dot his brow but he doesn't attempt to take his hoodie off. His right leg bounces as he taps his heel in rapid staccato.

"Okay. But first, how do you know William Porter?"

"I don't know him. A mate of mine, who works in the court building, told me William knows someone who's in the horse racing business and does investigations, and that's what I need. So, I texted him. All he did was give me your name and number. I'd hoped he'd maybe set up a meeting or something, but he's probably super busy."

"He is." It doesn't sound like William. Why didn't he at least give me a heads-up? "To be clear, I'm not a licensed private investigator."

"But you do investigations, right?"

I want to put lip balm on his dry lips.

"Yes, but unofficially."

"And you're in the horse racing business, right?"

"Yes."

"That's okay then." He sighs and leans back in the chair and grasps his hands behind his head. "And I want to make it clear that I'm innocent." He leans forward again and puts his forearms on the table.

"I'm listening," I say, to encourage him to tell us his story as quickly as possible.

"You must know Barnaby Caldermat."

"I don't."

"Oh. Then I guess you don't know he was murdered in his house."

"Sorry to hear that. Melissa, have you heard anything?"

"The name's familiar, but I don't think I've ever come across him."

"The point is the cops have been asking questions and I don't have a strong alibi. I live alone in a condo, and I can't prove I couldn't have done him in. I hired a lawyer, but he seems close to useless if you ask me. So, I fired him. I want someone to find out who the murderer is. It's not me, but I think the cops want to prove my guilt. They're not interested in taking the time to find other suspects."

"So, you're a suspect in this man's murder?" I ask.

"It's looking that way, but you can see they haven't arrested me yet. I'm sort of expecting it any minute. It's so bloody stressful." He rubs his hands through his hair and hangs his head.

"I need more information. I'm confused. What would your motive be?"

"I'll go back to the beginning."

I smile at Melissa as she places three mugs of hot chocolate on the table and sits down. Noah doesn't thank her, but I excuse him because he's obviously tense and it's as if he's looking through the mug and not registering it's there.

"I should explain I'm a gambler. I'm not professional, but I'm a pretty good poker player and make a reasonable amount. Yes, I'm one of those spoiled rich kids who hasn't had to earn my money. It was handed to me when my dad died. I don't remember him, but that's another story." He picks up the mug and puts it back down without taking a sip. "Where this guy Barnaby comes in is he claimed he could pick the winners in horse races using a secret statistical formula. A fellow poker player told me he'd doubled his money by investing in Barnaby's scheme. It's called the Caldermat Gambling Circle. Horse racing sort of intrigued me. I thought it could be lots of fun. So, I gave Barnaby a wad of cash. He'd only take cash, but I got a receipt. And, although he wouldn't reveal what horses or what races, I was hooked because I almost doubled my money with the first payment. So, I put a lot more in—over time, of course."

"I think I can guess the next bit."

"Yeah, well. After the first payment, lots of promises, but nothing. Zero. My poker buddy told me he hadn't heard from Barnaby for a month. We tried getting hold of him. This is the bad part. My buddy found out where he lived. It's a fancy place in Blackloch Estates. He broke in and stole Barnaby's laptop. He wanted to get the formula, find out where his money was, or something. Not sure if he even had a plan."

"I assume it wasn't helpful."

"No, but when he was leaving, he tripped over Barnaby's body. He screamed and ran."

"He's the most likely suspect, then."

"You'd think so, but he has a tight alibi for that morning, which is the estimated time of death. I don't."

"And I presume you lost a lot more money than he did. So, the police think it's revenge?"

"I did lose a packet. I was greedy. It's crazy. I should know better. But what's the point of killing the bastard? It makes more sense to steal the laptop than to kill him."

"You didn't have anything to do with stealing the laptop?" Melissa asks.

"Mm. I suppose I'd better come clean. I waited outside on the road with the car running. My pal was hysterical when he jumped in."

"You don't think he killed him?" Melissa asks.

"I'm sure he didn't."

I explain to Noah I don't know much about how wagering is managed at the track, I just put a few dollars on my horses when they race. And I've not heard of the Caldermat Gambling Circle, which must be illegal. But he insists he believes I can find out what happened, not because I know about betting, but because I know horse people. He's convinced that someone involved in horse racing is the murderer, but I don't give him a chance to explain. I'm too tired to continue the discussion any longer and tell him that Melissa and I will talk and get back to him. He wants to continue his story, but I need matchsticks to stop my eyelids from gluing themselves together.

"We must find William," Melissa says as she follows me up the stairs carrying my bag.

"That's a job for tomorrow. I can't stay awake a moment longer."

* * *

8

It was a joy to do the barn chores this morning. Spring at the farm is my favourite time. My mood is lightened by the chirpy birdsong and the perky green shoots. The two retired racehorses, Eagle and Bullet, graze in the field and all would be well in my world if it wasn't for William and Jake's mysterious absence.

And something else isn't right. I haven't seen any sign that Melissa is leaving for university tomorrow. She discovered she needs ten credits from a recognized university to be admitted to the Doctor of Veterinary Medicine program and was gung-ho in September, but I noticed a change when the snow began to melt, and the racehorses left the farm to start their training for the new season.

Kelly and I quicken our pace towards the house.

"I've made tea for you," Melissa says. Her blond hair is dishevelled, and her eyes are puffy.

"What's wrong, Melissa?" Her eyes drop down to peer into a mug of coffee. Kelly sits next to her. "Melissa, please tell me what's bothering you. Is it William?"

"No. Well, yes, a little." She looks up and tucks her hair behind her ears. "I don't know how to explain."

"You've changed your mind and don't want to become a vet."

"How did you know? Why didn't you say something before, and put me out of my agony?"

"That's not fair. It's only just dawned on me."

"I'm sorry. I'm not myself."

"The admission requirements are tough—I'll give you that. I'm surprised you didn't get more credit for your vet tech credentials and experience."

"It's not even that so much. I get homesick for this place, for you and William, Kelly and Jake, and Cooper of course."

"That's not all, I'm guessing."

"I think you're more in tune with what's going on in my life than I am." She shifts in her chair. "I don't mean that in a bad way."

She looks up and takes a sip of coffee while watching me over the rim of her mug.

"I know. It's okay. Whatever you do, I'll always love you. You're my sister."

I shouldn't have said that. Tears drip down her face and dark spots appear on her red sweatshirt.

"I don't deserve to be part of this family. I know I don't. You've done so much to help me get organized and on the right path to be admitted into vet college, and I've blown it by deciding I can't do it. I don't want to do it."

"You miss the horses and working at the track."

"Yeah."

We agree she'll do what's necessary to unregister herself for the courses she was soon to start. As I get up to leave the kitchen, I ask, "Will you try to get your job back with Edwin?"

More tears erupt.

*　*　*

Kelly and I are on our way to the racetrack. We left Melissa curled up on her bed with Cooper and his loud purrs. Perhaps it's his way of trying to soothe her. I wasn't successful, although she was obviously heartened when she realized I wasn't trying to change her mind. I respect her decision. She'll talk to me later when she's not so overwrought.

William texted me at last. He's okay and hopes to be home soon. He's having to deal with a difficult situation. I asked what, but no answer. I told him I was relieved to hear from him and attached a couple of heart emojis which I hoped would make him laugh. I'm not into those quirky symbols and he knows it. But I secretly hoped he'd send a heart emoji back—nothing. He's not into them either.

Kelly waits in the truck as I walk towards the barns in the back-stretch. I'm surrounded by sonorous bird song as sparrows fly, hop, and peck—almost touching me at times. A flock of pigeons lands in a flurry of multi-coloured feathers and then swoops up onto a metal barn roof to watch the busyness below.

Our racehorse trainer, Neal, sits in his office with the door open. He stands up and says how glad he is to see me. I decline the offer of a cup of coffee from a carafe holding a charcoal-coloured liquid that smells burnt. Besides, coffee isn't my thing.

"How is everyone, especially the horses?" I ask.

"We're all good. I have a big race picked out for Hector."

"Oh?"

"It's the Connex Stakes Race."

"You don't sound as excited as all that. Is Hector under the weather?"

"Not at all. It's just that there's another horse I know will be entered, and he'll be ridden by Cliff Ryman."

"Is that a problem?"

"It could be."

"Why?"

"Last season he won over thirty percent of his races. That amount of winning is just plain crazy."

"What are you saying? He's a brilliant jockey, or he cheats?"

"I don't know for sure. We get pretty upset if we reckon a race isn't fair. And that's what Hector could be up against."

"A jockey with that winning percentage is going to be in just about all the big races. He'll be in demand. And you're sure it's not the trainer who's cheating?"

"He doesn't ride for just one trainer, but his stats are pretty consistent."

"Oh. Do you have an idea how he could cheat? I can't think of anything."

"I can. But I'd rather keep it to myself until I've got more to go on."

"Hector wouldn't be at risk?"

"No."

"Let's enter and see what happens."

Fay watches me walk down the shedrow, and nickers. She knows I have mints in my pocket and paws at her stall mat in anticipation. She had a good winter at the farm and receives lots of tender loving care here. Linda is an excellent groom and Neal has assigned her to all my five horses. Fay's coat gleams and her soft eyes shine. She crunches on the mints and nuzzles me, asking for more. I can only give her two more, I have four other horses to give treats to.

The others look great too, as expected. I'm disappointed that I don't see Linda and hope I will next time.

As I get back into my truck, Kelly raises her head and wags her tail as much as the lack of space allows. She lies behind the front seats to be as inconspicuous as possible. I'm sure she understands dogs aren't allowed.

I start the engine and my mobile rings. It's Noah. I'd almost forgotten about him. I meant to ask Neal if he knows anything about Barnaby Caldermat.

"Any progress?" Noah's voice sounds raspy as if his throat is dry or sore.

"No, not yet."

"You're going to help me, aren't you? I've got no one else to turn to. You're it. I could spend the rest of my life in jail for something I didn't do."

"I prefer to help with investigations where horse welfare is an issue." I'm not sure I'm interested in helping a gambler.

"But who says it doesn't involve horses? Barnaby owned a string of racehorses. His murder could be something to do with his racing stable. It could have nothing to do with the Caldermat Gambling Circle."

"Perhaps." I have my doubts.

"I don't know who else to ask who understands the horse racing business." His voice has degenerated into a pitiful whine.

"I'm willing to chat with you again about it."

"Cool. Sure. When?"

I tell him I'll get back to him as soon as I can. He wants to meet now, but I have other things on my agenda.

* * *

Home at last. Cooper rubs against me and stands on his hind legs to rub his face on Kelly's snout. We all trot up the stairs to check on Melissa. She's not here. I'll text her later.

Our current mission is to find William and Jake.

William doesn't answer my call. I send a text asking him to contact me. Now I don't know what to do. I gaze at my mobile wondering if I should connect with his assistant, Ramona, but I won't take it well if he's told Ramona where he is and what he's doing, and not me. It hurts that William hasn't let me know himself. And why he took Jake is especially curious.

2

The Video

Kelly and I are in my truck, parked behind William's office. Ramona's car is here. I take a deep breath and walk to the front door of the tastefully restored old brick house.

"Hello, Meg. I thought you'd come."

"Oh."

"You're wondering if I know where William is."

"You know?"

"He asked me not to tell you and he's my boss." She gets up from her chair behind the desk and walks towards me. "But I think you should know."

"This sounds ominous."

"It really isn't. Let's sit down at the table in his office, just in case someone comes in."

I've become conscious of my stomach as it grumbles. It makes me feel more uneasy, and it keeps growling as we each select a chair and sit down.

"Would you like a coffee or tea?" Ramona asks. "No, I don't suppose you do. It's not that bad, really."

"Please, just tell me." I try not to sound exasperated or impatient, but the tone of my voice may have betrayed me.

"Sorry. William is with his sister."

"I didn't know he had a sister."

"They're estranged, I think that's the right term. She's a devout religious something or other, but I don't have details. You know William went through a rough time a few years ago and was taking drugs."

I nod.

"I guess that led to the estrangement. But circumstances have changed because his sister's dying of cancer. William's dealing with the legal and financial matters. She's a widow and didn't have a will and hadn't appointed an executor."

"Oh."

"I expect you're wondering why he didn't tell you?"

I nod. Now my stomach is churning to the point of nausea and my cheeks are flushed.

"Because that's not all."

Is Ramona revelling in knowing more than I do about what William is doing and where he is?

"His sister, Elizabeth, has a son. And he has to arrange care for him."

It takes me a full second to swallow my sizzling rage.

"Where are they?"

"Sorry, I can't help you there."

"Thanks." I stand up and get out of the office, nearly tripping over my own feet in my haste. I don't mean to slam the door, but it happens. As soon as I scramble into the truck, I tell Kelly all about it. I'm furious with Ramona and even more furious with William.

The hurt runs deep. I've been humiliated. The cause of the deepest pain is William's secrecy and deceit. He's shut me out when I should be at his side. He should want my support and help.

I ask Kelly how I should interpret William's behaviour. Why did he choose not to tell me? Kelly licks my hot cheek. I stroke her silky head and look into her soft brown eyes. She's the one who stands by me whatever happens in my life. She's always here for me. I stroke her ears and we go home.

Both Melissa and Cooper greet us this time.

"You look better, Melissa." I give her a quick hug and breathe in the sweet smell of citrus. Her blond hair hangs like a shiny curtain as she bends down to cuddle Kelly.

"I feel tons better. I went to the track and talked to Edwin."

"Have you got your job back? I know you filled in at his equine clinic over the Christmas break and during reading week, but that doesn't mean he'd have a permanent job for you."

"That's exactly what I was stressed out about. I wouldn't want to work for anyone else. Well, guess what? I start next week!" She does a few little jumps up and down on the spot. We have another hug as Cooper weaves around us and Kelly wags her tail.

"What about the university?"

"I don't get all the money back. Sorry. I feel bad about that."

"That's no problem. We're not short."

"We should thank Frank, I suppose."

"Yes, it was his money. I have to tell you about the strange and upsetting meeting I had with Ramona just now. And if you're not going back to work for a few days, you can help me find William."

While I put the horses away for the night, Melissa buys a few groceries so we can eat. Our supplies are low again.

*   *   *

17

We sit at the kitchen table with my laptop open and wonder how to make a start on the search for William. The screen loses patience and goes black. Melissa gets a drink of water.

"Do you know where William's birth certificate is?" I ask. "Actually, don't worry, I have an idea." Kelly and Cooper follow me into the office (I've finally stopped calling it Frank's office) and open the bottom right-hand drawer of the desk. The folders are labelled in clear, neat handwriting. I grab the two yellow ones marked 'personal' and, at a glance, they look promising.

My mobile rings just as I sit down at the kitchen table. The number isn't in my contact list, and I'm on the verge of cancelling it but it could be something to do with William.

"Hello?"

"Hi. Meg Sheppard?"

"Yes."

"Great. Noah, my boyfriend, gave me your number." She sounds as if she's had six cups of strong coffee.

"Is this about Barnaby Caldermat then?"

"No. It's about something different. But I know Noah didn't do it."

"You were with him when he went into Barnaby's house?"

"It's not about that." I visualize her stamping her foot. "I'm in danger. I need your help."

"What sort of danger and how do you think I can help?"

"I must talk to you. I'm at the end of your driveway. Will you let me in?"

It seems I don't have any choice since she's on our doorstep and in apparent danger. I tell her to shut the gate behind her and park at the side of the house. Kelly's hackles are up but I tell her it's okay—the woman's allowed to come into our house.

"Thanks," she says as she springs into the kitchen. "What a lovely dog. Name?"

"Kelly."

"I wish I had a dog like you, Kelly." She rubs Kelly's ears vigorously. When she stops, Kelly shakes. She may be relieved that the attention is over. "Boy, am I glad you're going to help me."

"I didn't say that. Let's start with introductions."

The petite, young woman scratches her head with both hands, and her short, black hair sticks out in random directions. After Melissa introduces herself, the woman tells us that her name is Elsa Lorenza and she's a jockey. She does some exercise riding for a trainer called Roxi Quentin as well as a few other trainers. She paces around the room at such a rate I get dizzy as I try to follow her with my eyes. I pull out a chair for her and she hangs her denim jacket on it but keeps on the move, like a bumblebee searching for a flower.

"Is this about Noah?" I ask.

"No, it's something different." She ruffles her hair again. She stands still for one second and then turns on the spot and throws her hands up into the air as if she's in one of Shakespeare's tragedies. "I took a video." Patience is not one of my strengths and I'm close to asking her to leave.

"Tell us about it and why it's put you in danger." My voice may have sounded curt.

"Sorry. I don't know what to do with myself I'm so crushed."

"Just tell us."

"Roxi's a tough trainer. She's hard on the horses. I don't like it. I talk to them and pat them when I ride. They do better with a bit of kindness is what I say. She's not that nice to people either. She's one of these half-empty people, you know, the glass." She looks at me without blinking.

"I understand. But I have no authority to do anything about tough trainers."

"What I really mean is she's cruel. And the problem is I videoed her abusing a horse and posted it on Twitter."

"She saw it, then?"

"I don't think so, but Vannersville Racing Authority officials found out about it. And there's going to be a hearing. Roxi yelled at me and yanked my hair. Look, I have a bald patch." She bends down and holds her head, so the left side is under my nose. Almonds, I think. I can't see anything.

"I don't see it."

"Well, it's there."

"That must have hurt," Melissa says. She's making more hot chocolate. It must be her favourite drink at the moment.

"Like hell. I pushed her away and she screamed obscenities at me as I walked along the shedrow. No one paid much attention. Interesting, that."

"I thought you said she threatened you?" I ask.

"That came later. She banged on the door of my new flat and shouted. I didn't open it. I'm not that stupid. She told me I must tell the VRA that the video's fake otherwise my life won't be worth living, or something like that, sprinkled with obscenities. She has a foul mouth, that one. I thought I'd heard it all, but she deserves the trophy. But the video is real."

"So, the reason you want to talk to me is that you're not willing to tell the VRA that the video's fake, and you believe Roxi will carry out her threats," I say.

"I admit I made a mistake posting the video. I should have taken it to the VRA. I suppose I shouldn't have made it." She throws herself onto the chair and drops her head into her hands and sobs.

"Meg," Melissa says. "I've found the video." We watch a woman repeatedly hit a horse that's tied up in a stall as she yells out curses. The horse suddenly spins sideways with his head still tied. I can't make out what she's hitting the horse with. The video ends abruptly as the woman backs towards the open stall door. Melissa and I look at each other with wide eyes. I witnessed the aftermath of human cruelty towards animal victims when I worked for the Vannersville Humane Society, and that was bad enough, but watching someone actively abusing an animal makes my skin crawl as anger and outrage build inside me. Melissa's hands tremble as she puts her mobile down.

"Why didn't you do something to stop her?" I ask.

Elsa raises her head. "You don't know Roxi."

"Nevertheless, it's hard to imagine Roxi would carry through on her threats to you," I say. "She'd be admitting her guilt. The video doesn't show her face, so she could claim it was someone else."

"That's great. But I could be dead." Elsa sits upright and wipes her cheeks on her sleeves. "She's a mad woman. Mad."

"Can you stay with someone?" I ask.

Melissa glares at me. I know what she's thinking. I have a bad reputation for offering shelter to people in my, our, home, during investigations. And Melissa has not enjoyed their stays for various reasons. She's right. And I promised her I wouldn't do it again.

"What about Noah? He's your boyfriend, right?"

"Haven't you heard?" She looks at me as if I've got two heads.

"Obviously not," I say.

"He's been arrested and charged with murder. You know—that creep, Barnaby Calder-what's-his-name." She jumps up from her seat. "This is like, awful. Can't you do anything?"

"Is there anywhere else you can stay?" I ask.

"What about the Vannersville Inn?" asks Melissa. "It would be safer there. You could tell the front desk there are to be no visitors and your room number is to be kept confidential."

"It'll be expensive if I have to stay there for the rest of my life." She's pacing around the room again.

"That won't happen," I say. "I'll talk to the VRA, and chat with Roxi. We'll see what we can do to diffuse the situation. But you should also report this to the police right away."

She grabs her denim jacket almost as if she's disgusted with us and slams the backdoor. She's left without drinking her hot chocolate. Melissa and Kelly venture out to check Elsa shut the gate.

"You were right. She didn't close it." Melissa joins me in the family room and we both lean back in recliners. Cooper jumps up onto Melissa's lap and paddles on her small stomach. Kelly sprawls on the floor beside me.

"I was tired before she showed up," I say. "Now I'm exhausted."

"We must find William. It's sort of hurtful, isn't it?"

"You could say that." I heave myself out of the recliner and go to the office to collect the two yellow folders I found.

"If you went any slower, you'd lose a race to a sloth." Melissa strokes Cooper who's settled on her lap, purring.

"Very funny." I retrieve the folders and sit down with a thump and a sigh. Kelly lifts her head and lowers it again. Melissa reaches over to take one of them.

"I've found his birth certificate, at least a copy of it," I say. "He was born in a place called Merton. I haven't heard of it, have you?"

"No."

"Ramona said his sister's a devout religious nut, perhaps not in those exact words."

"I'll Google Merton and look for nutty churches then. I'll get my laptop. Sorry, Cooper." She places Cooper on the floor who stretches and yawns. He ambles towards Kelly.

"Good idea. We'll start with nutty churches—if there are any. But just because she's religious doesn't mean she's crazy or a fundamentalist."

"I know," Melissa shouts, as she disappears up the stairs. Cooper follows, probably hoping she's going to bed so he can curl up with her.

I disturb Kelly again as I gather up the papers and put them back in the folders and return them to the drawer. Even though

William is my partner, I don't feel comfortable going through his private documents.

"Okey-dokey. Let's do this," Melissa says.

Although it doesn't take more than a few seconds for Melissa to find something, my eyelids feel as if they're magnetized together.

"Wake up!" Melissa says. "I've hit the jackpot." She kneels on the floor next to me. Kelly sits up and licks her face, which makes me smile, but Melissa is so wrapped up in what she's found that she doesn't react to the slobbery token of affection.

We both read. There's a church called the Holy Waters Church of the Faithful and it looks promising.

"Click on 'newsletters'," I say. We scroll through a couple. The third one has a brief notice at the bottom of the second page stating Elizabeth Beck, a faithful Church member, and widow, is sick, and prayer will be the cure.

"I'm going to text William," Melissa says, "and tell him we're coming to Merton whether he likes it or not."

"Good."

"Wow. I didn't think you'd agree."

"Well, I have."

*   *   *

Because I've not adjusted to Eastern Standard Time yet, I woke up before daybreak. Kelly didn't share my enthusiasm for a pre-dawn start, but she's with me in the barn as I clean the stalls. Eagle and Bullet didn't seem fazed by an early breakfast, and each sauntered out with me as the sun lit up the horizon in pinks and oranges. The trees were stark silhouettes against the colourful sky.

But it's now daylight. The crisp, fresh, spring air is invigorating.

Melissa received a text from William just as we were going to bed last night. My guess is he realizes he won't be able to stop us, so he suggested we visit tomorrow. Apparently, a lot's going on today. I miss William in so many ways. I miss his warm arms wrapped around me in an embrace. His touch makes my body tingle. He's the only man I've allowed to get so close to me. There's a hole in my life and it's growing bigger with each day he's not here.

And I miss his help. He usually hears from his contacts what police services are doing and what the autopsy results are, or at least the gist. I'm less effective as an amateur sleuth without William's connections and insight.

I've given Noah and Elsa some thought and wonder if and how I can help them. I have virtually nothing to go on about the murder of Barnaby Caldermat and I'm not sure where to start. And the video of the apparent horse abuse by Roxi Quentin played over and over in my head during the night—that's another reason I was up early.

Melissa is meeting someone for lunch and doing some shopping, so I just have me and Kelly to think about. Oh, and Cooper, but he doesn't need us around all the time.

It's probably a good thing I have work to do.

Having discovered which house in Blackloch Estates was the home of Barnaby Caldermat, I want to see it. I may be lucky enough to find someone to talk to who knew him.

* * *

The house is imposing. Perhaps it looks more so because it almost fills the frontage of the half-acre lot and has a wide, tarmacked drive leading to a four-car garage. The front door is set back and protected by part of the second floor which overhangs the steps. The roof has three large gables. I'm not sure if the third floor is lived in or if the windows in the gables are just for aesthetics. The front lawn is well-manicured, but the landscaping is meagre.

The doorbell chimes for several seconds with just one press. A voice comes out of nowhere and asks who I am. I give a garbled response, but it's enough to be granted admission.

"I'd like to see some identification," the woman says as she opens the door. Fortunately, Melissa suggested I make some business cards even though I'm not a licensed investigator. They simply have my name, academic credentials, and contact information. I stand outside as she asks questions. "Are you representing that man, Noah, who you mentioned?"

"That's not how I usually operate. I investigate cases involving horse racing. I'm primarily concerned with horse welfare."

"I don't see why I have to talk to you, but you may as well come in. I'm taking bereavement leave. God knows I've earned it, and I don't just mean because Barnaby's gone."

"I'm sorry you've lost your husband."

She leads the way to the back of the house. Large patio doors open onto a deck that's surrounded by tall dark spruce trees. She walks out and we sit in two chairs that face the wooded area. She has a laptop on the table.

"He wasn't my husband. He still has a wife, Zoey. I've been with Barnaby for two years. We met soon after he split up with Zoey. My name's Olivia Matterson, by the way."

"I've seen your name in the newspaper."

"No doubt. Then you'll know I'm the President and CEO of Vannersville Hospital and Medical Centre. And that the union is a royal pain in the neck. And the doctors drive me crazy."

"It sounds like you don't enjoy your job."

"Enjoy? God, no. But it's better than being out of work with no money coming in."

"How did you meet Barnaby?"

"What's that got to do with horse welfare?"

"I'm in information collection mode."

"I don't know much about anything."

"Where did you meet him?"

"I suppose it's no secret. I was in between jobs just over two years ago when I met Barnaby through an online dating service. I was bored and thought I'd see what came of joining. It was for a lark. But Barnaby interested me, and he soon asked me to move in. He missed his wife, he said. We didn't have a close relationship. But neither of us left. We just sort of lived our separate lives."

"He lived an exotic lifestyle, I hear."

"That's no secret either. I don't know where he got all the money to do what he did. And I don't know all that went on. But he told me he bought this house for cash. He has two fancy Mercedes. He used to own a Mercedes-Benz dealership, and he may still have it. See, I don't even know that."

"Did he own other properties?"

"Not sure."

"What happened on the day he died?"

"I've talked to the police. But I suppose you won't know about that. They think it was a burglary gone wrong. I suppose they must suspect that Noah guy you mentioned."

"You don't agree?"

"Oh, god yes. I think that's exactly what it was. But he didn't get much. Only a laptop which would be pretty useless, I guess. Although perhaps Barnaby was involved in something. How would I know? We hardly ever talked."

"Did you see or hear anything?"

"Not a thing. I was at work. When I came home the house was dark. And there Barnaby was, sprawled on the floor. I called the cops. I don't know how he died. They haven't told me that, but there were signs of an intruder they said."

"Do you know what the signs were?"

"Just the laptop gone—that was obvious. They think Barnaby must have let the person into the house in the morning—probably someone he knew."

"And you found him later that evening?"

"After I got home from work. I've got nothing more to add. Even though I'm on leave, I'm still working my rear end off. The board is getting far too hands-on. Too many reports. Too many meetings."

"I have some understanding of governance issues. I was the Executive Director for the Vannersville Humane Society."

"Not such a large organization."

"No."

"You can leave now. I've told you all I know."

"Thanks for your time." She ushers me out as if she regrets talking to me.

3

Thirty Horses

The afternoon brings spring showers and melodic birdsong. The birds sound as optimistic as the backstretch feels. Everyone's upbeat at the start of a new racing season. Memories of losses and hard times are forgotten and replaced by dreams of potential wins and success.

Neal is chatting on his mobile as he stands in the shedrow. I visit with the horses for a few minutes, and he catches up with me.

"Nice to see you, Meg. The horses are good. Hector's in fine form."

"He looks well."

"He's ready. I've looked at the nominations, and the competition isn't all that tough. Ontario sires only, as you know. But I'm not happy we'll be racing against Cliff."

"That's Cliff Ryman, the jockey who could be cheating."

"Don't let's talk here. I've got a few minutes if you can come to my office."

"Sure."

After some chat about the Connex Stakes Race, I remember I want to ask him about Barnaby Caldermat.

"I heard he's dead," Neal says. "Big owner. Over thirty horses, I think. Imagine what he's forking out each month." He lets out a long, slow whistle. "He must have been filthy rich."

"Who was his trainer?"

"His wife, Zoey."

"That's surprising."

"Why?"

"Because they've been separated for about two years."

"Doesn't mean you can't continue a business relationship."

"You have a point. Do you know anything else about Barnaby or Zoey?"

"No. Best if you talk to Zoey, I guess. She's in barn fourteen."

"Thanks. And thanks to you and Linda for taking such good care of the horses."

"Pleasure."

It's a pleasant walk to barn fourteen. I have to watch where I put my feet, though, because the pigeons and sparrows are all over the place picking up scraps of straw, hay and grain, and bathing in puddles. And someone must have turned up the volume—which is fine with me—I enjoy the cheerful chirps and coos.

A man bent over a bucket directs me to Zoey. At a glance, she looks more like a model for a gym than a horsewoman. She's writing on a whiteboard. It seems she's planning the exercise times for about forty horses.

"Hello. Zoey?"

"That's me." She turns and smiles, revealing perfect white teeth and bright blue eyes.

I introduce myself and explain that I'm an amateur sleuth. She shakes my hand with a firm grip.

"I've heard about you. Frank Sheppard's wife, right?"

"Yes."

"He did quite a lot to improve the welfare of racehorses. Good guy, Frank."

"He did. I'm sorry about your loss of your husband, Barnaby."

"Oh, goodness. No need to be sorry. We've been separated for about two years."

"You have his horses here, so you must have continued a business relationship."

"No. They went after we split up. Even when I had his horses, I never saw him here. He was an absent owner. Just came to the races with a couple of pals of his. If the horse won, I'd see him briefly in the Winner's Circle. That's all."

"He didn't consult you about the horses, their health, vet bills, or the races they were to be entered into?"

"Nope. Left it all to me."

"Do you know why he took so little interest? It costs a lot of money to train about thirty racehorses."

"Oh. That's funny."

"What do you mean?"

"He still owes me over a quarter million in training fees and vet bills. I refused to run up the tab any higher. He managed to strike some kind of deal with Roxi Quentin. She's had his horses for quite a while."

"Was that the reason you left him? Because he didn't pay his bills?"

"You make it sound as if I was the one who caused the separation. He did it entirely by himself. That's private." Her smile disappears. "You asked why he took so little interest. He revelled in the prestige of having a string of racehorses. He loved being in the Winner's Circle. He wanted to win the big races. It wasn't about the horses at all. It was all about money and image and status and pride."

"Have you heard of someone called Noah Pestel?"

"He's a suspect in Barnaby's murder, isn't he?"

"Not confirmed."

"Don't know him. My guess is there's a load of people who'd like Barnaby out of their lives."

"Oh. Who?"

"I don't have names."

"Do you know Elsa Lorenza?"

"She's a decent jockey. I've used her a few times to exercise horses. Good communicator, which I like since I can't ride the horses myself."

"She's Noah's girlfriend."

"Didn't know that. Doesn't mean anything to me. Elsa and I don't talk about anything other than the horses. Well, I must get on. I have a load to do. And yes, if I think of something, I'll let you know. Thanks for your card."

I turn away with reluctance. I'd like to know more about her relationship with Barnaby.

She keeps a neat shedrow. Each horse has a clean leather halter—with a shiny brass name tag—hanging beside their stall door. The ground has been freshly raked, and the feed buckets—which are hooked onto the rail across from each horse—look like new. There are fewer busy birds since there's little available to scavenge.

*   *   *

Why is my stomach fluttering? Melissa, Kelly, and I are on our way to Merton. We don't know what to expect. It's a dreary day with intermittent drizzle. Visibility is impeded by smears of grime that partially obscure my vision until I squirt windshield washer fluid. Then the wipers give me a clear view for a few seconds. I hold back from vehicles in front but can't avoid the spray thrown at us by oncoming traffic.

We reach the modest bungalow without any difficulty. We didn't need to look at the numbers pinned over each garage since William's car is parked on the narrow single-car driveway. Now I'm shaking. This is ridiculous.

I park on the road. There's no room to do otherwise. As we get out of the truck, William opens the front door. I notice a child holding a piece of paper and standing behind him, half hidden. Then Jake's face appears. William grabs his collar and beckons us to go in. He slams the front door behind us. Kelly must be disappointed that we've left her in the truck.

William wraps me in his warm arms. My fluttering stomach relaxes, and I soak in the feel and smell of him.

"Enough already," says Melissa as she pats an enthusiastic dog. Just in this short time, Jake looks as if he's put on weight. He hasn't had to keep up with Kelly or chase squirrels. William hugs Melissa, and then she jumps up and down on the spot. The young boy stays behind William and has hold of his Uncle's pants as well as a piece of paper.

"Did you draw that?' asks Melissa. The boy nods but looks apprehensive.

William picks the boy up, although he must weigh at least forty pounds. He introduces us to the boy and tells us he's called Gabriel and is his wonderful nephew. William knows we want to ask a lot of questions, but he puts his finger to his lips.

"Can I make some tea?' I ask.

"There's not much in the house. I need to shop."

"Let's go to the grocery store and get takeout on the way back," I say.

"Gabriel's never been to McDonald's. I promised him we'd go sometime soon."

"Would you like to meet Kelly, my dog? And would you like to have a drive in my pickup?" Gabriel turns his head away.

We decide to bring Kelly into the small back yard which is just grass so that she and Jake can burn off some pent-up energy before we all load into the truck. Gabriel stands on the tiny deck and watches. Then he giggles. The dogs chase each other around and around, then roll on top of one another, get up and run the other way around. Jake barks. They both lie down—their front legs flat on the lawn and their upright tails wagging. I'm convinced they're putting on a show for Gabriel and he's loving it. After several minutes, Jake flops down with his front legs and back legs stretched out, panting. Kelly is panting too, but her tongue isn't lolling out as much. She ambles over to Gabriel who's sitting on the step leading down from the deck. He doesn't move. She sits by his feet and looks at him. As he reaches out to pat her, she stays perfectly still. Then she gives him a lick. It's against the rules, but Gabriel smiles.

"Now we can go," William says. Melissa and Gabriel sit in the back seat with the dogs on the floor. Gabriel is on his booster seat that appeared from somewhere. Melissa and Kelly keep Gabriel's attention while William talks to me in a muffled voice. He tells me that his sister, Elizabeth, was transferred to a hospice yesterday. She's in palliative care. He says he can't possibly tell me everything in the few minutes it takes to get to McDonald's, but his main concern is Gabriel's care. He's been home-schooled by Elizabeth, is unsocialized and has no friends. William thinks, though, that Gabriel was scared to see his mother so sick and that he's been a bit better today, although he's missing his mother dreadfully. I ask William about the Holy Waters Church of the Faithful and what services they offer their families. William tells me not to go there. It's a long story. In a nutshell, there's nothing.

McDonald's is overwhelming to Gabriel, but he's more relaxed once we find a table in a corner away from the bustle. The constant beeping of timers for the friers stresses him at first, but he gets used to it. He's ecstatic with the silly plastic toy that comes with his meal.

None of us know what it's supposed to be, but its head bobbles and that makes Gabriel giggle. He's not said a word since we arrived at his house.

Once we get back and the groceries are stashed away, William says he doesn't know how much longer it will take to get things settled. He implies he won't leave until Elizabeth dies and Gabriel is settled somewhere. The expression in his eyes tells me a lot more. I need to think, and must talk to Melissa.

*   *   *

Melissa is back at work at the track and I'm doing my best to ignore Noah's texts and voicemail messages.

The house is too quiet. It seems so much larger when I'm alone, although Kelly and Cooper do their best to fill up the space. I've finished the morning barn chores, I'm drinking my second cup of tea, and I'm moping. We all miss William.

To divert my thoughts, I scroll through some social media. Barnaby Caldermat's name comes up a few times. It seems several people thought they could get rich quick by giving him their hard-earned money. It should be obvious to anyone who knows anything at all about horses that there couldn't be a statistical formula for predicting winners. Why do people fall for these things? But they did, and their money funded his extravagant lifestyle. And how did Barnaby think it would end? It's inevitable the gambling circle would eventually collapse and there'd be some very angry people. Consequently, there must be quite a few suspects for the police to check out, unless, as Noah thinks, they're just out to prove his guilt. But I don't want to believe that.

The spring sunshine dances on the kitchen floor as its rays are scattered by the fresh green leaves on the trees. Cooper pounces on the playful shadows while Kelly sits by the backdoor as if to say we should be going somewhere or doing something. She's right.

The video Elsa taped of Roxi—apparently hitting a horse while tied up—has been lurking in the back of my mind. It's about time I did something about it. Elsa has left two voicemail messages. I listen to them. They're almost the same. She's afraid to go back to the track but she needs the money. She can't afford to lose her rides and the momentum she's built up as a jockey and exercise rider. But she says Roxi has threatened her again and she's scared. I reply that I'll meet with her after I've talked to the Vannersville Racing Authority and Roxi.

Kelly and I leave Cooper lying in the largest patch of sun on the kitchen floor, and head to the racetrack.

*   *   *

The day is warming up and several horses are getting sudsy baths outside. One has a bucket of water poured over his head to wash the soap off. He must be used to it because he doesn't even flinch but just blinks his large eyes a few times. I keep walking until I reach the barn where Roxi Quentin has her stalls.

Roxi's shedrow is a mess. Behind the rail that runs across from the stalls is a tangled muddle of dirty polo bandages, saddle pads, towels, baling twine, and other stuff I can't make out at a quick glance. The feed buckets that hang on the rail are old metal ones and look as if they've been kicked along the shedrow a few times. They may have been dark blue in their distant past. A woman leads a horse out to the wash pad.

"Hold this horse, will you?" she yells at a young man who's lugging a couple of bales of straw into the barn. Her voice is high-pitched and edgy. She must be Roxi.

The horse looks in good condition, perhaps a little on the thin side, but appears to be as edgy as Roxi's voice sounded.

"Hold her still for god's sake." Roxi is aiming the hose at each of the horse's feet in turn so they're clean when she's returned to her stall after being walked around the shedrow to cool off after her workout.

"Hi, I'm Meg Sheppard," I say.

"I don't know you, and I'm busy." There are deep vertical lines between her eyebrows that look as if they're carved into her face.

"Elsa Lorenza," I start to say.

"Don't mention her name!" Her eyes are almost pinched shut and her thin lips barely move as she spits out the words.

"I want to give you the opportunity to tell your side of the story," I say, as I back up a couple of paces. The horse turns sharply away from her, so she grabs the lead-rein and gives it a couple of yanks as the hose lies on the rubber mat spewing out warm water. The young man also backs away.

"It's a story all right. That damn video is fake."

Worried the horse will get the brunt of her growing rage, I thank her and leave. The young man seems to have disappeared. He's probably not coming back. There's plenty of work for grooms and hotwalkers so he won't have any trouble finding a decent, humane trainer to work for. Unfortunately, the horse can't choose its trainer and can't move to another barn.

*　*　*

Bill Price, one of the racing officials with Vannersville Racing Authority, remembers me.

"Come in, Mrs. Sheppard. It's been a long time since we talked last."

"Please call me Meg. Yes, it's been a while."

"You've had some success with your horses." He leans back in his chair. I've always thought he has a kind face and the integrity to go with it. I'm not sure if the two are linked, but perhaps they are. His hair is now completely white, but his face doesn't look more aged.

"I'm happy with my trainer. Last time I spoke with you, my horses were with Shane Parrington, and that didn't go well."

"It certainly didn't. Is there something you want to ask me?"

"Yes. I'm sure you've seen the video that apparently shows Roxi Quentin hitting a horse tied to a stall wall."

"I have."

"I'm sure you know who took the video, Elsa Lorenza."

"I do."

"Elsa tells me she's been threatened by Roxi and she's asked me to help her. She appears to be genuinely scared and has moved out of her flat temporarily."

"Ah. Your question?"

"Is the VRA investigating the abuse?"

"I assure you the alleged abuse is being investigated."

"There's more to this, isn't there?"

"There are usually two sides to a story."

"Is Elsa being investigated as well, then?"

"Yes. That's all I can tell you officially."

"Is there anything you can tell me off the record?"

"Just that Roxi Quentin is a complex woman. She invites dislike but she's her own worst enemy. I've had occasion to talk to her several times." He leans back in his chair which squeaks an objection to the movement. "And Elsa has come to our attention more than once. That's all I can add."

"This helps a lot. You've essentially told me I need to keep an open mind."

"I'm glad I've been helpful. I wish you good luck in the Connex Stakes Race."

"Thank you."

As I walk out of the administration building, I almost bump into the young man, a groom I suppose, who was holding the horse for Roxi.

"Are you okay?" I ask.

"Yeah. Why wouldn't I be?" He turns his baseball cap around as if to see me more clearly.

"I just wondered. I angered Roxi and you seemed to get the brunt of it."

"Nope. We're good."

"Great." I walk past him and consider what he and Bill Price have said.

4

Beaten

Elsa isn't staying at the Vannersville Inn. I checked. I text her and she says she can't meet me right now. She's tied up.

Noah's messages can't be ignored any longer. I skip over them—since I'm pretty sure they all say the same thing—and text him to suggest we get together today. He replies that he can meet me in the garden at the back of his condo building in ten.

I arrive five minutes late.

He sits on a black metal chair with his arms resting on a small glass-topped table set in dappled sunshine. Two bird feeders hang from a low branch of an old maple tree and there's a flurry of feathers in competition for the seeds. Noah's leg bounces as he peers at his mobile.

"Hi, Noah."

"Hey." He turns his head and his shiny ginger hair shimmers in the scattered rays of the sun.

"You're not in a cell at least."

"It turns out they haven't enough evidence to charge me. But I'm a person of interest, whatever that means."

"Elsa said you'd been charged and arrested.'

"Whoa. What?" He slams his mobile down onto the table and I cringe. I hope it's made of tough stuff.

"She's your girlfriend, right?"

"No way." He rubs his hand through his hair.

"Oh. That's what she told me."

"She's a pathological liar, that one."

"Talking about the truth. I don't think you've been honest with me."

"About what?" He looks down at his hands which are firmly clasped together.

"You said your poker buddy told you about Barnaby Caldermat and gave Barnaby a lot of cash over a period of time."

"Well, yeah."

"Tell me more."

"It makes me sound like a real dolt. I should've known better. If my dad was still around I'm sure he'd have a conniption. His hard-earned money down the drain. Mind you, I didn't know my father." He hangs his head and I almost want to put my arms around his shoulders, but not quite.

"So, you lost a lot of money. Now, why would you think the formula was worth having if you were losing so much?"

"That's a good question."

"I try my best to ask only good ones."

"Yeah, well. The trouble was I still wanted to believe in the formula. Yeah, that's stupid. I've had to face up to it—it's not possible to pick winners using a formula—that's why we use the term 'horse race' when anything can happen because it's not predictable."

"You said it."

42

"It might help to look at each racehorse's past performance, though. And even then, the favourites win only about thirty percent of the time."

"You must have done some research, but too late."

"Yeah."

"But before you did this research, you still believed in the formula."

"Barnaby must have been cheating and keeping the cash for himself. I don't even know if he put any of it on the horses, all I know is he kept the money we effing idiots gave him."

"Let's go back to what happened in Barnaby's house. If I'm going to find the murderer, you must tell me what really happened."

"As I told you in my texts, I'm sure the coppers want to prove my guilt. They reckon they've got their man. They had to let me go, but I could tell they sure didn't want to."

"You still believed in the formula, so what did you do?"

"I had to have that formula. I'd lost so much, and I needed to recoup."

"So?"

"I think you've guessed it. I stole the laptop."

"That took courage. How did you know where to find it?"

"Barnaby invited me to his home office when we first met. I reckon he did it to impress me and have me believe he was making lots of money. It worked. He had a fancy house and two new Mercedes in the driveway."

"Did you ask if he would sell you the formula?"

"I did, as a matter of fact. He told me he wasn't selling, and, in any case, no one could pay him enough. Anyhow, he had his laptop out and he showed me a graph and some tables. I didn't look at them carefully, of course. Dollar signs were blurring my vision."

"What made you think he wouldn't take the laptop with him wherever he went?"

"I don't know. The way he had it set up, I think. He had it plugged into something and had sticky notes on it."

"How and when did you break into his house?"

"I texted him the day before to ask if I could see him in his home. I had some questions. He said he'd meet me in the garden on the deck. I could go in by the side gate. I was disappointed, but then I thought it might work because I could say I needed the bathroom and could grab his laptop from his office and put it in my backpack. I was a bit surprised he wanted to meet outdoors but, hey, it was a nice day. Perhaps he watches birds or something. Anyway, I got there a bit before the time, and I had an old laptop in my bag so he wouldn't suspect I'd taken his. I thought it would be clever to switch them."

"What if you'd met in his office? Wouldn't it have been impossible to steal his laptop from under his nose?"

"I thought I could switch laptops when he got us a drink or something. It sounds like such a dumb idea now."

"What about his partner, Olivia?"

"I know she works at the hospital. I reckoned she'd be out all day."

"What happened when you arrived at his house?"

"I sat on the deck for more than ten minutes. Then I knocked on the patio doors. They were open about a foot or so. I thought that was strange. I called out. No answer. But I was determined to get that laptop. So, I decided to seize the opportunity and grab it, and get the hell out of there."

"He'd know it was you who stole it, though."

"I didn't think of that at the time. I'm not good criminal material, obviously." His face flushes rosy pink.

"Your plan had a lot of holes in it."

"I was desperate. He owed me a lot of money and now I have no hope of getting it."

"But you gave him the cash."

"It was a scam."

"But you fell for it."

He coughs.

"Is there somewhere I can get you some water?"

"I can't go in. The condo's on the market and two couples are booked to look at it about now."

"I'm sorry."

"I'll pick myself up."

"Good. So, you grabbed the laptop and left?"

"When I trotted in, calling Barnaby's name, I didn't notice anything wrong. I rammed his laptop into my backpack. I didn't even substitute it with the old one I brought. I thought it best to go back out the way I came. No fingerprints because I could get in without touching the patio doors with my hands. But when I trotted back into the kitchen I stumbled and nearly lost my balance. There was something big on the floor. It was semi-dark because he was in the shadow of the kitchen island, but I could tell it was Barnaby. He didn't react. Nothing. I figured he must be dead. I freaked. I mean, I really freaked."

"Why didn't you put the laptop back and phone the police?"

"Another good question. I didn't. What can I say? I ran."

"What now?"

"Please find out who killed him. I'm sure those coppers are hell-bent on charging me."

"Why would they have you in their crosshairs? How did they know you were there?"

"My text about the meeting. They checked his mobile of course. I'd forgotten all about it."

"It puts you at the scene of the crime."

"Exactly. And they found his laptop in my condo."

"I agree—you're not good criminal material. I assume there was no formula?"

"No, but there were spreadsheets with names and amounts. He got a lot of money from us idiots."

"They'll be some very unhappy people now they realize they can't get their money back."

He hangs his head. His leg isn't bouncing anymore.

*   *   *

Streaks of yellow, pink, and orange hang over the horizon as if reluctant to fade. The beauty of the sunset captivates me as I close the barn doors. Kelly wags her tail and wonders why we aren't going inside the house. I pat her and tell her she's a good dog.

Melissa joins us and smiles as she hands me a mug of tea and sips her coffee.

"It seems that you're glad to be back working at the track," I say.

"I am. I don't regret taking those courses though. It gave me a chance to think about things and figure out what makes me happy. I love my job."

"And you like working for Edwin."

"I do." She peers into her coffee.

"We need to talk."

She turns her head sharply towards me and frowns.

"It's nothing bad," I say. "At least, I don't think so."

"Uh oh."

"Don't go 'uh oh'. It's about William and Gabriel."

"I agree."

"What do you mean, you agree?"

"We should."

"Should what?" I know, but I want her to say it.

"We should suggest to William Gabriel live here, at least temporarily, to see if it works out for everyone, especially that poor little boy."

"It's a huge responsibility."

"But I know what it's like in foster homes. I'm the product of that broken system. He's been so smothered by his mother and that stupid church that he wouldn't survive a week. He's got no clue how to stand up for himself. He doesn't know how to get along with other children or how to relate to adults—other than his controlling mother."

"You don't know she's controlling."

"I see the signs. My heart goes out to him and he's William's nephew. We can't turn our backs on him if we love William."

"Right. That's decided. I'll call William tomorrow."

I put my arm around Melissa, and she rests her head on my shoulder as our tea and coffee swirl precariously in the mugs. She mutters that so many childhood memories are flooding back, and she hasn't been able to stop thinking about Gabriel since we saw him. I'm thankful Melissa isn't bringing our mother into it. Neither of us wants to stir up the turmoil of emotions she evokes.

We walk back to the house and Cooper rescues Melissa from her memories. He rubs against her legs, and she picks him up, sniffing as a couple of teardrops run down her cheeks. She smiles at him as he tickles her face with his long, white, whiskers, and takes him upstairs to her bed where he loves to curl up for the night. Melissa's tired after a long day at the track and has to get up before dawn to go back to work. But she's much happier, and that makes me feel warm inside.

Kelly and I go into the family room so I can finish my tea while I catch up on my emails. I seem to have quite a few.

It's a surprise to have one from Bill Price, the VRA official I met with. It includes two links. I click on the first and I'm led to a decision by the stewards to suspend Elsa Lorenza, jockey, for the whole of this year's racing season at the Vannersville Racetrack. Bill has noted by the second link that this race led to the VRA's decision.

I start the video. The horse being ridden by Elsa is called Shooting Stars and the trainer is Roxi. That's interesting. Shooting Stars is a 25:1 long shot. As far as I can tell, the horse looks in good shape and loads into the gate without incident. She breaks well but is trailing the field as the horses enter the first turn. Most of the time she's not far behind—just a length, sometimes two. As they reach the final turn, she suddenly finds a second gear. Her stride is longer and there's more energy in her effort. She steadily overtakes the pack on the outside, and wins by a nose.

Roxi stands at the rear of the horse in the winner's circle, as trainers usually do. Elsa has a broad smile for the photographer and leaps off the horse. Roxi appears to ignore Elsa. It's as if Roxi's face is smaller. She's not smiling. Something's not right with this picture. But I can't figure out what it is. I must ask Neal.

* * *

Spring showers sprinkle the horses and riders as they go to and from the training track. Most of the horses have their tails tied in a knot to help keep them clean, but the sandy track surface has sprayed their legs and chests without mercy.

After I've enjoyed five soft muzzles each taking treats out of the palm of my hand, I join Neal in his office.

"You've heard Elsa Lorenza's been suspended for the rest of the racing season?" I ask.

"I think everyone knows."

"I received a link to a race she rode in, and I can't see what the issue is." I bring it up on my mobile and hand it over to Neal. He watches, brow furrowed, until the horses reach the final turn.

"Ah, I know. At least, I think I do."

"What?"

"She's an electric jockey."

"What does that mean?"

"I bet she uses a machine or device to give the horse a surprising shock, usually at the top of the stretch. The stewards must have evidence. Perhaps they found the device on her."

"What sort of device? It sounds cruel."

"I'm not sure it's cruel. If it really hurt, most horses would bolt. I saw one of these things once, years ago, and they probably haven't changed much. They have batteries and two prongs. The rider has it hidden in his glove, the prongs poking out so that he can touch the horse's neck."

"It sounds awful to me."

"Looking at that race, I can't think what else it could be. Elsa keeps her whip in her right hand all the time. Usually, riders will change it up. That's another sign she could have something in her other hand. And the horse suddenly changes pace. Some horses do that without much urging—they're finishers and like to pass other horses as they race towards the wire. But the way Shooting Stars reacted, my bet is Elsa used an electrical device."

"Is that what you suspect Cliff Ryman of doing?"

"I'm unsure about him. It's rare for jockeys to use electrical devices. If they get caught, they could face years of suspension, perhaps even lose their licence, so it's a huge risk to take. It's just his winning percentage is up there."

On my way out I find Linda rolling up clean bandages that have just come out of the dryer. The bandages would have been filthy today. They protect the horses' legs while they're exercising, but in these conditions, they get caked in training-track sand.

"Hi, Linda. How are you?"

"Not bad." Beads of sweat glisten like tiny sequins on her brow and upper lip. She overheats with the least bit of exertion.

"Have you heard about Elsa being suspended?"

"That news spread fast."

"Do you know why she's suspended? Neal thinks she may have used an electrical device."

"The rumour is Roxi Quentin, she's a trainer, saw Elsa drop something onto the track after a race. It happened a while back."

"Was that the race where Elsa rode Shooting Stars?'

"Yep."

"You must have heard about the video of Roxi taken by Elsa?"

"Saw it."

"What are people saying about it?"

"That it's a setup, in retaliation for Roxi reporting Elsa to the VRA."

"Interesting. Thanks for this, Linda, and thanks for taking such good care of the horses. They look great."

"No problem." She places the last rolled purple bandage in a large storage container.

I join Kelly in the truck. She's waited patiently for me while hidden behind the seats. I click on Shooting Star's race again. I watch the horse making its way to the Winner's Circle, but I don't see Elsa drop anything or Roxi pick up anything, although Roxi's left hand is clenched. Her right hand is the one on the horse's hind when the winning photo is taken. It could be she's holding something small. If so, perhaps it's the device. That would explain her grey pallor and stern-looking face.

Kelly looks disappointed when I get out of the truck and leave her again. I walk towards Roxi's barn. As I get nearer, raised voices grow louder. I wonder if Roxi is lashing out at someone or a horse or both. I hesitate and consider turning back. She didn't want to talk to me last time, and I don't suppose she will this time, especially if there's an altercation in progress. But I don't catch her voice among the two or three other high-pitched and agitated voices.

"I'll call an ambulance," says the young man I met before.

"No," says someone who's lying on the floor of a large metal storage container—it's like a large shed, where the hay is stored. "I can't leave the horses."

"You need a doctor," shrieks an older woman who must be one of Roxi's staff.

"I'll make sure the horses are looked after, with the help of your staff," I say. I have no idea where that came from, but one look at Roxi is enough to convince me she needs medical attention. One eye is swollen shut, blood is dripping from her nose onto the floor, her arm is lying at an odd angle, and her legs are covered in bits of hay and dirt.

"Roxi, you should go to hospital," I say, as I crouch down beside her. "You can't do anything for the horses in this condition. You'll be doing the horses a favour if you do your best to recover quickly. I'll make sure everything's looked after." I turn to the young man. "It's okay to call an ambulance and please call security." I keep talking to Roxi while I place her head on a folded-up saddle pad that the woman has brought. We put a thin horse blanket over her and wait. Roxi refuses to let me take pictures. She doesn't want me to investigate what happened.

It takes about five more minutes for the ambulance to show up. Security is a couple of minutes behind. I hope they look into what's happened to Roxi. Somebody must.

Despite Roxi's wishes, after she's left I take photos inside the storage place and look around for a couple of minutes. I find no clues as to who hurt Roxi.

I phone Neal and ask if he'll help. I know he's busy, but he has a great crew. I talk to Roxi's staff. It seems that all the horses have been exercised, including scheduled timed workouts. It's just regular care of the horses for the rest of the day. Neal says he can keep an eye on things for Roxi, although he's not one of her fans. He'll do it for the horses. I knew he would. And Linda says she'll pitch in as well. Before I leave, I double-check that the staff know what they need to do for the rest of the day and promise I'll be back tomorrow.

On our way home, I drive through Blackloch Estates. I'm banking on Olivia being at home since she's likely still on bereavement leave.

"What do you want?" she asks, as she opens the door to the end of its chain. She has a glass of white wine in her hand. Something moves towards the back of the house. I think she has a visitor.

"I was hoping to talk with you."

"About what? They know that guy Noah did it. So, case closed. No need for you to be snooping around." She waves her wine glass around. Her voice is snippier than the last time I was here.

"There's some doubt as to Noah's guilt. Surely you want to find out what happened to your partner?"

"Don't give a damn what happened to him. Good riddance is what I say." I hear someone call her name. Does the voice sound familiar? I don't have a chance to find out. The door is slammed in my face. "Go away!" she shouts from behind the closed door.

That didn't go well.

5

Deflated

Both Kelly and I are relieved to get home. We wander to the barn and get Eagle and Bullet settled in for the night. The kitchen is quiet and empty. No one is here. Melissa texted me to say she was out for dinner.

Cooper saunters over to us. He stops, spreads out his front paws, digs his sharp claws into the mat, and stretches back with his tail in the air as if he's doing a downward dog. His yawn reveals a cavernous, pink mouth. He must have had a tough day.

Getting my priorities straight, I feed them both and plug in the kettle. Jake's empty feed bowl sits by Kelly's full one and I have a panicky thought. Will William and Jake come back to live here? I wish Melissa wasn't out. Kelly's off her food, so she must be as discombobulated as I am.

"Never mind my tea, Kelly, I need a walk. Let's explore the big field."

Kelly's keen. She got some exercise when we put the horses to bed, but she enjoys a run around the large back field.

Clouds have moved in, and the spring colours have faded, leaving us in a black-and-white world. I should have brought a flashlight. Kelly follows scents along the fence line but I'm not taking in any of the smells or sounds around us. My mind is flitting about but landing over and over again on the hole in my life that should be filled by William. I've scared myself by wondering what his plans are, and if they include me.

Kelly pricks her ears. She barks and takes off towards the house. Someone must have come up the driveway. I can barely make out a vehicle in the semi-darkness. Perhaps I can see the silhouette of a man standing by the back door. Kelly rushes back towards me, followed by Jake. My heart leaps. The three of us run back to the house.

"William!"

"I'm so glad to see you," William says, as he puts his arms around me. He's crying.

"What's wrong? It's Elizabeth, isn't it? Come inside for heaven's sake. Where's Gabriel? How is he?"

"Oh, Meg. I'm at a loss to know what to do. He's in the car and refuses to get out."

"I'll get him. Kelly, I need your help."

Gabriel's pale face is almost luminescent. It's as if he's a ghost. He doesn't move or make a sound. His limp hands sit on his still lap. I want to check that he's breathing. Of course, he is. I tell Kelly to get into the car and sit next to him on the back seat. She sits close to him and gives him the gentlest and slowest lick I've ever witnessed.

"She loves you," I say.

His eyelids flutter as if he's gaining awareness of his surroundings. He turns to Kelly and puts a hand on her head. She stays perfectly still except for her silky tail. She sweeps it backwards and forwards on the seat in slow motion. Her eyes are fixed on his but he collapses into sobs, his chin on his chest. Kelly noses her head onto his lap, and he hugs her neck. My eyes well up. I pinch my arm to stop myself from crying.

William stands next to me with his hands in his pockets as his eyes gaze up at the blurry moon. He looks as if he's lost out at sea.

"Meg, this is overwhelming. What should I do?"

I nudge him away from the car, out of Gabriel's earshot.

"It's simple," I say. "Gabriel's family. He should stay here."

"But he's not part of your family. I don't want you to do this. I must figure it out. I would have preferred you didn't know about him. I reckoned you and Melissa would want to do something, and it wouldn't be fair on you. And what's more, he's been raised by a religious fanatic."

"William! You're making no sense and it's hurtful. Just because we're not married doesn't mean we aren't family. Don't ever say such ridiculous things again."

"What about Melissa? She loathes other people staying here.'

"Gabriel is not 'other people'. He's your nephew and that makes him our nephew. And before you spout any more nonsense, Melissa and I agreed Gabriel should stay here with barely a word spoken between us. Don't forget, Melissa was shuttled from one foster home to another—she knows what it's like to be abandoned. She couldn't bear for Gabriel to go through the same thing. While we wouldn't dream of forcing our position on you, that's what we both believe makes sense and what we'd like to do. So, it's up to you. In any case, we need to get Gabriel inside. Have you brought his clothes?"

"Some. He was worrying me so much I just got us in the car and came here. I didn't know what else to do."

"You did the right thing. Thank goodness you're home." I put my arms around him again and he holds me tight.

Cooper loves Gabriel at first sight. He waltzes over with his tail in the air and rubs against him. Gabriel strokes him but Jake isn't too happy about the attention being given to the cat and pushes himself up against Gabriel, almost knocking him over.

"He's a jellybean," I say. "Jake thinks you should give him all the attention."

* * *

William and I didn't get much opportunity to talk yesterday evening mostly because we were busy getting Gabriel settled in. Melissa drifted through the kitchen at a late hour on her way to get some sleep before work early in the morning. I'm not sure she registered that Gabriel's in the house.

William has his hands full today. The priority is Gabriel, and there's much to get organized, not only the legal adoption process presumably, but registering him for school, buying clothes, getting some toys, decorating his bedroom, and so on. He has little of his own to bring to the farm. William insists that he'll get it all under control and he'll take Gabriel with him to the office, at least for now. Meanwhile, he has some work to catch up on. Ramona called him from her home three times yesterday evening. Despite all the pressures, he's taking Gabriel out for breakfast when he wakes up. We didn't hear a peep from his bedroom all night, so we hope he slept. Cooper moved from Melissa's bed to his, curled up beside him, and kept him company. Jake was in two minds and eventually slept outside Melissa's door.

My hands are full today with matters of a different kind.

The first stop is Roxi's barn. I arrive later than I hoped even though I got up earlier than usual to do the barn chores.

As I step into the shedrow, I almost turn around. I must be in the wrong barn. But I recognize the old beaten-up metal feed buckets hanging on the rail. Otherwise, the place is immaculate. The shedrow is raked, clean bandages are rolled, dirty saddle pads are in a tub, and clean ones are hung over the rail. There's no garbage on the floor.

There's only one person I know who could perform such a miracle and I go searching for her.

"Meg," Roxi says as I pass a stall.

"Roxi, what are you doing here?"

"It's broken, well, I suppose that's obvious," she says as she lifts her arm which is wrapped in a fresh white cast and supported by a blue sling. She winces. "But I'm fine otherwise and I'm not damn well sitting at home when there's work to do. I can do quite a lot with one arm."

"You're made of strong stuff."

"I expect you're looking for the miracle worker."

"Linda, yes."

"She got here about 4.30 this morning and hasn't stopped until two minutes ago when I told her she should take a break and then go back to her barn. She still has all her regular work to do."

"I expect Neal has arranged some extra help."

"She also whipped my small team into shape. I've never seen them scurry around so fast. Quite funny really."

"We need to talk. Let's go somewhere you can sit down."

* * *

We find a small, rickety table and two plastic chairs in a corner of the cafeteria.

"How are you feeling?" I ask.

"Better than I thought. There's life in the old gal yet."

"Who beat you up and why?"

"I don't know who."

"I think you have a good idea."

"Perhaps."

"You know why?"

She sips some coffee from a shaking polystyrene cup. "Who are you working for and what do you want?"

"You think I'm working for Elsa."

"I do. She made a point of telling me. And said you'd prove she's innocent and that I'm a horse abuser."

"Innocent of what?"

"You must know that story by now."

"Enlighten me."

"She's not innocent. And that's why she's suspended. That action isn't taken lightly."

"Tell me about it."

"I want to know who you're working for first."

"Elsa asked me for help. She said she was in danger. But I'm not working for her. If I'm working for anyone it's Noah Pestel. He's a person of interest in the murder of Barnaby Caldermat."

"Oh, god, that slimy excuse for a human being."

"Barnaby?"

"Yes, him. He's ruined me."

"How?"

"I'm going home for a rest and coming back later." The swelling around her eye is much the same as it was and her face looks as if it could do with some moisturizer. The wrinkles crinkling her cheeks tell the story of many years of hard work and a lot of it outside in the elements.

"Good idea. When can we continue our chat?"

"Come to my house in about an hour. It's a dump. And bring me some lunch. I don't care what."

*　*　*

Linda's back in Neal's barn looking after the horses with her special tender loving care. She tells me again that the video of Roxi must

58

be fake, and Elsa couldn't have buzzed Shooting Stars. Linda says they are both liars, but she would have helped out anyway. The horses must be cared for whatever the humans are up to. I agree with her.

Linda's so busy I can't chat with her for long, so I don't know her reasons for believing the video is hokum and that Elsa didn't use an electrical device in the race. Linda's so passionate about horse welfare that she wouldn't come to these conclusions lightly.

Kelly gets a short walk along a trail near the track, then we pick up lunch and drive to Roxi's farm.

I double-check that I've arrived at the right place. Unless I entered the wrong property number into the GPS, or the incorrect concession road, I'm at Roxi's farm. The long driveway looks as if it has a disease. Water-filled potholes pepper the way up to the house. Some of them are perilously deep, which I don't find out until my truck bounces in and out of them. Scrubby, spikey, buckthorn bushes have invaded the front of the property. The dense tangle of twisted black branches speckled with small green buds darkens the entrance, and it seems sinister, almost menacing.

After the bumpy ride, Kelly's glad to get out of the truck. I let her have her freedom because I can't see any signs of other animals on the farm.

The house is disappointing. It's old but without character. It has dirty white siding and peeling brown paint on the window frames. The storm door has lost its screen and the concrete step has crumbled to half its original size.

I knock on the door and hear a yell from somewhere inside to come in. I shout back to ask if it's okay for Kelly to be with me. The storm door creaks as if it's not been opened for several years, and Kelly hesitates. I take off my shoes just as Roxi yells again, this time to tell me to keep my shoes on. The floor is gritty. Not liking the sensation on my feet, I slip my shoes back on. The kitchen is at the end of a short, dark passage. I find a couple of chipped but clean plates to put the lunch on.

"I'm in here," Roxi shouts.

Her voice comes from a room leading off the passage. It's in semi-darkness, although there's enough light seeping through the closed drapes to show up the threadbare patches on the area rug. A dull, yellow glow surrounds a lamp which stands by Roxi's armchair. A couple of flies dance around it and fling themselves at the shade now and then.

Roxi rests her cast on the arm of the chair as I put the plate on her lap.

"Thanks," she says. "I like your dog. I've always wanted a border collie. Couldn't cope with my crazy work schedule. I'm either not at home or exhausted most of the time."

"Kelly's special." I sit on a low sofa that sinks even lower under my weight. It's probably a good thing I can't see the grimy upholstery, but I can smell the musty dust I've disturbed.

"Before we get into the video, can you tell me what you know about Barnaby Caldermat?"

"He's the reason I live in this hell hole. I own a nice farm. I worked darn hard for years on end to own that place and now I have to rent it out so I can keep going." She moves her arm a little and winces. "Damn flies."

My eyes adjust to the lack of light enough for me to see her long, fine, white hair which hangs straight to just below her shoulders. Her face is almost the same colour as her hair, except for her right cheek that's tinged with yellow from the lamp. The light isn't bright enough to show up the effects of the beating, except for her swollen eye.

"Tell me about Barnaby."

"I had some good horses in the day," she says. She bites into the sandwich which is proving hard to manage with one hand. "Then I had a run of bad luck. Injuries, mostly."

"It's a difficult business."

"It's a shitty business, but it's all I know."

"Where does Barnaby come in?"

"It started with that conniving bitch, his wife, Zoey."

"Oh."

"That damn video is worse. I want to talk about that. Have you looked at it? I mean have you studied it?"

"Why?"

"No, you haven't. If you look at it carefully, you'll see that the stall is not at the track. It must be at a farm somewhere. It's sure as hell not here. I've got a run-down barn that's about to collapse. Not safe for horses. I can show you."

"I've seen the video and it does look like you."

"It might look like me, but it's not me. It's blurry. It could be anyone. They could have staged it with someone wearing similar clothes and a wig. It wouldn't be that difficult."

"I'll have a closer look. What are the VRA officials doing about it?"

"I wrote to them. I don't know. If I lose my licence, I lose everything."

"Elsa admits to taking the video and posting it on social media. Why would she do that?"

"You know, I'm sure you do. She rode Shooting Stars to a win. I was excited but I wanted to check the horse was okay. He doesn't usually close like that. I walked over to them as Elsa rode him towards the Winner's Circle. When I was about two horse lengths away, I saw it lying on the track. So, I picked it up. I was furious. I was so angry I thought I'd throw up right there."

"It was an electrical device or machine, right?"

"It's called lots of things. Yeah, it's a device designed to give the horse a shock. No horse deserves that. And it's cheating. I don't cheat. I never have and never will."

"Did you confront Elsa?"

"No point in that. And I was too angry. I might have hit her right off the horse. I reported it to the stewards and handed them the device after taking a photo of it just as insurance."

"I can understand you being mad at her."

"I have a temper, as everyone knows. And you're now going to ask why I use her to ride my horses. It's because she's a decent rider—she's a jockey which many of the exercise riders aren't. There's a shortage of riders and she communicates what she feels when she's on the horse. I like that. But I don't trust her anymore."

"Let's move on to Barnaby."

"Isn't that your phone ringing? I've heard it twice."

"It probably isn't important, but I'll check." One call from Melissa and one from Neal. Uh oh, the horses. "I think I'd better call back. It could be about one of my horses."

"Hope not," Roxi says. She takes another large bite of her sandwich.

Melissa sounds as if she's trying to catch her breath when she answers.

"Meg, oh, it's awful."

"Are the horses okay?"

"Yes. But Elsa isn't. It's all over social media that she's been found dead in her flat. The rumour is that Roxi did it."

"What are the police reporting?"

"I don't know. Can you find out what happened?"

"Roxi, I have to go."

I'm not about to repeat this shattering rumour to Roxi. It could be inaccurate. I hope it is. So, Kelly and I step out of the house and are almost blinded by the sunshine. My eyes take a couple of minutes to focus properly, and I don't like what I see. My tires are flat. All four of them. As we get closer to the truck, Kelly picks up a scent that leads to tracks made in the driveway which hasn't seen new gravel in many years. The heavy pattern left by tires with a deep tread must belong to a large SUV or pickup.

My tires appear to have had holes drilled into them.

"Roxi?" I call, as I re-enter the house.

"I'm still here. What's up?"

"Where's your truck?"

"The old guy from the next-door farm borrowed it. His truck got stuck in the back field and he had to get feed."

"Someone's drilled holes in my tires."

Despite her arm and obvious exhaustion, she almost leaps to her feet and follows me outside. Kelly's still sniffing around.

"No one around here has tires like these monsters," Roxi says, as she peers at the tracks. "Who would want to do this to you?" She stares at the flat tires.

"Or you. We don't know if the person was targeting you or me. There's only one vehicle here."

"I can't take any more of this shit." She strides back into the house. I make some calls, take some photos, and wait outside. Roxi needs time to cool off. I regret suggesting she may have been the intended target. Anyone could have followed me here—anyone who doesn't want me digging up the truth about Barnaby or Elsa, or even about Roxi's video.

6

Burned

My hands tremble as I sit at the kitchen table. Kelly is next to me and presses against my legs. It's as if she feels my angst. She probably knows better than I do why this wave of apprehension has engulfed me. It doesn't want to come to the surface of my consciousness, but I must let it break through and face it head-on.

Will I be able to rise to the occasion and take at least some responsibility for looking after an angel, an innocent? My role model, my mother, was on the opposite end of the spectrum of empathy and compassion than I wish to be. Her lack of protection of me and her abandonment of Melissa are clearly not good parenting qualities. Animals are easy to care for. Their unconditional love means you're forgiven if you mess up, and their resilience means if you make mistakes they can handle it, most of the time.

"What's the matter?" Melissa asks, as she walks through the backdoor and dumps a couple of bags on the floor. Jake appears out of nowhere and wags his fat, black tail with such vigour I can feel a breeze. Kelly stays sitting by me. Cooper must be asleep on Gabriel's bed.

"Just thinking," I say.

"I hope you're going to find out who killed Elsa. The gossip is it was Roxi."

"She has a broken arm."

"But we don't know how Elsa was murdered. Might have been possible for someone with one arm."

"But Roxi can't drive right now. One of her staff drove her to the farm. And a neighbour borrowed her truck."

"Where there's a will, there's a way."

"Mm. And someone drilled holes into all four of my tires."

"Where? Here? That's serious. Are you okay?"

"I'm fine, honestly. It seems a stupid thing to do when the victim doesn't know who they are or why they did it. And to confuse matters, it happened at Roxi's place. They may have thought it was Roxi's truck."

"Doubt it. She doesn't have wheels. She must have lied about the neighbour borrowing her truck. Her barn staff always drive her. If I know this, then the person who wrecked your tires would also know. It's obvious—they wanted to get at you. Like what always happens when you start digging stuff up. Make sure Kelly and Jake stay safe. What do kids eat?"

"I have no idea. You'd know better than me."

"It makes life more complicated when you have to prepare meals on time that are nutritious and something he'll eat. I bought groceries, but who knows?"

"I haven't even thought about food."

"I knew you wouldn't. Growing boys need food." She flicks her long blond hair over her shoulders and unpacks the bags.

"Thanks, Melissa."

"It'll be okay. The three of us can do it. We make a good team."

William and Gabriel burst into the kitchen as if chased by a fiery dragon out of one of Gabriel's many new books. William's mouth looks as if it's been turned upside down.

"And what's the matter with you?" asks Melissa. She hugs Gabriel but keeps her eyes on William. Kelly and Jake get pats from Gabriel as they wag their tails and smile with their shiny eyes. But tears are glistening on Gabriel's cheeks.

"Why are you crying?" I ask Gabriel. He runs upstairs to his room with Jake close on his heels.

"Let him be," William says, as Melissa makes a move to follow. "I need a coffee." He walks towards the counter.

"I'll make some," Melissa says. "I think I'm the only capable one at the moment."

The room darkens as the early evening sun vanishes behind a bank of clouds. The gloom reflects the sombre mood that surrounds us.

"You look upset," I say, as William pulls out a chair.

"I am. Gabriel is too, which makes it even worse."

"It takes a lot to rattle you, William," Melissa says. She smiles, but her attempt to lighten the mood doesn't work.

"A man from that disreputable church called at the office today. Gabriel was in the room next to mine, so he heard everything the man said. He and his wife have no children, but they always knew God intended them to have at least one. According to them, when they found out about Elizabeth's illness, they approached her, and she agreed they could take care of Gabriel. They said they prayed with Elizabeth, and they received God's blessing."

"Do they have anything in writing?" I ask.

"Yes. This is a copy." William hands me a crumpled-up piece of paper. "It's on Church letterhead." I unfold it and flatten it out on the table.

"Oh, the house and all Elizabeth's assets go to this couple," I say. "That's suspicious."

"It's obviously not what's stated in the will Elizabeth drew up while I was there, and we had witnessed, and is on file with our office."

"What does her will state?"

"The proceeds from the house and so on are to be kept in trust until Gabriel's eighteen. Elizabeth confided in me that her belief was shaken. It wasn't strong enough, she confessed, to withstand the premature death of her husband, her terminal cancer, and the fact that her child would be left without either parent when he was only seven. No child deserves to be orphaned."

"Poor Elizabeth," I say.

"Yes," William says.

"So," Melissa says, as she hands a mug of coffee to William and a mug of tea to me, "I guess you reckon that piece of paper's fake."

"It is, but that couple are zealots and are adamant that Gabriel should remain in the fold of the Holy Waters Church of the Faithful. And that God has sent this as a test. It's a test of the faith of the virtuous, or something equally preposterous. They say they have the whole congregation behind them."

"But," I say, "it's really about the money. It shouldn't be that difficult to prove this is a scam."

"Perhaps," William says. "But in the meantime, it means emotional stress and disruption and time wasted. And, most troublesome, adds to the insecurity that Gabriel is already feeling. It's a reprehensible thing to do to a child."

"Which proves the point that it's all about the money and not about a concern for Gabriel," I say.

* * *

Roxi calls about five minutes after I get up. The birds aren't even awake and the sun's a distant misty glow peeking through the trees. She says she's been awake all night because she couldn't stop thinking about the attack. She knows the tires couldn't have been flattened by Elsa. And now she doesn't believe Elsa was the one who beat her up. She's convinced her attacker was a man, even though security found one of Elsa's riding gloves in the storage container. Roxi can't think of anyone who'd want to hurt her.

"What if it was someone trying to frame Elsa?" I ask. "It seems that somebody doesn't want her around. But leaving the glove didn't result in action. At least, it didn't appear to. I think I would have heard if Elsa had been questioned. And I bet Elsa would have contacted me if she had been. So, it could be that the person who wanted Elsa out of the way didn't succeed and resorted to more extreme measures."

"What do you mean?" Roxi hasn't heard the rumour.

"Elsa's missing."

"That doesn't surprise me. It's happened before. And it's madness to think anyone, other than me right now, wants Elsa gone. Anyway, I'm at the track and must run. Good luck in the Connex Stakes. I hope that blasted cheat doesn't win, you know, Cliff."

"Thanks." The attack on Roxi probably has nothing to do with Elsa. Roxi could have been targeted for a reason she's not willing to share with me.

By the time Kelly and I get back into the kitchen after having completed the barn chores, the house is empty except for Cooper. William takes Gabriel and Jake wherever he goes. He says that Jake is like a therapy dog for Gabriel, but I rather think the dog's helping them both. Gabriel and Cooper are best buddies which surprises me. I underestimated Cooper's ability to give affection and faithful companionship, and Gabriel's tenderness towards the cat is such that it makes Jake jealous.

Cooper doesn't bother to stay in the kitchen with Kelly and me. His favourite person left, so he's off to find a warm and comfortable place for a nap.

It was a pointless exercise, but I reported my flattened tires to the police and sent photos. They said they plan to visit the scene but warned me that, even if they could spare the resources, they'd be unlikely to find evidence leading to the perpetrators. But that's the least of my concerns. The biggest question is who would murder Elsa? Just as I begin to organize my thoughts, Noah calls.

His voice is high-pitched, almost whiny, as he asks me who would kill Elsa and why. He catches his breath and asks if he can come to the farm and talk. I tell him he'll have to meet me somewhere else because it isn't convenient for him to come here. A young boy shouldn't hear the sort of conversation I anticipate we're going to have—and I don't know when Gabriel and William will return.

Noah and I arrange to meet on a bench outside the racetrack with a view of the horses being exercised. It's one of the several seats along a new trail that follows most of the fence encircling Vannersville Racetrack, and the section where we'll meet runs beside the training track.

He's early and his leg is bouncing so much that I wonder how he manages to hold his cup of coffee. Kelly and I can see him from about a quarter of a mile away. I park the truck, with its brand-new tires, at the opposite end of the trail so that Kelly and I will have a pleasant walk. Walking usually helps me to think things through, but I have little success this morning.

Scattered sparrows are perched throughout the chain-link fence, chirping. They don't react as a horse gallops by on the sandy training track a few yards away, puffing through its nostrils in rhythm with its footfall. I soak in the comforting sounds for a couple of minutes before we reach the bench.

Kelly ignores Noah and sits beside me. I sip my lukewarm tea.

"Noah, you want to talk."

"It's about Elsa. It's like I'm living in some kind of sick horror movie." He runs his hand through his shiny ginger hair and looks at me with a deep frown.

"You told me she wasn't your girlfriend."

"The police think she was. They've already had me in for questioning."

"Well, was she?"

"What does it matter?"

"It matters to the police. Why are you so cagey about it? Was she, or wasn't she? If you want my help, you must cooperate."

"I saw her a few times, but it didn't work out. She was seeing someone else, and I told her I didn't like it."

"Any idea who it was?"

"I don't want to talk about it. I'm freaking out because the police are harassing me. Once the police decide you're guilty, you're a goner. They can plant evidence, they can force you to confess, and other stuff. They want to prove I'm guilty of both murders. It makes them look good if they can say they've caught the guy." He leans his elbows on his knees and looks at the gravel under the bench.

"They haven't charged you. You wouldn't be sitting here."

"But they're going to. They just have to set it up, make it happen, so they can."

"Have you found a new lawyer?"

"Your guy, William, gave me a couple of names. I'm meeting with one of them this afternoon."

"That's good."

"But a lawyer isn't an investigator. I need someone to get these cops off my back. A lawyer is just someone who'll be there in court after I've been arrested. I don't want to be arrested in the first place."

"You don't seem upset by Elsa's death."

"I'm not. I told you. She's a pathological liar."

"What makes you say that? Aren't you also a liar? You said she wasn't your girlfriend, but you've just admitted you saw her a few times. You're not telling me everything. I can't help you if you keep secrets. It's up to you."

"I thought you were in cozy with the police and could get me cleared—that they listen to you. But I bet you're in their pockets because you're not using that influence to help me. I bet they pay you to help them get their man and, I see it now, you're working with them to help get me arrested. And William's given me names of corrupt lawyers—ones cozy with the cops. Just because I'm not stinking rich anymore, people think they can take advantage. Go to hell." He chucks his half-full coffee cup over the fence and jogs off.

That was a nonsensical outburst I didn't see coming. Kelly gazes up at me with her big, brown eyes. I imagine her saying 'I told you so', as I put my cup in the garbage bin and stand up.

"You don't like him, do you?" I ask as we walk back the way we came. Another horse canters along the track and we stop to watch for a couple of seconds. Melissa's face pops up on my mobile. She's ordering Lego for Gabriel and wants to know my opinion on which one of three sets she should get. I haven't a clue. What does a little boy who's lost everything he knows, want? Love. Security.

Kelly leans against me as if she can sense the tremors of doubt. The fear of inadequacy and ineptness ripples through me. I'm not parenting material and won't be able to give Gabriel what he needs.

My shivery thumbs suggest the Lego set which has some animals in it. Just because.

Our next stop is Roxi. I want to know why she said that Zoey is a conniving bitch. Those are strong words. I didn't get a chance to follow up when I was at her farm.

"I see you got new tires," Roxi says, as she leads a horse back into his stall from the wash pad with shiny clean hooves.

"How's your arm?"

"Not as painful but bloody annoying."

"Still think it was Elsa that beat you to a pulp? Because I don't. She's a petite woman, a jockey. There's no way."

"I can't deal with Elsa's disappearance on top of everything else. It's too much."

"Roxi, we need to talk."

"I can't right now." She sniffs and as she leaves the stall, she abruptly turns away from me. I follow as she shuffles along the shedrow. "Linda helped again this morning, but I told her not to come anymore. I can't afford to pay her. I don't want any more charity and I'm getting better at doing things one-handed".

"When can we talk, then?"

"Look, I've got work to do. Come to the farm at about three. I'll take a break then." Her voice is trembling. She must be exhausted.

"I'll be there."

"Park your truck behind the house."

She continues to walk away from me. I don't know where her staff are. I can't see anyone.

Kelly stays hidden behind the front seats of the pickup as I leave Roxi and stride towards barn fourteen.

The third person I ask tells me Zoey's having a smoke in her truck which is parked on the other side of the barn.

Zoey beckons me to join her and rolls down the passenger window. Bluish cough-inducing smoke wafts out of the door as I open it. Zoey's smart appearance, athletic build, and soft complexion don't mesh with the cigarette-puffing habit. But sitting next to her in the confinement of her truck gives me a closer view of her face when she turns to talk to me. There are distinct furrows between her brows and premature vertical wrinkles lining her cheeks.

"You're here to ask me more about Barnaby, right?" Her smile isn't reflected in her cool blue eyes.

"And to find out more about Barnaby's horses."

"I'll start with that, then." She flicks cigarette ash as she extends her arm out of the window. The smoke is nauseating, but I don't want to miss this opportunity. "Barnaby was living the high life when we met. I'd just got my trainer's licence. I was pretty proud of that. My dad was an owner and breeder of thoroughbreds, as well as a successful businessman. He took me to the races and the backstretch whenever he could. I loved it all. His passion for this crazy world rubbed off on me to the extent that I dreamt of being a trainer. I don't suppose you want to hear all that stuff. Anyway, I was introduced to Barnaby by an owner I'd worked with when I was an assistant trainer. I needed more horses to make up a viable training operation, so I agreed to meet with Barnaby. He wanted desperately to be a racehorse owner. He didn't have a farm and knew diddly-squat about horses, but that doesn't stop you from being a racehorse owner, does it?" She turns to me and raises one eyebrow. I shake my head and hold back a sneeze. "Before you ask, he bought horses and claimed horses, without any advice. As soon as I said I'd be his trainer, he was off like a racehorse bursting out of the starting gate. Nuts. But what do I do? I marry him and take on thirty-one horses, most of which were of poor pedigree and had mediocre prospects. That's how my nightmare started."

"So, it didn't go well?"

"What, our marriage or training his horses? The answer is both were disasters." She throws her head back and blows out a cloud of smoke. I turn towards the open window and breathe in. "He blamed me for everything. Everything. He got desperate. I didn't know he was involved in an illegal gambling ring that was failing. Not back then. I do now. It explains some of his off-the-charts behaviour. Doesn't excuse it, but at least there's a reason. Because he went mental. He wanted me to use drugs on the horses. He needed wins. Money, money, money, was all I heard about."

"Did you use performance enhancers?"

"No. Are you kidding me? I love horses. I couldn't do that to them. Not even with what Barnaby put me through. No way."

"What did he put you through exactly?"

"That'll have to be another chat. I've got to go. I've got too much to do."

"Just tell me how Roxi came into the picture."

"I truly haven't got time, but I will say she's a good person. Crazy, like most of us, and with a fiery temper, but she's not an abuser."

Kelly sneezes as soon as I get settled in the truck, so I open the windows halfway. After a brief walk on the trail by the training track, past the bench where Noah and I sat earlier, we drive to Roxi's farm.

Nothing's changed. I don't know why I expected anything to look different. The same tangled branches, the same bumpy ride up the driveway, the same dingy house. But we don't have to go inside. Roxi's sitting on an old plastic chair by a round rusty patio table, just outside the backdoor. She points to another plastic chair that has traces of lichen and perhaps moss on it. I wonder how long it's been around. I'm not sure of its original colour. She has a pot of coffee and two mugs. I decline the offer and sit down on the cool, rickety chair that wobbles on cracked, uneven flagstones. Kelly lies on the emerging weeds, with her head between her paws.

"You didn't have the opportunity to explain what you said about Zoey when I was here last," I say. I move my chair a little to make it more stable. It's not much better.

"I called her a conniving bitch."

"Something like that."

"It's the Connex Stakes race tomorrow. What about security for Ginger Victor?" Her eyes are both bloodshot, not just the one that was hurt when she was beaten.

"Neal told me that he's hired a reliable company to keep a careful watch over Hector. We've had issues with security before, so he's being more diligent this time."

"That's good."

"Are you asking for any particular reason?"

"I hear stuff. Most of the time it's nonsense."

"What have you heard?" It seems that she's reluctant to talk about Zoey or Elsa. She must regret inviting me to visit.

"That someone doesn't want your horse to race."

"That's not unusual when you have a good prospect in a high-level race. Hence the extra security that many trainers use in the same circumstances, as I expect you do."

"Mm." She takes a gulp of coffee. "But it's more than that."

"Tell me what's being said and whether you think it's true or not."

"The little birds at the track are saying Cliff Ryman, you know, the jockey on the big favourite, doesn't want you or your horse near that race."

"Sounds like it's not just about the horse then."

"Just watch your back."

We both turn our heads—surprised by sudden cracking sounds. They stop, but there's someone in dark clothes crouched down in the spiky buckthorn. Perhaps it's just a neighbour and his clothes are stuck on the thorns. But Kelly turns towards the noise and growls. She senses danger and her hackles are up. I grab her collar because I see flames. It's as if the man's hand is on fire.

He runs, hood shielding most of his face, and throws whatever it is, with its flames, into my truck as he dashes past. I wish I hadn't left the window down.

Deafening explosion.

Fire and shrapnel.

Kelly yelps.

I hit the soft, damp ground.

Roxi screams.

Heat. Putrid smells. Brilliant flames spreading. Grit in my mouth.

Relief that Kelly is pressed against my side, breathing. Her teeth are chattering. I place my arm over her but stay lying on the ground.

Where's Roxi? I can't lift my head to look.

My mobile has fallen from the table onto the ground just in front of me. But I can't reach it. The ground sways. For the second time today, I'm nauseated—but this is more intense. The heat is unbearable, but I can't move. Kelly and I are stuck to the weedy patch as if it's Velcro.

How long have I been here before there are sirens? Sirens. From two directions.

*   *   *

"Meg, are you okay?" William asks. How did I get into this cold, white room?

"Kelly! Is she alright?"

"She's here. I brought her. She's okay. I put her therapy vest on and carried her in here—I knew she wanted to be with you. Don't tell anyone, but I nicked a blanket and she's lying on it beside your bed."

"Kelly, oh, Kelly."

William lifts her, including the blanket, and puts her on the bed as I shuffle over to make room.

"Whatever you've poked your noses into this time has smoked out some particularly nasty characters." William holds my cool hand in his warm one as I stroke Kelly's silky head with the other. "Kelly's okay. But she's shaken up. And you have bruising. You have some mild burns on your right arm. That's why you have those bandages. The doctor told me you need rest and lots of fluids. And he prescribed antibiotics. From what the police tell me about the scene, you're lucky to be alive, let alone in one piece."

"If Kelly hadn't growled, I would have moved towards the person. It looked like his hand was on fire. But what about Roxi? I heard her scream."

"Roxi who? I haven't heard anyone mention her."

"That's where it happened. At the farm she rents. She's a trainer at the track who got beaten up by someone. She trains Barnaby Caldermat's horses, you know, the racehorse gambler who was murdered. I'm investigating his murder, Roxi's beating, Elsa's murder, and now this explosion."

"Do you mean Elsa Lorenza? A jockey?"

"Yes. She's missing and assumed dead, but I've not told Roxi that because I think they've been close."

"She's missing and what I've heard is the police are not treating it as a homicide. The reports in the papers were inaccurate. A small quantity of blood was found on the floor of her apartment and the first responders on the scene jumped to the conclusion that she was murdered, but no body has been found. I knew you'd be asked by someone to follow up on that one, so I asked some questions, in between all the garbage I've been dealing with because of those zealots from the Holy Waters Church of the Faithful."

"How is Gabriel?"

"When I left him at the farm, he was building a Lego set with Melissa. He's never played with Lego before. I'm not sure he's been permitted to play with anything. I can't contemplate what my sister was thinking." William purses his lips and slowly shakes his head.

"Oh, William."

"I'm worried about you, too. I can see it in your eyes. You're afraid of the prospect of looking after a child. You don't think you can do it."

"I'm not made of the right stuff. The role models I had nearly destroyed me. I've nothing positive to go on."

"You won't be doing it on your own. We're a team. And I include Kelly, Jake, and Cooper, as well as Melissa. We're in this together." He sighs and holds my hand with both of his. "I'm doing what I vowed I wouldn't. I'm putting pressure on you. The trouble is I can't think of any alternative. Gabriel needs us." He looks at me with his dark, watery eyes just the way Kelly does when she wants me to show her how much I love her.

"William."

"I can't live without you, Meg. If you don't wish to take on this responsibility with me, and I admit it is an audacious request, I will understand and respect your decision."

"You sound like a silly lawyer." I smile but that doesn't stop the salty tears running down my cool cheeks.

"I suppose that's what I am." He sits up.

"William, of course we must take care of Gabriel. It's just that I'm scared. I don't want to damage his life as my mother scarred mine. And thinking about my stepfather makes me want to wretch."

"You're you. You're not your mother. You're the woman I love who has compassion and empathy, who cares about animals perhaps a bit more than people, but that's okay with me." He winks. "The three of us can give Gabriel the love and security he needs. And the three animals will help, and probably the horses will in some way as well. I am confident that we'll give him a wonderful home full of warmth, tenderness, support, and forgiveness. None of we three have been nurtured by loving families, but our experiences with various forms of dysfunctional family life have taught us a lot. We know what not to do and what would have helped us to flourish and develop into well-adjusted people."

"Instead of the three shipwrecks we are, you mean?"

"Meg! I'm being serious."

"Well, I can't take any more of this," I say as I adjust the scratchy, white sheets. He leans back with a frown. "I can't handle you wearing your emotions on your sleeve. I'll be making Kelly wet with my tears if you don't shut up." I'm relieved to see him smile. "What about school? Shouldn't Gabriel be going to school?"

"Yes, for sure." His frown has disappeared. His eyes are brighter. He sits upright. "I've managed to get him registered at the school near us and he starts in a couple of days. He's terrified, but he's been assigned a volunteer grandmother for at least the first week. I think that's a brilliant idea."

"Good."

"So, you have a murder to solve, two missing persons to find, and a beating to investigate. And, I almost forgot, an explosion."

7

Shock

Neal trots towards me. His face is grey, and his mouth is turned down, aging him about ten years.

"I'm okay, Neal. Honestly," I say.

"Well, you don't look it. Shouldn't you be resting? I'm glad Melissa let me know you were home from the hospital. Rumour has it that you and Kelly were blown to pieces."

"We're fine. But another truck has bitten the dust. I'm sure my insurance premiums will go up tenfold. Have you heard anything about Roxi?"

"No. One of her staff came over first thing this morning and asked for help. They can't find her."

"You must know the explosion happened at Roxi's place?"

"I didn't know. So, are you saying Roxi was there when your truck blew up but wasn't around afterwards?"

"That's right."

"Odd."

We turn towards Hector's stall.

"I don't want to disturb him before the race," I say.

"He's pretty chilled at the moment. But he's picked up on the cues and knows he's going to run."

"I'd rather not see him. I'm so jittery—he's bound to sense it."

"I'm going to have my office door open so I can keep an extra pair of eyes on who's coming and going. As you know, I've good reason to not have complete faith in security guards. Are William and Melissa here?"

"No. Neither of them can make it. Edwin has an emergency at his clinic, so Melissa's working. And William has an important case and's in court this afternoon. He hopes to come later."

"It's a nice, cool day for racing."

"Have you heard anything recently about Cliff Ryman? He's still on the favourite, I assume?"

"Yep. I haven't heard any more. According to the handicappers, Hector's the only one in the field with a chance of beating him."

* * *

Neal and I stand by the racetrack and lean on the rail. The Connex Stakes race is the first to run on the turf this season, and the surface could be yielding. I'm not sure if Hector will mind if his feet dig into the soft ground, or if he doesn't care what condition the surface is in.

I check William's camera again. Even though it's digital, it's large and too obvious, but I need to be able to zoom in. I'm determined to capture close-up videos and photos of Cliff Ryman. I want to know how he cheats, assuming he does. But it may be nothing to do with how he rides, it could be that he dopes the horses, or rigs the races in some other way. Perhaps someone pays other jockeys to hold their horses back or something else I can't think of right now. I hide the camera under the jacket that's draped over my hand and arm.

My photography work means I'll not be able to follow Hector's progress in his race. I'll only be able to hear the track announcer. I'll watch it later.

As Hector appears on the track, his chestnut coat is so shiny it reflects the sunlight and appears almost iridescent. The cool breeze ruffles his short mane and long tail. He's in high spirits and is almost dancing on his toes. He wants to gallop.

Cliff Ryman's on a powerful-looking horse that's almost black. The jockey and horse look confident and relaxed. We watch all the stunning horses trot past us as the names of the horse, trainer, owner, and jockey are announced during the post parade. Hector stays under Jaden's control with the help of the pony and his rider at his side. But Cliff and his mount leave his pony behind and canter off.

A heavy silence hangs between Neal and me. The hum of the track buzzes around us as we wait for the horses to be loaded, one by one, into the starting gate that's the furthest distance from us it can be. One horse rears up and has to be backed out. Fortunately, the horse must be okay because the veterinarian hasn't scratched him from the race, and he's reloaded into the gate without incident. The jockey and gate personnel are okay too. I look through the zoom lens of the camera to check on what affect this commotion has had on Hector. Focusing under the gate I see his feet dancing around a little.

At last, they're off.

I can't follow what Hector is doing as I take a video of Cliff. But I register some of what the announcer is saying. Cliff is letting his horse relax behind the three front-runners who are just about level with one another. The announcer reams off the order of the horses and Hector is in the middle of the pack, behind Cliff but making up ground. Hector appears in my view as he gallops past Cliff's horse and joins the front-runners. There are now four horses in front of

Cliff. I don't have a clear view of Cliff for a few seconds as one of the horses loses his momentum and fades—falling back along the rail as Cliff keeps his horse going at a steady pace.

Hector must be one of the three front-runners and just as I'm tempted to scan the camera towards him, the order of the race is announced again. Hector is in second place. They enter the final turn.

Cliff doesn't change his whip from his right hand to his left at the top of the stretch. He's held the whip in the same hand for the whole race. I can see Hector, still in second place, as Cliff hits his horse with the whip and gets a good response. My hands are shaking, partly from the effort of keeping this large camera focused on Cliff, and partly because I may have at least some evidence of jiggery-pokery. I brace myself on the rail so that I can steady the camera. This could be the most crucial time to get good, clear photos.

My camera angle allows me to see Cliff cross the finish line closely followed by the number six horse and then Hector. I keep my camera focused on Cliff. After galloping out for about a furlong, he turns his horse around and trots back towards the grandstand. As the groom and trainer greet him, he throws his whip up in the air in triumph. But I keep my lens focused on his other hand—his left. He slips this gloved hand into the top of his riding pants for a little over a second. I'm pretty sure I know why.

I put the camera in the large bag I've brought with me and stuff my jacket on top of it.

"There's an inquiry," Neal says.

"Why?" I missed the incident.

"Jaden claims Hector was bumped by the number six horse before the first turn. I couldn't see it from here, but we'll watch the replay and it'll show the early part of the race from the front."

We walk onto the track to greet Hector and Jaden. Hector's nostrils are flared and he's breathing heavily, but he's not exhausted. The jockey whisks the saddle away so he can be weighed and get ready for his next ride. Neal walks with him to hear what Jaden has to report about the race.

Hector tosses his head and rubs against Linda as she sprays him with a fine mist from one of the hoses at the side of the track. I hold the lead-rein while she throws a thin blanket on him.

"Thanks, Linda. You do such an excellent job. He looked great out there and did so well."

"He should have won."

"Well, I know you'll treat him like a champion, so he'll think he won anyway."

"That's not the point. I don't like cheats." She and the horse turn and walk back to the barn. Why can't people play fair? Greed, I suppose. And, as Zoey said, it's about money, image, status, and pride. I wonder if the owners know their horse won by cheating.

As Neal and I walk back to the grandstand he asks me if I captured what I wanted on film.

"I'm not sure I have enough proof, but I've enough to raise suspicions. I'll have to study the footage."

"I thought it was classic. Cliff hit his mount with the whip just as he was coming home, and I thought the horse reacted too suddenly, just as if it was a surprise, which the whip wouldn't be."

"I suppose the horses are used to a few strikes with the whip when they're heading for the finish line."

"And whips have been improved. They have a softer end, are cushioned, and there are strict rules on how they're to be used. No one wants to see wounds or welts from the use of the whip. In any case, some horses back off if they're beaten. The crop should be used to urge them on, to encourage them. Otherwise, it can be counterproductive."

"What about an electrical device?"

"As I've said before, I'm not sure it's cruel. But the shock surprises the horse, and some react strongly to the stimulus, just like

Cliff's mount seemed to—if that's what he used. And they win races when they shouldn't. It's cheating, plain and simple. I bet Cliff put a lot of money on his horse."

"Here's the replay," I say. We watch in silence for several seconds. "Wow, Hector sure got bumped. He very nearly hit the number eight horse. It set him back. I can see that."

"They're replaying another part of the race. Look, the number six horse bumps Hector again on the far turn. You'd almost think it was deliberate, but perhaps he's just a difficult horse to handle."

"But he shouldn't be allowed to race if he's a danger on the track."

"Agreed. And look, they've disqualified him. That was a quick decision."

"Hector's second then. That's great! And to think he was brave enough to keep running and not back off when he was bumped. He must have lots of confidence."

"He's been training well, and this means he placed in a big stakes race."

"Thanks, Neal. This is great."

"You're welcome. It's a pleasure. But I'm not happy he's second to a cheat. He deserved the win."

*　　*　　*

We've all had a long day. Gabriel is asleep in his bed with Cooper. William tells me he had a trial day at school with the volunteer grandmother. According to the teacher, it went better than expected. He showed interest and was able to focus on work which are good signs. However, the teacher mentioned that he didn't utter one word the whole day.

"William," I say, "I assumed Gabriel just didn't want to talk to me, for some reason. Does he talk to you and Melissa?"

"No. But I know he can talk because I've heard him say a few words to Kelly, Jake, and Cooper. And he talked before Elizabeth left."

"Should we get help for him or something?"

"Let's give him some time. We know he can talk. I think it'll work out. However, it won't be resolved if I can't get that church off the case. They've gone to the media. There's an online article and it's been picked up by some other media, such as vannersvillenews. com. They're not only willing to fight this in a court of law, they're fighting it in the court of public opinion."

"Surely, they won't get anywhere?"

"Read it. They've done a significant amount of research into my past and not only my estrangement from Elizabeth. They have a surprising amount of information on my struggle with drugs, embellished somewhat. They've made it sound as if I had nefarious dealings with those businesses, you know, the ones that hired John Nelson to follow and intimidate Frank. They even suggest I had something to do with Frank's murder"

"You've got to be kidding. That's preposterous. Isn't it libel?"

"Yes. So, in order to protect my reputation and my career, I must hire a top-notch lawyer and take them to court. This is not something I want to do right now, or at any time for that matter."

"What about attack?"

"I don't know. Anyway, what about the camera? Did you get some good video?"

"Where did I put it? I can't remember bringing the bag into the house. I'll check the truck." Kelly and Jake dash out of the door with me as if they're sure there's something that should be chased off. I check that the horses are okay in the barn and go back to the truck I rented today. It's the biggest one I've ever had.

No bag.

My heart beats faster as I try to recall where I had it last. I remember putting it down on the track when I held Hector as Linda threw a thin blanket on him. But I don't recall picking it up.

The three of us trot back to the house and I text Linda.

She replies right away and says she doesn't remember a bag at all.

"Did you have anything else in the bag?" William asks.

"Just my jacket. And there was nothing in the pockets. But the videos and photos I took! That's so frustrating. I'm angry with myself." I slump down onto a kitchen chair. Kelly nudges my arm with her head, and I fondle her ear.

"Perhaps the jockey saw something?" William suggests.

"I'll text him."

Jaden calls almost immediately.

"Hey, Meg."

"Jaden. Thanks for calling. Did you see the bag I had? I seem to have lost it. I had the camera in there with the video and photos I took. I put it down when Linda hosed Hector."

"Oh, geez. Had to run. Didn't see anything. But check this out. I'll send you the link. It's on my YouTube channel. Could be helpful."

"Thanks. And I should have asked you before. Can you tell me what you know about Cliff?"

"Now, that's a big ask."

"Oh."

"It's okay. Sure. Not on the phone or by email. Has to be a private meeting."

We arrange to meet tomorrow at Neal's barn, after the workouts. I point out to Jaden, in case he's apprehensive about being seen with me, that it would be expected for me to chat with him about the race afterwards. And he's okay with Neal being there.

"Where's Melissa?" I ask as I accept a steaming mug of tea from William.

"She went to bed at the same time as Gabriel. She said she was exhausted."

"I hope she's okay."

"I think so. It sounded like Jaden didn't have anything helpful to say about the camera."

"He didn't. He's sent me a link. I suppose I should check it out, but I can't see how it's going to help." I click on the link and sit up.

"Something useful?"

"He wore a Jockey Cam during the race. You never know. He may have captured something."

The video is wonky at first as the horses come out of the gate, but that's probably caused by Hector's sudden surge as the race starts. Then he veers to one side—I suppose that was the first bump. As the race unfolds, we watch Hector's large ears bouncing up and down and the white rear-ends of four jockeys up out of their saddles. Three of them are in a row at the front and Cliff is behind them, all four are in front of Jaden. I feel a bit seasick as I watch all the ears and behinds bobbing. We lose Cliff as Hector passes his horse. But can I see something in his hand? I'm not sure. It's a bit blurry. Then another wonky bit of video. That must have been the second bump as they entered the far turn. Later, the head of another horse appears, presumably as Jaden moves to see how he's placed as they leave the final turn. The video is now of Hector's ears and the green stretch ahead. He's up with the front runners. Hector was second at that point in the race. And then a horse appears to charge up on the outside. That's Cliff with his whip still in his right hand, but Hector is on his left-hand side. I'm still not certain but I think I see something sticking out of his glove. The movement of the horses makes it hard to tell.

Jaden must have made a deliberate attempt to capture Cliff after the race because he turns Hector around at the same time Cliff turns his horse, and trots alongside Cliff on their way back to the grandstand. The video captures Cliff throwing his whip in the air as his gloved left hand slips into the top of his riding pants. Then it goes back to the start of the race.

"You said Hector was bumped?" asks William.

"The bumps were clear in the replay and almost looked deliberate. At least the second bump did. Both bumps were caused by the same horse, and I guess that's why the video went wonky a couple of times."

"Are you going to have someone analyze this footage for you?"

"I'm going to try to do it myself. It'll have to wait until tomorrow, though. Then I'll see Bill Price. He'll know what the next steps should be."

"Bill Price is a steward, right?"

"Yep."

"By the way, I had time to connect with a couple of my contacts today and there are some interesting findings relating to Barnaby Caldermat's murder. Would you rather I told you tomorrow since you've had such a fun-filled day?"

"You know the answer. Stop teasing. But let's take a glass of wine into the family room. I wouldn't mind putting my feet up for a bit."

"I'll pour."

Kelly and Jake follow me and lie down on either side of the recliner. My eyelids want to close as a sudden wave of dizzy dreaminess comes over me. I must be very tired. I haven't had any rest since my truck blew up and I got injured. The burns are healing well, though.

"What you found out had better be good," I say as I accept a glass of red wine. "I'm liable to fall asleep at any moment."

"I guarantee this is not sleep-inducing information." William smiles and his eyes twinkle. I sense he has some dramatic news. "Minute traces of blood were found on two large kitchen knives kept in a block on the counter in his home. Yes, the blood matches Barnaby Caldermat's. And their shapes match the stab wounds."

"Why two knives?"

"Good question. However, what's really interesting is that he was already dead when he was stabbed. The coroner's preliminary findings are that Barnaby had a lethal mix of alcohol and barbiturate in his system. The big question being asked is: did he commit suicide, or did someone administer the barbiturate to him, and if so, how?"

"Did he leave a note?"

"I think that's part of the puzzle. No note."

"He died in the morning, right?"

"The time of death is based on someone's statement," William says. "They say he was alive early that morning."

"That's probably Olivia Matterson, his partner. I wonder if it's the truth."

"I see. Why?"

"I talked to Munro, you know, Dr. Milton at the hospital."

"And?"

"I asked him if he knew anything about Olivia. He said she's been confrontational with the medical staff to the point that the Chief of Staff wrote a letter to the board. The official line is that she's on vacation for two weeks while they look into specific allegations of harassment and intimidation. Munro said that these allegations involve administrative support staff as well as the medical staff. So, I'm wondering when these two weeks started. Perhaps she wasn't at work when she said she was."

"I expect you can find out." William smiles.

"I've asked Munro and he says he'll unearth what he can. So, if Barnaby was murdered, who gave him the barbiturate?"

8

Over The Edge

Soaked to the skin, I sit in the kitchen and text Neal. Kelly and Jake are both lying under the table having had the worst of the rain rubbed off with old towels. As I was leading the horses out of the barn this morning, Jake took off into the back field despite the downpour, and Kelly, much to my surprise, followed. She usually takes every precaution to stay dry. The horses were smarter. They went straight over to the run-in shed.

The smell of wet dogs is too strong for Cooper. He's disappeared. The odour closest to my nose is from my rain-sodden clothes—it's almost stronger than the stench from the dogs. I'm chilled and looking forward to a warm shower, but I kept thinking of Roxi when I was cleaning out the stalls. I text Neal.

He replies that Linda is over at Roxi's barn again this morning. So, Linda must be back there despite Roxi claiming she's managing with one arm. He adds that Roxi hasn't shown up, it's a mess, and the extra work is stretching Linda beyond human limits. No wonder Neal is irritated.

I leave the dogs to steam up the kitchen and go upstairs to get ready to drive out to Roxi's place.

By the time we're all in the truck, we smell a lot better. I can't spend long at Roxi's because I've agreed to meet with Jaden in Neal's office this morning.

Having parked the truck behind the house, I let the dogs out. I don't see a vehicle. Have I ever seen a vehicle here? Melissa must be right—Roxi doesn't have one. The back door is ajar, so I push it open and call Roxi's name. I tell the dogs to stay outside. They both sit by the crumbled doorstep in a misty drizzle. I hope I won't be long.

"Roxi?" The lamp is on in the living room, but it's still so dingy in here I can't tell if she's around. After scanning the room, I decide she isn't, and go to the stairs. The light from the open backdoor shows the frayed stair carpet with its loose threads—easy to get snagged on. It's impossible to know what colour the carpet had been when it was laid.

There are two bedrooms. The bathroom must be downstairs. The first bedroom has a decrepit, sagging bed covered in horse paraphernalia and other miscellany. I don't bother to take it all in.

Roxi is in the second bedroom. The drapes are closed but are so thin I can see she's propped up on a pillow in bed. Her white hair is matted and there's no cast on her arm.

"Roxi, are you hurt from the explosion? How are you?" There's no sign of food or drink. "Have you eaten?"

"Go away." She turns her head towards the window so I can't see her face. Dead flies are scattered on the dark wooden floor beneath the narrow sill.

"I'll get you some water."

"I don't want anything. Go away."

"You need help. What about your horses and your staff?"

"I don't care."

"What about your arm?"

"It's fine. Go away."

"I'm not going to leave until you have some help."

"I don't want help."

"You're going to get it whether you like it or not." She grunts. The trouble is, I don't know what to do. "I'm going to get you a drink."

I walk, with caution, down the stairs and look around the kitchen at the dirty surfaces, gritty floor, and grimy window. I turn on the light. The illumination makes the place look worse, but it helps me to find a kettle and a mug, and a jar of instant coffee. I rinse the mug and dry it while the kettle comes to a boil. There's nothing in the fridge that looks as if it's not growing something, so she'll get black coffee.

As I mull over the condition Roxi's in, I risk her wrath and call for an ambulance.

Not being sure of the safety of her well water, I don't add cold water to the coffee but pour the mug's contents into another cold, rinsed mug, and walk back upstairs.

She doesn't register my entrance.

"Roxi, I've made some coffee. Why don't you try it?"

"Why don't you go to hell! You interfering bitch. I don't want you here. Go away!" She yells obscenities at me and hits the mug with her fist. The coffee sloshes over my pants and shoes. While hot, it doesn't scald me.

The dogs scramble up the stairs and almost skid to a stop when they reach the bedroom. They must have thought I was in danger. Jake barks but Kelly slinks around the bed towards Roxi's face and sits, just looking at her. I don't do anything. I can't imagine Roxi would hurt her.

The bed shakes. Roxi is sobbing. A trembling hand reaches out and pats Kelly's head. I can't find any tissues. Kelly sits there for several minutes while Roxi talks to her and pets her until the para-medics arrive.

I'm concerned about what reaction they'll incite from Roxi, but she doesn't yell and acquiesces without complaint. She's too weak to stand so they use a gurney. I stand in the unrelenting drizzle and watch them pull away hoping I've done the right thing.

"Kelly, you're a hero again. I love you so much." I squat down to hug Kelly, and Jake nudges me. "You're a good boy too." I fondle his soft ears.

* * *

Wet for the second time this morning and smelling of coffee, I'm glad to have a quick shower and put on dry, warm clothes. We pile into the truck again and once we arrive at the track, I park in the lot by the security office since I'm not sure I can rely on Jake to keep a low profile in the backstretch. Kelly is a pro at staying quiet as she lies behind the front seats, but Jake is liable to bark.

The misty drizzle persists but I'm dressed appropriately. I plan to avoid getting wet. Jaden didn't seem to mind the delay—it's about half an hour later than we originally agreed to meet.

Neal's leading a horse in the shedrow and they're coming towards me. Neal's face is flushed, and his mouth is a straight line.

"Can't stop. Short-handed."

He must be filling in as a hotwalker and I sense stress. I make a note to check in on Roxi's barn after meeting with Jaden.

"Hi, Jaden."

"Hey." He's leaning against the doorjamb. We go into Neal's office and sit down.

"Thanks for riding Hector so well."

"Yeah, well, he's a good horse. He gave me an honest ride. But being beaten by a cheat feels bad."

"We all feel rotten about it. Thanks for the link to your Jockey Cam video. I'm sure it'll be helpful. I'm going to look at it more carefully."

"Yeah, well, good." He crosses his short legs and folds his arms.

"Jaden, tell me what you know about Cliff."

"I don't rat on my mates, but I don't consider him one of the mates."

"I'll be using any information you give me for my own purposes and won't be telling anyone how I obtained it. Your name will stay out of it."

"That's good, 'cause he's sure good at retaliation."

"So, what's he like?'

"Winning's everything to all of us, right? But Cliff's a bad loser. He's worse than anyone I know. He's so competitive. The rest of us are pals even though we race against each other."

"Have you seen how he cheats?"

"We jocks think he uses a machine. You know, an electrical device. That's why I tried to stay with him on the way back to the grandstand. I thought I might get it on video."

"You might have. As I said, I'll be checking it out more closely. Why do you think he does it? Is it money?"

"It's money, the share of the purse he gets when he wins, but it's also the glory. He loves it. And he gloats over us. You know, he's smug. He's pumped up like a bloody peacock spreading his feathers out. Showing off. We can't stand it when he comes back into the jocks' room from the Winner's Circle."

"What do you know about his personal life?"

"Yeah, well, you probably know more than me. He beat up his girlfriend. And he got into a fight in a bar. Those things hit the papers. He got off. But the track suspended him for a while. Come to think of it, I think that was 'cause he hit a horse or something. We jocks don't want the likes of him around. He gives us guys a bad name. We don't like cheats or abusers."

"Does he have a girlfriend now?"

"Don't know. He had something going on with Elsa Lorenza. The one that they thought was murdered. You must have heard about that?"

"Yes."

"They reckon she's missing and not murdered. I don't know. She used a machine, like Cliff. Roxi reported her."

"I know. She took a video of Roxi apparently abusing a horse."

"Yeah, well. That's a fake, isn't it? I feel sorry for Roxi. She works hard but she's had a ton of bad luck. That Barnaby guy stuck it to her. And then she caught Elsa, and that video was put out there. Then she got beat up."

"Any ideas on who beat her up?"

"It wouldn't be Elsa, would it?"

"Why do you say that?"

"It's too obvious and Elsa's so small. Roxi's older, but she's feisty. Elsa's not a bad person, not like Cliff."

"So, you think Cliff beat her up?"

"I don't know. I don't think he'd do that. He wants to be the top jockey so bad. If he was found out he'd lose his licence. And why would he want to beat up the old lady? What for?"

Jaden has to leave. He's late for a meeting with his agent. I ask him to let me know if he thinks of anything else and thank him again for the video. He shakes my hand and says how grateful he was for the opportunity to ride Hector. His hand feels curiously small but strong. Jockeys need to be super fit but must keep their weight low. It's not easy. As if he's read my mind, he says, "Cliff has a problem with keeping his weight down. Many of us do. But he really struggles. I've heard he uses the sauna a lot. A couple of the jocks say he's bulimic. He's got issues."

"Well, it's a tough job being a jockey, isn't it?"

"Sure is. You got to be disciplined—have a good fitness routine and a strict diet. I don't mind. I love riding so much that it don't matter to me."

"You've been a great help."

Neal is walking a different horse and looks even more frustrated.

"Can I do something?" I ask. Neal walks the horse out to a patch of wet grass in front of the barn so that he can graze for a while.

"You can do something about Roxi and her horses. We can't run both operations, especially when no one's paying the bills." The horse decides the blades of grass nearer to the road are tastier, so the three of us move. Neal has the horse on a lead-rein.

"Roxi is in hospital."

"I'm sorry to hear that, but there are horses to look after and we can't do it anymore, not without money to pay staff."

"Her staff aren't being paid?"

"No. And at least two of them have moved to other barns. You can't expect them to work for nothing however much they love the horses. They've got their families to think of."

"I'll talk to the staff, and I'll see if I can talk to Roxi. She's not doing well."

After I've visited each of my five horses and given Hector a couple of extra mints, I walk over to Roxi's barn, hoping that Kelly and Jake are okay.

"Meg, this is a mess," Linda says. She sounds breathless and sweat drips off her face creating a dark patch on her t-shirt.

"I'm not sure what I can do about it. Roxi's in hospital and seems to be in a bad state."

"She shouldn't be a trainer then."

"Part of the problem, I'm sure, is Barnaby Caldermat didn't pay his bills."

"What about his estate?"

"What with owning so many horses and his failing gambling venture, I don't think there'll be much left."

"There should be rules about who can own horses."

"There are some."

"But they don't have to prove they have enough money."

"Do you have any ideas?"

"Me?"

"Yes."

"Zoey used to be the trainer and she's the widow, isn't she? She should do something."

"Can I do anything for you?"

"Get someone to take care of these horses."

Zoey's in her office talking to a jockey, with the door open. I keep my distance and watch for him to leave.

"Meg, right?" she asks once he's left. "I didn't expect to see you. I thought you'd been badly burned in some kind of explosion. Are you okay?"

"I'm fine. The rumours are greatly exaggerated." I smile, but she averts her gaze. "Zoey, I was hoping you've a few minutes to chat about a couple of things."

"Sure. Not for long, though."

"Thanks." She beckons me in. Her office is small, as they nearly all are, but it's well organized with a desk and small fridge, coffee maker, and whiteboard, as well as a couple of padded metal chairs. It's cleaner and tidier than most trainer's offices I've been in. There's a horsey odour mixed with the aroma of coffee and the unpleasant smell of stale cigarettes.

"Last time we chatted, you mentioned Barnaby put you through a lot."

"He sure did."

"Was it about money?"

"And pride and ego. And greed. I didn't know about his illegal gambling business until recently—when it went sour. He had a Mercedes-Benz dealership, so I assumed that's where he got his wealth. He loved expensive clothes, fancy wine, and flashy cars of course."

"So, how did his lifestyle affect you?"

"It wasn't so much his lifestyle as his personality."

"In what way?"

"The only person who mattered was Barnaby. He could be charming but underneath that façade was a man who wanted control. He didn't have an ounce of compassion or empathy in his body. It was all about his success, power, and mostly wealth."

"You're still not telling me how this affected you."

"You get the condensed version. He was a wife beater." She turns her face away and stares at the whiteboard which has horses' names listed with a time of day noted by each one.

"I'm sorry to hear that. Did you report him to the police?"

"No. I thought it would just make matters worse." She turns her pale face towards me. Her mouth is a colourless, hard line and her long, fine fingers are tightly curled. "I thought I could change him. Honestly. I thought I could draw out some tenderness and empathy by encouraging his involvement with the horses. I believed it would make a difference. They are such incredible animals, and they can have an enormous influence on troubled people. Look at Roxi, for example. But it didn't work with Barnaby. He wasn't interested in the animals, only how this game could get him on a pedestal and make him money." An enormous sigh shudders through her.

"What do you mean about Roxi?"

"Well, you must know she's a mixed-up woman?"

"I don't know much about her."

"I'm not telling any tales out of school when I say she suffers from bouts of depression. We all know that. But for quite some time her work with the horses kept her going until Barnaby sent her off the rails. And added to that, Roxi found out Elsa's a cheat, then she was beaten up, and then there was that explosion at her place. Wow, no wonder she went over the edge again. I hear she's in hospital."

"Why didn't you warn her about Barnaby being such a scoundrel?"

"She came to me hungering for some horses. She'd lost a good owner—I don't know why. I'd finally left Barnaby despite his threats and attempts to intimidate me. Actually, it was my dad who alerted me to Barnaby's gambling fiasco. He was worried I'd lose everything because of Barnaby. He never liked him. But it was already too late. So, when Roxi showed up I was looking for someone, anyone, to take Barnaby's racehorses. He hadn't paid me for a couple of months, and he didn't care a hoot about the horses. Roxi's suffered more than I did because she's not had a penny out of him, as far as I know. I heard Barnaby gave her a minority share of the ownership in exchange for free training for several months, which would have made it worse. She's only managed to get one or two claimed. Most of them need to find new careers as riding horses. Everyone would be better off. Another thing, Barnaby blamed everyone else for his failures. So, he was mad at me, furious with Roxi, and livid with Olivia."

"Why Olivia?"

"Because she wouldn't give him any more money, despite being knocked about by him."

"So, how are you managing financially?"

"My dad came to the rescue. I hate that he had to help me. Part of my reason for marrying Barnaby, to be frank, was so I'd never have to worry if my racing results went into a slump. The irony is I was doing well as a trainer until I let Barnaby into my life. He ruined everything for me. And the trouble is, Dad warned me. He said he was no good. He thought he was smarmy and fake and not to be trusted. He never did like car salesmen though." She smiles, but it's more like a grimace. She unclenches her fingers and lays her hands flat on the desk. "I made a big mistake getting involved with Barnaby. But I'm getting back on my feet now."

"He sounds like an all-round unpleasant character, prone to violence. I wonder how come anyone invested in his gambling scheme?"

"As I told you, he can put on the charm. I was seduced by his grace and, I'm ashamed to admit, his flashy lifestyle."

"What about Barnaby's will? What do you know about it?"

"I've seen it. Thomas gets the Mercedes-Benz dealership and I get the house and the remainder. But Barnaby had bought shares in a pharmaceutical company that launched a new painkiller called Bandroxamide, or something like that, but it's killed a couple of people, so it's been banned by Health Canada even though it was originally approved, and I think there's a class action suit. He lost a large investment and had to pay back a big loan. He asked my dad for help—and that was after I'd left him—so he was desperate. That's how Dad knew. His gambling thing was already falling apart. By the way, why Olivia moved in with him after I left is something I'll never understand. He must have told her a pack of lies."

"Do you know Olivia?"

"She's a good friend. That's how Barnaby met her. She came to the house at least once a week for a chat and a glass of wine. When I left, I suppose Barnaby went after her. He thought she had money. But she doesn't. She works hard though, and gets a good salary from the hospital, so maybe Barnaby thought her income would ensure he wouldn't starve. I don't know, really. I tried to warn Olivia, but she fell for his put-on charms I guess, just like I did."

"Roxi's horses are in urgent need of a trainer."

"Oh no, you won't see me getting involved in that one."

"Do you have advice? She may not be around for a while and the bills aren't being paid, and it sounds as if Barnaby's estate has no funds to pay his debts, so what happens to the horses?"

"How many are there?"

"About thirty, I think."

"Are they all owned by Roxi and Barnaby, or are there other owners?"

"I don't think so."

"If there are other owners, they can move their horses to other trainers, but I suppose that won't help with the outstanding bills. You'll have to talk to Roxi about the ones she co-owns."

*   *   *

Kelly and Jake need a run and a drink, so I drive straight home. I walk around the back field as they dash from one fascinating scent to another. While I can't appreciate the odours to the same extent the dogs do, I enjoy the vibrant colours of the glistening green grass and the dandelions' sunny faces refreshed after the rain. A bright red male cardinal flies across my path and a red-bellied woodpecker hammers at one of the trees at the edge of the field.

It was tempting to divulge to Zoey what William found out about Barnaby's death. But I don't think that information should come from me. And William has only been told about the provisional, verbal reports, and probably off the record. There's nothing official yet, as far as I know. I'd like to follow up on Barnaby's murder, but Roxi's horses are much more of a concern at the moment, including the toll their needs are taking on Neal and his team. Especially Linda.

Back in the kitchen, I wonder if the dogs can tolerate another hour trapped in the truck, when Melissa arrives.

"Melissa, are you going to be around for a bit?"

"I'm not going anywhere. I'm tired. It's been a long day. Edwin had several ultrasounds to do and there's a skin disease going around. So, we've been busy."

"I'd like to leave Jake here, but I'll take Kelly because I plan to visit Roxi in the hospital. I have quite a few questions to ask her. I don't know if she'll be willing or able to answer them, but I'm going to try."

"Good luck. I'm having a hot shower. See you later."

"William's picking Gabriel up from school, right?"

"As far as I know. I think he's taking Gabriel back to the office because he has a client meeting."

9

Missing

As I pull into the hospital parking lot my mobile rings. I'm surprised to see Detective Sandra Valeska's name.

"Hello, Meg?"

"Hello, Detective Valeska."

"I need your help. Noah Pestel is missing. We haven't been able to trace him. We want to bring him in for questioning again."

"He was in the process of selling his condo. He's probably moved."

"We're aware of that. What concerns us is that the blood on the carpet in Elsa's flat has been analyzed and is a match for Noah."

"Oh." I wasn't expecting this.

"As you can imagine, there are various possible scenarios."

Detective Valeska explains that her boss believes Noah was living with Elsa. They were partners. But the guilt Noah felt as a result of murdering Barnaby Caldermat and beating up Roxi was too much, and he attempted suicide. Since there's no body, her boss is convinced that Elsa must have stopped him in time, and now he's on the run.

"I have clear instructions to find him asap. I thought you might have seen him or have some ideas."

"I can't believe that Noah beat Roxi up. I can't think of a motive."

"Anger. Our intel is that Barnaby's horses weren't making money. She's the trainer."

"They weren't and aren't. But Noah wouldn't have benefited if they had. Barnaby was taking everything. He was greedy. And I expect you know Barnaby owed a substantial amount to a failed venture in a new drug called something like Bandroxamide?"

"I was informed of that yesterday. Do you have anything on Noah that might help us locate him?"

"I'm not sure he's guilty of Barnaby's murder."

"My boss believes Noah is guilty. He wants him off the streets and has told me it'll give Vannersville Police Services' image a much-needed boost when they catch this murderer. You haven't answered my question."

"I don't have information on where Noah is."

"You'll let me know?"

"I will."

She says to call her any day. If I prefer, I can call when she's at home, usually after eight in the evening. I read into this that she doesn't agree with her boss and that she'll be freer to be frank with me about her own theories. Detective Valeska has asked for my assistance in the past. She's told me she believes in engaging with the community and sees it as a win-win arrangement.

The memory of my last meeting with Noah darts into my mind and leaves little space for other thoughts. I can remember some of the words he used. He said he was freaking out because the police were harassing him. He was sure they were on a mission to prove his guilt. He also said he thought I was cozy with the police, and they'd listen to me and get him cleared. And he was obviously angry and embittered about losing his wealth and believed he was at an unexpected disadvantage because of the change in his financial circumstances. Now I wish I'd done more to help him.

I'm facing a more complex puzzle with lots of pieces I can't put together. Is his disappearance connected to Barnaby's murder? And why is his blood on Elsa's carpet? The attempted suicide theory doesn't work for me.

What about Roxi? Is her beating linked to the murder and the disappearance? And what about my tires and burned-out truck?

And where is Elsa?

Kelly is eager to enter the hospital and wears her therapy vest with pride. She receives so much attention from both staff and patients in this place that I fear she's not good for productivity. But I'm certain she's a welcome distraction and it gives me pleasure to see so many pairs of eyes light up when she's visiting. No one would notice if I had two heads, which is fine with me.

Roxi is sitting in a chair with her hands clasped in her lap as she stares out of a grimy window at treetops losing their colour in the waning light. The fluorescent brightness in the room makes her hair appear whiter and her face more lined. Her arm looks awkward in its splint. Her elbow sticks out over the hard arm of the chair.

"Hi, Roxi. It's Meg. I've brought Kelly to visit you."

Kelly puts her head on Roxi's lap. Roxi strokes her silky ears with her unencumbered hand. She looks frail and must be quite a bit older than I realized.

"That's nice." She keeps her eyes focused on Kelly.

"Roxi, you need to be straight with me. You're holding back."

"I don't know what you mean." But her hand wavers over Kelly's head for a split second.

"You know exactly what I mean. Let's start at the beginning. The electrical device you picked up. Tell me more."

"I'm not well. I don't want to talk about it. I'll call the nurse."

"I reckon you'd feel better if you shared what's really bothering you, what's gnawing away at your heart. I think it's something very significant."

"No one can help me."

"You can help yourself, but only if you face the truth and do something about it."

"I can't."

"Let me guess then, and you correct me when I go wrong." She stops patting Kelly, but my beloved dog doesn't move away. She keeps her big brown eyes focused on Roxi's face. I move my plastic chair a little closer so that I can talk with a quieter voice. At least she hasn't insisted I leave. "Elsa is related to you."

She turns her head towards me. "How did you guess?"

"There has to be more to what's going on between you. Is she your daughter?'

"Granddaughter."

"I can see it would have been very upsetting to you when you saw that electrical device on the track after the race."

She places her hand on Kelly's head.

"It must have been even more distressing for you when you saw the fake video."

She doesn't answer but hangs her head. Her fine white hair drapes over Kelly's muzzle as her chin sinks onto her chest.

"I believed you when you said you don't cheat. So, not only were you very disappointed in your granddaughter, you were ashamed the horse won because Elsa cheated." Roxi doesn't say anything. So far, I must be right.

"But what makes this so difficult is that Elsa cheated because she wanted to help you. She knew Barnaby wasn't paying his bills and the horses were doing poorly. She wanted you to be grateful, not angry. The fact that you lashed out at her and not only that, you reported her to the VRA, made her furious. I think she has a similar fiery temperament to yours. So, she produced a fake video of you abusing a horse. She thought it would be believed because it's well known that you have an anger management issue. I'm right, so far, aren't I?" It's as if she's been frozen, along with Kelly. "Perhaps she didn't think through the consequences." No response.

"Roxi, would you like a cup of tea? I'll leave Kelly to keep you company."

She lifts her head as if in slow motion, hesitates, looks at Kelly, and says, "coffee would be better. Regular." Her voice is gravelly.

"Be right back. Kelly, stay." Roxi needs time to contemplate—to decide whether to trust me with her story.

It doesn't take long for me to pick up the drinks and get a croissant for Roxi. They look and smell fresh.

"Roxi, are you ready to talk to me?"

She sips her coffee. The croissant is in the drawer of her bedside cabinet. She says she'd rather eat it after we've left.

"I'm not sure I've got the strength." She glances at me with small, piercing eyes.

"Tell me about Barnaby, to start."

"Zoey sent him packing, in my direction." She mumbles into her lap, but I can hear her. "But she wasn't honest with me. She didn't tell me he doesn't pay his bills and the horses were poor performers. Yes, I should've done my research. I could've found out. But I took her at face value. She seemed nice enough. Chatty. Looks after her horses. Has a neat and tidy barn. I'm angry at myself, but I blame her too."

"So, things get harder to manage. Did you confront Barnaby?"

"He's, he was, impossible to get hold of. He had no interest in the horses. He only wanted to be around if one was likely to win. I only met him once."

"And you couldn't sell the horses or even give them away because Barnaby was the majority owner?"

"I've been stuck with them. I love horses, but I have to live. I must pay for feed, bedding, staff, vets, farriers, exercise riders, wormers, supplies—the list is so long. I owe a lot of people a ton of money and I see no way out."

"Elsa saw things were going badly and tried to help."

"She made matters worse by cheating."

"With the electrical device."

"Not just that."

"Oh. What else?"

"Drugs." She puts her hand over her mouth and looks at me. Telling me this has literally left a bad taste in her mouth—her face is scrunched up as if she's eaten a lemon.

"Performance enhancers? How did she manage that?'

"I don't know." She puts her hand on Kelly's head again. My wonderful dog must be providing Roxi with some comfort. "I caught her with a syringe in her hand."

"She's missing and you're worried about her, aren't you?"

She coughs, picks up her cup, and splutters on a sip of coffee. She puts the drink down on the bedside cabinet and sits up as she takes a deep breath. "She's got mixed up with some bad characters, and it's all because I got myself in such trouble. I sure regret taking on Barnaby's horses, but I regret even more that I turned that electrical device into the VRA—stupid thing to do when Elsa was trying to help. I should've talked to her, but I was as mad as hell. I'm seeing the whole damn mess more clearly now and I don't have the energy to be angry anymore."

"What about the syringe?"

"That horse she was with was vet scratched because he came up lame later that day. I don't know if she drugged any of the other horses. None of them have had a positive test—only a few have been tested, as it happens. But there are drugs out there that can't be detected, so I'm told. The short answer is I don't know what Elsa's been doing."

"Do you know where Elsa got the drugs from?" I drop my empty cup into the small stainless steel garbage bin.

"I suspect." She slouches and pats Kelly's head. "I only suspect. I have no proof. Dr. Berzinski. He's the only dishonourable one I've heard about."

"A veterinarian. Who told you about him?"

"One of the grooms who works for your trainer Neal, told me to watch out for him. She heard a rumour that he sells supplements claiming they improve fitness and are legal, but they're really PEDs. She thinks innocent trainers could be caught out and don't realize their risking their licences. And she wants the bad apples to know she's onto them."

"Why didn't she report Dr. Berzinski to the College or the VRA?"

"I asked. She said there's no evidence, just hearsay. Linda's a good horsewoman. She's always looking out for the horses. She's the one that saved the day when I was beaten up."

"She's the groom for my horses. She's an incredible woman. Roxi, who beat you up? I'm sure you know." Silence. Her hand trembles as she strokes one of Kelly's silky ears. Kelly has hardly moved an inch while we've been talking. "I'll find out anyway. You might as well tell me."

She turns to me with an imploring look in her eyes and doesn't blink as she speaks. "Can you find Elsa? I'm worried about her, and it's my fault. My anger took over, but she was trying to help. I can't bear this feeling of guilt." She holds her head in her hands, albeit awkwardly because of the splint. I can't tell if she's crying.

"I'll do what I can. And I'll try to get Barnaby's horses out of your barn somehow."

She turns her face to look at me again and this time her eyes are a little brighter. "That would be such a huge relief." She sits up. "But you have to promise they won't go to Quebec to be slaughtered."

"I wouldn't even consider that as an option."

Kelly and I leave the morose and guilt-laden woman and visit a couple more patients on our way out.

Just as I'm about to leave the hospital I remember I want to know if Noah is, or has been, a patient here. I'm sure Detective Valeska has checked, but I want to confirm for myself.

I go searching for Dr. Milton. After asking three people, I'm told I'll probably find him on the third floor. As we exit the elevator, I catch sight of him walking towards us from the end of the long, brightly lit corridor.

"Well, hello Kelly," Dr. Milton says. "What brings you here?" He rubs her ears, and she wags her tail.

"I was hoping you could give me some information," I say.

"Let's go into this case conference room. We'll be able to talk here. He pushes open a door which happens to be beside us. A large round table and six chairs sit in the centre of the small, square room. A whiteboard with nothing on it and a couple of pictures of flowers that don't inspire me, hang on the walls.

"You can call me Munro, you know." His large dark-rimmed glasses magnify his green eyes. They make me feel as if he can see into my brain. If so, it would be a disappointment.

"Thanks for taking the time."

"No problem. I remember you asked me if Olivia was at work on the day that Barnaby Caldermat was murdered."

"Yes."

"She was not. It was one of the vacation days I mentioned to you. She's back now, but things are tense. I'm willing to wager she won't be around much longer. The board is no doubt consulting with lawyers to determine the size of the package to offer in exchange for her resignation. It'll be a package that would match anything she'd get by going to court if they fired her for cause. Oh, I forgot, you know all about that hiring and firing stuff."

"That's good information. So, she could have been at home. Thanks. I have another question. How can I find out if Noah Pestel was treated here in the emergency department?"

"Give me a moment." He retrieves his smart phone from his top pocket. Kelly lies down and I rack my brain to think of anything else I should ask him while I'm here.

"No. He's not been here."

"Thanks. Another quick question. Barnaby, Olivia's partner, died of a lethal mix of alcohol and a barbiturate. Obviously, that means he could have committed suicide. But he was also stabbed after he was dead. The police are treating the case as a homicide for now at least. My question is, could someone have given him the barbiturate somehow?"

"That's an interesting twist. I didn't know about the barbiturate. Do you know if he suffered from epilepsy or cluster headaches?"

"I've not heard that."

"It's just that barbiturates aren't prescribed as much as they were in the past, except that phenobarbital is an excellent anticonvulsive medication and is used widely for that purpose and can be used to treat cluster headaches—migraines."

"He could have obtained the drugs illegally."

"Of course. He could have used them for sleeping. If his life was in the turmoil I'm guessing it was from the news I've read—his gambling business collapsing and his pharmaceutical venture imploding—he probably needed something to help him sleep. Now, to your question as to whether someone could have administered a large enough dose to kill him, the answer is yes. And, before you ask, yes, it can be injected. But it would be useful to know if he was prescribed a barbiturate and if there was any trace of the medication in the house."

"If not, then someone else most likely was involved."

"Someone who had access to barbiturates, probably phenobarbital, as I mentioned."

* * *

Kelly and I are glad to get home. We're late putting the horses in. As I pour the feed into Bullet's bucket raindrops start to thump on the barn's metal roof making it sound as if a tempest is unleashing its fury.

Jake runs out to greet us as we head back to the house. He licks Kelly's face and wags his thick black tail, but Kelly pays no attention. She's on a mission to get inside the house as speedily as possible. I am too. The wind has picked up and the rain is stinging my face. Even though I'm bent over and quickening my pace, I sense that Melissa is anxious. She stands with the door open, hugging herself.

"What's wrong?" I ask as I step onto the mat. Both dogs shake before I can grab the towels to rub them down. Fortunately, they're not soaked. The kitchen is spared a drenching.

"Oh, Meg. It's awful. William went to pick Gabriel up after school and he wasn't there."

"Where's William?"

"He's on his way to Merton. He thinks Gabriel was abducted by those loony church people. And he thinks they might be stupid enough to go to Elizabeth's house."

"Why would they do that?"

"Because, William said, they believe it's theirs. They're completely bonkers. William said he's done some research into them. He discovered they've been living in the church basement, for one thing. William's in a terrible state."

"We have to help him. Let's go." Melissa doesn't argue. "Did he notify the police?'

"I don't know."

"I think we should." One favour deserves another. I phone Detective Valeska. First, I confirm I'll look for Noah, and then I tell her about Gabriel as we clamber into the truck. Kelly doesn't look keen, which is unlike her. But we've already had a long day. And I was looking forward to a warm bath. It'll have to wait.

The rain lashes down as Melissa opens the gate. She smells of wet clothes and lemon when she gets back into the truck.

"I should've put my hood up. I've just washed my hair."

"Send a text to William to let him know we're on our way," I say. "I don't think we should surprise him."

"Okay."

I have the windshield wipers swishing backwards and forwards at top speed, but visibility is still hampered by the torrents of rain coming towards us. The road markings have mostly worn out over the winter months, which makes it harder to gauge where the middle or the sides of our country roads are.

It's a relief to hit the main highways.

"William hasn't responded," Melissa says, as she swipes strands of damp hair off her face. The smell of wet dog has overtaken her lemon scent.

"William mentioned earlier he's been in touch with the minister of the church," Melissa says, "and he was somewhat helpful."

"Perhaps we should connect with the minister and let him know what's happened."

"I'll try to track him down."

"But perhaps that's not a good idea. They may not have gone to Elizabeth's house. My guess is they'll be in the church basement. And perhaps the minister is harbouring them."

"Let's risk contacting the minister," Melissa says. "Whatever nutty church it is, surely he can't condone abducting a child? Stealing him from his uncle?"

"You're right."

We don't speak for what seems like an eternity as Melissa peers down at her phone and moves her thumbs frantically. Her face is lit up by the eerie glow emanating from the screen. Jake has given up on the potential for an exciting outing and lies down with Kelly on the floor behind the front seats.

Melissa looks up.

"Anything?" I ask.

"Not yet. I've got directions to the church, though."

"Good."

We find the road where the church is located. There's a car parked at the side of the building. I drive up beside it. I let the dogs out and we put their leashes on. The rain continues its relentless attack, and we're close to being soaked within a couple of minutes. Neither of our jackets is adequate for this deluge. The streetlight is reflected in the puddles, but it's almost ineffective. I'm sure there's a flashlight in the truck somewhere, but I can't remember where. So, we stumble into the water-filled potholes that are scattered throughout the parking lot and find a side door. Just as I'm about to try the handle, a car pulls in. It's not William's Jag.

A man, dressed in black raingear with a wide-brimmed hat, heaves himself out of the small car.

"I'm the minister here. What's going on?"

"Our nephew Gabriel has been abducted," I say. Actually, I have to shout. The wind is carrying my voice away.

"Elizabeth's son?" He holds onto his hat as the wind threatens to take it airborne.

"Yes. William Porter's sister's son. William is my partner." I can't see his face and can't read the tone of his voice. "Please let us in. We think he's being held in the basement."

"Oh dear." He rummages in his pocket and pulls out a key. It shines as the water hits it and the feeble light finds it. He fumbles with it and eventually unlocks the door. It's dark until the minister finds a switch to the right of the entrance. A flight of stairs leads from the small landing down to a paint-chipped door framed by light.

"You may be right," the minister says. "Oh dear. Oh dear." Now I can see his face, he looks as if he's about ninety. His lined, papery skin is bluish grey and his eyelids sag over his bloodshot eyes.

Melissa and I unleash the dogs and we all descend the stairs, with the minister several steps behind us.

I fling the door open.

They must have heard us coming. Melissa and I almost skid to a halt just inside the door. I tell the dogs to sit. The minister catches up and mumbles "Oh dear. Oh dear." We're all dripping water onto the floor and our hearts are thumping in our chests.

The man, I don't know his name, holds a small kitchen knife at Gabriel's throat. The woman leers at us as she stands at his side. Gabriel's teeth are chattering, and his watery eyes are full of terror— he stares at us without blinking. The minister grabs my arm to steady himself, lets go, and takes two erratic steps towards them.

"Percy, this is not what God wants you to do," the minister says in a shaky voice. His body sways. He collapses onto the floor in a wet, black, mound.

"Melissa, see if you can help him," I say. "Percy, it doesn't make sense to hurt the boy. Your plan depends on him being around. You want access to Elizabeth's money and house. This is what it's all about, isn't it?"

"We got a message from God. It's God's will," the woman says in a whiny voice that grates on my nerves.

"What's God's will? That you take Gabriel by force and keep him prisoner? It doesn't look like he wants to be with you." As if to prove the point, Gabriel wretches. I'm afraid the knife will hurt him as he tips his head forward. But as he throws up, Percy takes a step away and the knife is no longer at Gabriel's throat. "Go!" I say to the dogs. Kelly knows what I mean, and Jake follows her—just a split second behind. I rush after them. Gabriel runs towards me and almost knocks me flying. He hugs my legs and sobs.

"Melissa!" She's already by my side. "Take Gabriel to the truck."

"No." Gabriel says. He won't let go of me. He's holding on for dear life.

Kelly and Jake bark and snarl at Percy and his wife. The noise is intense as it reverberates off the breezeblock walls. The couple must be frightened of dogs because they're clutching onto one another and aren't making any attempt to move. I can't see the knife, but I don't want any of us to turn our backs on them. I'm wondering what to do to get out of the situation when loud, clomping footsteps come from the stairs, loud enough to be heard over the racket the dogs are making.

"I'll take it from here," a police officer says in a deep, authoritative voice. William is right behind him as they enter the room.

"William! I'm so relieved to see you." We wrap our arms around each other. Melissa joins us and we have a warm, but damp, group hug with Gabriel in the middle still holding onto my legs.

"You've been crying," William says to me.

"Have I?"

The minister has apparently regained consciousness and is sitting on a chair at the side of the room. My guess is that he was over his head with this couple and didn't know what to do about them. His problem has been solved. The police officer has handcuffed them, and they'll be charged with abduction, at the very least.

"I've called for an ambulance and for back-up," the police officer says. "The boy should be checked out, and it looks like that old man needs to see a doctor as well."

"No, I'm fine," the minister says, as he sways in the chair. "Oh dear. Oh dear."

"No doctor," Gabriel says, as he looks up at my face.

"No doctor," I say, as I choke on those silly tears. "We'll go home as soon as the back-up police officer comes. Then Kelly and Jake will be off duty." They're snarling at Percy and his wife, and the police officer seems fine with that. We tell him about the knife, and he says he'll retrieve it for evidence once he has support.

The minister leaves in the ambulance. I'm glad he'll be checked. This may be a nutty church, but he seems to be a decent human being.

* * *

Two more police officers have shown up and Percy and his wife are seated in the back of a police vehicle. We're glad to leave the basement with its fluorescent lights, cold floors, and peeling paint, as well as its strange characters.

As we walk across the parking lot avoiding the puddles, William tells us he explained the situation to the police officer as they stood outside Elizabeth's house for about fifteen minutes. He thought the couple would go there. Then William went inside the house to double-check they hadn't already arrived and hidden somewhere. But there was no sign of anyone having entered since he and Gabriel left. He checked his phone as he came out, and picked up three texts from Melissa, which prompted the two of them to drive to the church.

We're all scrambling into my truck because I told William to leave his car. He's soaked to the skin and obviously exhausted. He didn't argue. He isn't wearing raingear and has no hat or umbrella. The police officer had a huge rain poncho and a cover for his hat. He kept dry as they stood outside Elizabeth's house talking and watching.

The odours are battling it out and I'm not sure which is winning. We all smell of poor Gabriel's vomit. A strong wet dog stink hangs in the steamy air. Melissa's lemon scented hair is drowned out by the horsey smell of her soaked jacket. William's jacket must have some wool in it because he smells like wet blanket. And I'm not sure what scents are escaping from me, but a faint whiff reminds me of our barn. I turn on the heater and fan at full blast. The dogs are panting, but the rest of us are shivering. It'll be wonderful to get home.

10

Debts

We're still tired this morning, but we're also thankful. It could have been much worse. Once we got home last night and Gabriel was tucked up in bed with Cooper, and Jake was lying on his bedroom floor, I could feel the tension dissipate as if we'd pricked a balloon that had swallowed us all. William's so relieved that Gabriel is okay. He also mentioned he doesn't anticipate any trouble in moving forward with the adoption process. It's almost a fait accompli, he says. I'm worried, though. Gabriel has been through so much and being held at knifepoint by those malicious characters must have added to his struggles. I know what it's like to be traumatized—it's not easy to put it behind you. It's harder to shake the experience off if you're a child since it affects your inner being. The trauma I suffered when I was sexually abused by my stepfather for several years is part of me. I hope that Gabriel is made of stronger stuff and is more resilient.

Yes, I cried yesterday when Gabriel hugged my legs. Because of my history, I have trouble with physical touch and intimacy, and I also have serious doubts about my ability to love people and show affection. But Gabriel's hug was the most amazing embrace I've ever experienced. And the fact that he wanted to be with me and saw me as a protector overwhelmed me. I still have watery eyes. But I continue to harbour serious doubts about my ability to be a loving and capable stepmother.

Gabriel's hanging out with William today. He may have to sit in the courtroom for a brief period, but William says he'll work from home for the rest of the day, so I have the freedom to follow up on things—I have lots to do.

Melissa has the morning off, so Kelly and Jake don't have to sit in the truck for hours. And Gabriel will go back to school tomorrow. One of us will be there, early, to pick him up afterwards.

Zoey let me know that Thomas Caldermat is the executor of Barnaby's estate. The priority is to do something about Roxi's horses. Thomas lives and works in Branderton, a town about an hour away from Vannersville. He's the Manager of Financial Services for the Town.

* * *

We agreed to meet in the tea shop on the main street. It was easy to find and there's parking close by. Yesterday's rain is today's drizzle. I have a better jacket to ward off the damp, but I don't plan to give it much of a test in any case. I'm early, but so is Thomas who's seated at a table near the counter.

"I guessed you'd be a tea drinker," Thomas says, as he holds out his hand. His smile is framed by a moustache and a neatly trimmed beard, but it's not reflected in his steely grey eyes.

"I am."

"Let me get one for you. What would you like? They have every-thing under the sun here."

After a bit of back and forth, I get my own tea, but thank him for offering.

"I'm sorry for your loss of Barnaby," I say.

"I'm not one for beating about the bush and I think it best you know where I stand. He's no loss. You'll be hard pressed to find one person who's upset he's gone." He tilts his head to one side and watches for my reaction.

"I can't argue with you. I haven't met anyone yet who's said they miss him."

"Exactly my point."

"Tell me about him."

"How long have you got?" He leans back as he places his hands flat on the table. "Barnaby's dad, my uncle, left his mother when he was about five. By the way, my uncle was a philanderer, and his leaving for a floozie was a scandal that hit the local papers. It wasn't easy for his mother. She doted on Barnaby. We all thought she was trying to make up for the failed marriage and his lack of a father. They weren't well off. His father didn't pay up and I'm ashamed to say that we did little to help—my dad could have stepped up. I didn't see a lot of Barnaby when we were growing up, but whenever I did see him, he was talking of big plans to make a lot of money. He wanted to be a millionaire by the time he was thirty."

"What were those plans?"

"I don't really remember. I didn't pay attention because I didn't believe him most of the time. My family considered him to be dis-honest. None of us invested in anything he got involved in, including the Mercedes-Benz dealership or the pharmaceutical business."

"What was he like as a person?"

"Callous, manipulative, devious, and smug. Do you need more?

Because I can come up with some more unpleasant adjectives to describe him."

"No, I get the picture. Have you met his wife, Zoey?"

"Yesterday. I met her before at their wedding, but only briefly. I agreed to be the executor of his will, but I didn't think I'd ever be called upon to act on it and didn't take it seriously. Zoey seems a decent woman. I have no idea what she saw in Barnaby, but there you go."

"What about Olivia?"

"I haven't met her yet. Now, you're looking into Barnaby's murder, or suicide. I wouldn't be surprised if it's the latter, by the way. You said you needed me to do something?"

"Barnaby owned about thirty racehorses stabled at Vannersville Racetrack. Did you know that?"

"Zoey mentioned she used to be Barnaby's trainer, but the horses were transferred to someone called Roxi?"

"And Roxi has a minority share in the ownership, which possibly makes things more complicated. What's more, Barnaby owed Roxi a lot of money and she can't afford to look after the horses or pay the staff. It's become a crisis. And Roxi is in the hospital at the moment—long story."

"I can see why this needs immediate attention. Roxi should submit a claim to the estate for what she's owed."

"But there isn't any money, is there?"

"How much is she owed? And how much does it cost to look after these horses?"

"I don't have a figure, but I can give you an idea," I say. "My understanding is she's been training Barnaby's horses for about two racing seasons. I don't know what her ownership percentage is. She's a minority owner, but for simplicity's sake I'll assume Barnaby and Roxi each owned fifty percent. As a ballpark figure, and these calculations will be conservative, the cost per day to train each horse is about $100. This does not include any extraordinary expenses such as ultrasounds or special medications or treatments but just the basics such as exercise riders, jockeys, grooms, hotwalkers, worming pastes, and so on, and Roxi's share as trainer. So, I'll make the math simple by assuming the racing season is April to November, or eight months. Rounding things off, for two seasons, for thirty horses at fifty percent, that's about $720,000. And I haven't included any winter care costs. Not only is Roxi working for free, she can't pay the bills and has had to rent her farm out and live in a hovel to make ends meet. And the horses need care."

"Shit. That's much worse than I thought. And Zoey's owed about a quarter of a mill." He squeezes his bottom lip between is fingers and thumb as a deep frown etches into his brow.

"I have a proposal."

"I hope it's good, because the house goes to Zoey and the only other asset I'm aware of is the Mercedes-Benz dealership. Olivia isn't mentioned in his will. The two new Mercedes are leased. Aren't the horses worth something? I thought racehorses were valuable."

"Roxi says they're poor performers. Zoey told me that Barnaby bought and claimed horses without the benefit of her advice or anyone else's in the business. They didn't do well with Zoey, and they've obviously got older and have won little money with Roxi."

"Shit. I was counting on there being something there. What's your proposal?"

"Assuming the aim is to stop the bleeding, the horses all need to go to Four Rs."

"What's Four Rs?"

"It stands for Racehorse Rescue Rehoming and Retirement Society. It's a registered charity."

"I see."

"Then Roxi could retire from training and sell her farm to pay off her debts, well, really, they're mostly Barnaby's debts. But since she's a minority partner, she doesn't have the authority to do anything with the horses without your okay as executor."

"I'll have to think about it. It doesn't look good. Barnaby's made a right royal mess of things. I can see why he'd want to bow out."

*   *   *

As I clamber into the truck holding a paper bag with two oatmeal raisin cookies for the dogs, I regret not thinking to pick up something for Gabriel. The fact that I don't know what he likes makes me feel worse, so much so that the corners of my mouth curl down. My emotions are getting the better of me today. Perhaps it has something to do with our unwanted adventure in the church basement yesterday.

The pickup's engine purrs, and I'm about to maneuver out of the parking space when my mobile makes a noise. Olivia has responded to me at last, but Noah hasn't replied to any of my six texts or two voice mails. But at least I get to see Olivia. She's home for a couple of hours, she says, working on a report. I wonder if it's another one lambasting the medical staff and pushing her nearer to dismissal by the hospital board—which may be inevitable in any case. She says she can spare ten minutes. I don't get the sense I'll be welcomed.

She answers the door and waves me in, but it's as if she's swatting at a pesky insect.

"If you've come to tell me Barnaby didn't die from the stabbing, I know. He was already dead."

"I'm glad you've been told. Are you aware of what they suspect is the cause of death?"

"It's obvious. He drank like a fish and took drugs to sleep. I guess the two didn't mix well."

"No, they wouldn't. Was he prescribed the drugs?"

"They've asked me that. I have no idea. They searched the house and nothing."

"But you say he took drugs to sleep? How do you know that?" A glass of golden coloured wine glints in the sun as it sits on the kitchen counter. We're standing in the wide hall.

"He must have done."

"Why do you say that?"

"Because he killed himself. His life was a fiasco—a total disaster I've since found out. Looks like I get nothing. Zoey at least gets the house."

"What will you do?"

"I reckon I have squatter's rights, so I'm staying. It's been almost two years."

"What does Zoey think of that?"

"Zoey's fine with us sharing the house, but it'll be in her name. I get that."

"How's work going?"

"I'm doing nicely." She purses her lips and half-closes her eyes.

"You'll get a decent severance package."

"That's the plan. Now it's time for you to go." She opens the door, and almost shoos me out.

My next stop is Elsa's flat. Both she and Noah are still missing. I've sent several texts to Elsa as well as to Noah, but that's got me nowhere. I want to talk with Noah before Detective Valeska takes him in because her boss is convinced that he's guilty and I'm not.

A police officer stands outside the entrance which is at street level although the flat is above a shop. I contact Detective Valeska and ask for permission to enter. After about ten minutes I'm given the green light, but the police officer on duty must escort me and I must not touch anything. This visit will be a waste of time.

The officer is non-communicative. He's likely perplexed about my presence. But he's polite enough.

We stomp up the wooden stairs and the officer unlocks the door to the flat by entering a code using the keypad. I wasn't quick enough to catch it.

When he opens the door my first impressions are of light and openness. It feels more spacious than it really is because it's open plan. The imitation wood flooring is a pale taupe and is in immaculate condition. There's a rug in the centre of the room and I can see a small dark patch. That must be the blood. The officer cautions me to stay at least three feet away from it. There's a sectional sofa in the corner beside a large archway beyond which is the kitchen and eating area. It must have been recently renovated. When I turn around to observe the whole living area, a bracket with four hooks catches my attention. It's attached to the wall behind the door to the flat. There are three jackets. The officer stands close to me, and I'm frustrated that I can't check them out. He says he knows nothing about them, but something is niggling at me. I take a couple of photos of the jackets, and of parts of the flat.

There's just one large bedroom which has a king size bed, an ensuite bathroom, and a walk-in closet. I walk around the bed as the officer's eyes follow me. I'm not going to find anything here, but I take a few more photos. The last stops are the storage room and the two-piece washroom. As I walk into the washroom, we hear someone pushing the keypad buttons, and then what sounds like a kick. The officer reaches the door in two long, quick strides and opens it. By then the man has turned, and when I get there all I can see is the top of his head as he disappears down the stairs and out of the door onto the street. I was too slow to take a photo and the officer has both of his arms stretched out to block my exit. He doesn't pursue the man. I would have gone after him.

The officer asks me if I know who it was, and I tell him I don't, which is true. I can only conjecture. He must have come back for some reason. And the keypad code has been changed.

Before I start the truck, I phone the hospital to find out if Roxi is still a patient. Apparently, she was discharged this morning. She doesn't answer my phone call, so I drive towards her farm. After a few minutes I change my mind and head for the track—although it's the middle of the afternoon and most of the day's work will be completed except for feedings.

In spite of my jacket being labelled as 'weatherproof', dampness has seeped in. My hands are cold. It's more like an English winter day than a spring day. The dreariness saps the colours out of the flowers and grass and darkens my mood.

Roxi is in the shedrow. Her white hair and pale face almost give the impression that she's made herself up to be a ghost for Halloween. Her posture is more stooped, and she seems frailer. She's deteriorated both mentally and physically. It's sad to see. I remember the first time I saw her—she'd lost her temper with a horse and her staff and wasn't happy I was around. I'd rather she regained some of that spunk and feistiness than see her like this.

"I suppose you can't bring Kelly here."

"No."

"Why did you put that Thomas guy onto me?"

"What do you mean?"

"He says you told him the horses are worthless."

"I didn't say that."

"Well, you must have said something. He's contacted an auction place and he's demanding I get the registration papers and give them to the shippers when they come in a couple of days. He says he's been told they'll fetch about $500 each. So, I know the horses are going to Quebec. I'm so upset I can't think straight. I told you—I told you I didn't want them to go to slaughter." She braces herself against the rail running along the shedrow as she sways. I'm afraid she's about to faint.

"Roxi, I did not suggest auction. I suggested they all be sent to Four Rs. You must know I wouldn't do that."

"Linda said you wouldn't. But how could he know about that auction place and what they get for each horse from the meat buyers?"

"I suppose it can't be that hard to find out."

"I'm frantic but what can I do? They may be poor racehorses, but they're beautiful animals and deserve a second chance at another career. I love them all." She splutters and coughs.

"I'm going to fix this. Go home. Get some rest. I'll deal with it. Let me help you to your truck."

"I haven't got a truck. I can't afford the insurance. I get one of my staff to drive me. I'll text him to pick me up."

"I'll take you. It's not far out of my way. Come on."

As we near her dreary farm, we enter a drive-through and I pick up a couple of meals for her, as well as three drinks. She's almost in tears with gratitude. I think about all her hard work over so many years, and how she's been reduced to a shell of herself and overwhelmed by the gift of a couple of free meals. Barnaby Caldermat has a lot to answer for. Perhaps it's not all his fault, but still.

I'm glad to get home but not happy to find Kelly, Jake and Cooper left on their own, shut in the kitchen. I get an exuberant welcome with wagging tails, a couple of soft woofs and a rub by a furry ball. There's a text on my phone I hadn't picked up. William and Gabriel have just left to pick up takeout food for the three of us. Melissa is out for the evening.

With my rubber boots on, the dogs and I walk to the barn. The drizzle persists and creates a soft grey mist that makes it seem as if someone has painted the scene with dirty grey watercolour paint. Everything is still. Not one leaf rustles. Not one daffodil bends. The birds aren't singing. It almost feels ominous, as if something bad is going to happen.

Kelly's bark startles me and my stomach quivers. Then Jake barks. Kelly sits in the doorway to the barn and Jake sits down next to her. It's as if they're waiting for me to tell them what they should do. Whatever it is, it can't be dangerous. They would be more aggressive. At least, I think so. Kelly is so smart.

Jake shows his white teeth in a snarl, but Kelly is just super alert. She won't pull her eyes away from the interior of the barn. I wonder if it's a coywolf. We've had a few around recently and I worry about the safety of the barn cats.

The lights reveal nothing. But a voice comes from Eagle's stall. The door is open about six inches.

"Is someone in here?" I ask. I stand by the dogs. We're all on high alert. Our eyes are wide open, and the dogs have their ears pricked as they sniff the air.

"It's only me, Noah," a muffled voice mutters from inside the stall.

"It's okay, guys," I tell the dogs. They trot towards the stall door as Noah slides it further open with caution. His ginger hair has lost its shine and his clothes could do with a wash. The smells of hay, wood-shavings and horse feed are not enough to overpower body odor.

"What are you doing here?" That may be a stupid question. The dogs have lost interest and wander about the barn.

"I have no one else to turn to. I'm sorry I lost my cool last time we met, but it's like I'm living on a knife's edge. Please get me out of this nightmare." He scratches his head with his fingers.

"If you're willing to be straight with me, then I can help. What's wrong with your hand?"

He looks at his hand as if he's just noticed the grubby piece of cloth wrapped around it. His legs appear to wobble, and he topples over as if in slow motion. He lands on his side, stretched across a bale of hay that's against the aisle wall. I know he won't want to go to hospital, but I should call 911. I hesitate for a couple of seconds. He stirs and moans.

"You need medical attention." I feel his forehead. As I thought, he's burning up. His hand is probably infected.

"I can't go to hospital. I just need something for this hand. It's so bloody painful." He moans again.

"What's going on?" asks William. I nearly jump out of my skin. I didn't hear him come into the barn. I explain as best I can while Noah sits up on the bale and rocks backwards and forwards, holding his hand out in front of him, his arm supported at the elbow by his other hand.

"I'll take you to the walk-in clinic," William says. "They might treat you without you having to go into hospital."

"I'll take him," I say.

"It's fine. I know the horses need to go in, and I have some clout with the doctors at the clinic. Most of them know me."

"That's kind of you. Where are you staying, Noah?"

"Last night I slept in my car in the condo garage. I didn't think anyone would think to look there. I couldn't face another night sleeping outside. It's like I'm a fugitive running from the cops." He leans to one side and lets out a deep, rumbling groan. My stomach churns as I imagine the pain he must be in.

"I'll bring my car to the barn," William says. "You be ready, Noah. Meg, Gabriel is by himself in the kitchen."

Somehow, we lever Noah into the car.

Kelly, Jake and I go into the house. Gabriel is playing with Lego in the family room. The bags of takeout haven't been touched. Why am I nervous? Why am I trembling at the thought of looking after Gabriel? He looks up. I smile.

"Where's Uncle William?" I haven't heard him say more than a couple of words before. His voice is soft and melodic. I sit down on the floor next to him and he tells me what he's building, although I don't understand much of his description.

"Gabriel, would you help me, Kelly and Jake bring the horses in? It's past their bedtime. It won't take long, and then we can eat whatever Uncle William got for dinner."

He jumps up, runs to the door, grabs his jacket and thrusts his arms into the sleeves while it's upside down, and tosses it over his head. Next, he snatches his boots from off the mat and pulls them on. I've got only one arm into a sleeve of my jacket whereas he's ready to leave the house.

We all trot to the barn. He wants to lead the horses in. The compromise is that he holds the end of the lead-rein and I have the halter as we bring each horse in. The dogs follow us wherever we go.

Back in the kitchen, I open the bags and I'm a bit confused.

"What did Uncle William get you to eat?"

Apparently mashed potato and gravy is a hit, along with carrot and celery sticks. What about protein? I pour him a glass of milk and make note that we must improve his nourishment.

11

A Plan

The backdoor bangs and the dogs scramble into the kitchen, barking.

"It's just me, you silly dogs," William says.

There's a heavy weight on me and in my half-woken state it takes me a second to realize Gabriel is lying on top of me with a throw over him. We're sprawled on a recliner.

"He should have gone to bed an hour ago," William says as he puts a takeout tea on the table beside me.

"I don't even know how he got here. We must both be exhausted."

"I'll carry him upstairs and get him into bed somehow."

"You don't have Noah with you. I thought you might have to bring him back here."

"Long story. I'll tell you in a minute." William grunts as he lifts the boy and I suddenly feel unsquashed and lighter. I set the recliner upright and sip some of the welcome tea. Jake has gone up with

William and Gabriel. I expect Cooper is on Gabriel's bed wondering why he isn't up there yet.

A sigh escapes from deep inside me. Perhaps I do have some capacity to be a mother to Gabriel. He's certainly giving me a chance.

"He didn't even wake up when I put his pajamas on." William says. "What did you give him?"

"Ha ha."

"I'll grab my coffee. I left it in the kitchen."

"What about the food you got?"

"I don't want it. Did you eat?"

"No, I didn't feel like it. So, tell me about Noah."

"The clinic was clogged up with people, but at least they have a triage system there. In other words, it's not a first-come-first-served basis. I was able to impress upon the nurse Noah needed immediate medical attention. He didn't have his health card, so that caused a hold up. We got that sorted out though. I went in with him to see the doctor because he was unsteady on his feet. The wound looked ghastly to me, and I've seen quite a bit over the years. His hand was swollen and red. I won't give graphic details, but they had to give him a local anaesthetic so that they could clean the deep cut. I'm almost certain it's a knife wound."

"That must be the source of the blood on Elsa's carpet. Did he tell you anything about what happened?"

"I'll get to that. He felt a lot better when the local anaesthetic took effect, although I don't think I've ever seen anyone look as green as he did. They gave him an injection of antibiotics because they said it would be fast acting, and he was given two prescriptions, so I got those filled while he had a nap in my car."

"So, where is he now? Still in your car?"

"No, of course not. I would have let him use the apartment above my office, but it's rented out, as you know. But when I left the flat to move in here, I transferred the sofa bed from the living room down into the extra office, just in case I needed it for some reason. So, I set him up there. I even had a set of sheets and a couple of throws."

"I hope you've let Ramona know. Otherwise, she'll have the shock of her life when she finds him there in the morning."

"I thought of that. I sent a text and left a message."

"I want to know what he told you."

"Not much. It wasn't the time to pressure him since he was considerably under the weather."

"Honestly, William, he must have told you something."

"I'm not trying to be difficult about this. It's just that he wasn't forthcoming, and I didn't like to push him."

"He must have told you who stabbed him."

"He wasn't clear about it. He mentioned both Elsa and a man called Cliff."

"I think it was Cliff who tried to get into Elsa's flat when I was there. I took some photos."

"Of him?"

"I wasn't quick enough. All I saw was the top of his head. But I took others."

"Let's see them." He perches on the arm of my chair, and I scan through the photos.

"The jackets caught my eye. Do you see what I mean? One of them has a masculine look. It's brown denim with dark brown shoulders and has studs around the bottom, as far as I can tell. Another is a red rain jacket and the third is a dark blue jacket and there's something embroidered on it." I zoom in. "The initials are RQR, for Roxi Quentin Racing. The brown jacket looks too small to be Noah's when I compare them to the other two," I say. William studies the photo for a couple of seconds.

"I agree. It looks slightly larger than Elsa's, but it's hard to determine."

"I don't think it's hers. It probably belongs to Cliff, and he was trying to retrieve it the other day. I'll let Detective Valeska know in case it's significant."

"I expect you want to determine how Elsa's connected to Cliff?"

"I do, especially since she's missing."

*   *   *

This morning, unwelcome white weather has dragged us back into winter. This spring is in danger of becoming one of the worst on record. The sound of the wind as it makes the tall trees sway reminds me of the rumble of waves washing up on the shore of the Devon coast near where I grew up. But it's a lot colder than I remember it ever being there. Spring has slunk away, and it was tempting for me to follow suit and go back to bed. But a couple of cups of tea and working in the barn revitalized me, thankfully. My chores are almost finished.

Rose will be running this afternoon. Neal asked me a few days ago if I agreed Rose should be entered into this particular allowance race. It's probably a bit out of her league, but Neal knows I don't want to lose her in a claiming race. We'd prefer her to run about six furlongs, but the right race hasn't come up. A horse could be in tip-top condition, ready to race, but the schedule doesn't include the race we're looking for. We end up putting our finely tuned athlete in a difficult spot just because the horse would go crazy if he or she didn't get a chance to run for another two weeks or so. It can be frustrating for everyone.

So, partly because I don't want to lose her, and partly because the right allowance race isn't running, Rose will face strong competition.

I'll watch the race alone because William is picking Gabriel up from school and I'm not sure where Melissa is—she's hardly ever around.

140

The bitter wind ignores my spring jacket. Even the dogs are glad to get back into the house and shake the wispy snowflakes off their coats. Cooper stands clear.

William's face appears on my mobile as I take it out of my pocket.

"Hi," I say.

"Noah left when Ramona came to work," William says. "I thought you'd want to know."

"Did he leave a number? He must have a new phone. I haven't been able to reach him."

"No. I must run. Sorry. Hope Rose has a good race."

"Thanks. Hope you have a great day."

Although there are several issues I should be following up on, the one that's concerning me the most is what Roxi said about Thomas' plans to ship the horses to an auction place where most buyers are in the meat business. The more I've discovered, the more disturbed I've become. My subconscious must have been processing this because an idea has popped up, out of nowhere, as I put my mobile on the kitchen table.

* * *

Kelly and Jake were a bit confused when I left them at William's office on my way to the track. Ramona gave them a chilly welcome and shut them in the spare office where Noah spent the night. But William will pick them up in about an hour and then collect Gabriel from school.

Neal meets me at the rail by the track to watch the race. I've got a thick scarf wrapped around my neck and a long, quilted jacket on. It doesn't seem right to have to bundle up in winter clothes when spring officially arrived more than three weeks ago. My mother made it worse by sending me a photo of a patch of tulips bathing in the sunshine in the grounds of her retirement residence in Devon.

Large flakes of fluffy snow dance in the wind as I watch for the horses to appear on the track for the post parade.

"It's a cold one," Neal says.

"It's brutal." Despite my gloves, my hands prickle as I grip today's program.

"I wish Cliff Ryman wasn't running in this race." He points to the program. "He's on the favourite as usual."

"I noticed. But we don't expect a win, do we?"

"Rose is in good form, but it would be a surprise if she won, cheat or no cheat."

"I wonder what she thinks of this weather?"

"Most horses prefer it on the chilly side when they're working."

The bugle calls the horses to the post as they enter the track accompanied by their ponies. Rose is in post number three. Her racing name is Alusio. It took me a while to figure out this is an anagram of Louisa, Frank's first wife who died of cancer. Her death devastated Frank. I don't know how much longer Rose will want to be a racehorse, but I'll never be able to part with her.

Even though the snow is swirling around it's obvious that Rose has a dappled coat—amazing for this time of year—and is in great shape. She's prancing alongside the patient pony.

An eternity goes by—at least that's what it feels like—until the horses are in the gate and the announcer proclaims "they're off!".

Rose is in the middle of the pack, with four horses in front and the other four behind. Cliff is third. I grip the program with my cold hands as Rose appears to hang back. The front runners are making good time, about twenty-three seconds for the first two furlongs. Rose isn't a sprinter, but she's still in the middle of the pack as they enter the far turn. Cliff's horse isn't starting to move up, which seems odd to me. The front runners aren't gaining. The time for four furlongs is forty-seven seconds. Cliff stays in third place, but Rose

142

starts to move as they enter the final turn. If it wasn't for the tracking system that shows the order of the horses on the big screen, I'd be confused as to where she sits. She's third. She passed Cliff's horse somewhere between the two turns.

As they approach the grandstand Rose is on the outside of the two front runners. Perhaps she's gaining, I can't be sure. Neal and I yell out her name and I smack my program on the rail. I'm much warmer now. The snow hits my face and melts.

Her hooves pound the ground and she's airborne as she lunges forward. Her ears are flattened, her neck stretched out, and Jaden is crouched down—his back level with her back. He's only used the whip twice to encourage her to put in her best effort. Her tail flies out behind as she passes us. She stretches and reaches and it's a photo finish. She's either first or second. Neal and I jump up and down.

"That was fantastic. She put her heart into that race," I say, as we make our way to the gate that leads onto the track. "I think she came second."

It takes a long time for the horses to come back to the grandstand. They galloped out for quite a distance past the finish line. Rose was one of the last to return. Her nostrils are flaring but she looks happy. She thinks she's won. Jaden doesn't look happy though.

"She won!" Neal exclaims. The official result has been posted and then the photo of the finish is on the screen. She won by a nostril.

Rose gets lots of pats and praise as we assemble in the Winner's Circle. After the photos are taken, Linda rubs the horse's face as Rose tosses her head. She puts a blanket on her and leads Rose to the test barn in the backstretch. Each winner of every race is tested for drugs.

Neal and Jaden chat as they walk towards the jockeys' entrance to the grandstand. Jaden has a ride in the next race and must change into the correct silks for the owner of that horse. I trot behind them but can't catch what they're saying. Jaden disappears through the door and Neal turns towards me.

"Let's get a drink," he says.

"Good idea."

We stop to watch the replay on the way to the owners and trainers' lounge. Neal doesn't say anything. He stands still with his hands in his pockets, and stares at the big screen that's just inside one of the doors leading from the outside seating. It's as if he's studying the race, looking for something. I hope he doesn't think there's anything wrong with Rose.

Several people pat him on the back and congratulate him as we make to a table, but his reaction seems a bit cool.

"What's up, Neal? Is it Rose?"

"No. Jaden's sure Cliff held his horse back deliberately. He wanted one of the other horses to win. It was planned, he's darn certain. But Rose upset the apple cart. He's glad about that, but he's not happy. Cliff's not only an electric jockey, it looks like he cheats in other ways too."

"Surely that isn't all that surprising, is it?"

"I suppose not."

"If he held his horse back, that points to illegal betting."

"Yep."

"Jaden's going to report it, isn't he? That's why you look so grave."

"Yep. You got it. Cliff isn't to be messed with. I'm worried for Jaden."

"You really think he'll retaliate?"

"Yep. Who do you think beat up Roxi?"

"You think it was Cliff? I've wondered but couldn't come up with a reason."

"Well, I can't come up with one. But that's the sort of thing he does."

"Right. Elsa's under suspicion, but I found out she's Roxi's granddaughter."

144

"Yep. Elsa's spirited, much like her granny, but she wouldn't beat someone up."

"She made that fake video."

"That's a joke. Everyone could see it wasn't the real deal."

* * *

Roxi called me first thing this morning. So, as soon as the barn chores were done, the dogs and I arrived at the track. I park by the security office. Jake is learning the routine and lies down with Kelly behind the seats.

Roxi's back in her barn—I'm sure she shouldn't be.

Linda's been here again this chilly morning, but it's still chaotic. She's being pulled in too many directions, even for her.

"Meg, that Thomas guy," Roxi says. "He's just left. He's worse than Barnaby. He doesn't care a cent about these horses. But I have no money to care for them anymore. I can't do it."

Her hair seems whiter and thinner, if that's possible, and her face is dry and flaky. A stooped posture makes her look as if she's been beaten down and defeated by life's challenges.

"I have a plan," I say with as much conviction as I can rustle up.

"And it's like I don't have any ownership rights, and he won't say he'll settle the outstanding training bills. He says the estate has to pay Zoey first. I'll get nothing."

"There must be records of what you're owed?"

"Mostly, but I gave up sending out invoices this year. There was no point. And I'm worried sick about Elsa. I haven't heard a word from her."

"That's next on my priority list."

"It should be the first."

"I know. But we can't let these beautiful horses go for meat."

"No, no. Oh hell. It's all my fault. I'm such a loser."

"Beating yourself up isn't going to help. Let's save these horses and then I'll focus on finding Elsa."

I explain to Roxi my plan to buy the horses for the $500 per head they would likely fetch at the auction. I just need to get Thomas to agree. Then I'll donate them to Four Rs. At least it would put an end to Roxi's expenses growing daily.

"Have Four Rs agreed? Is it that retirement place?"

"I've already arranged it. The Four Rs farm is on a large piece of property with great pasture. The horses will live outside with access to run-in sheds for shelter. But the really important thing about Four Rs is they'll give each a chance to find a new career, as a trail horse or in dressage, show jumping, hunter, eventing, or just as a companion for another horse."

When I finish explaining the plan, Roxi touches my hand. There are tears in her eyes. She says if this works, she'll sell the farm, give up training, and move to a retirement community. I'm sure that would be harder for her to do than she realizes.

Roxi tells me Thomas walked towards the cafeteria when he left her barn.

12

Assault

It's fortunate I haven't left the track because I want to meet with Thomas as soon as possible. He doesn't answer his phone at first, so I text to tell him I have a plan for the horses.

The temperature has risen to a few degrees above freezing, but sleet stings my eyes as I stride towards the cafeteria. The bitter cold of yesterday has moved on and the smells are more pungent. All the ditches have water in them, and what isn't road is either a squelchy area of grass, or mud. I keep to the road.

The birds are as tuneful and cheerful as if it's a beautiful spring day. They flutter around picking up nesting, and peck at tasty morsels on the ground that I can't see. One bathes in a dirty puddle near the road. They reflect the busyness of the backstretch as riders and their mounts leave and return to the barns, people heave wheelbarrows or tubs of manure into dumpsters, grooms wash their horses' feet (it's too cold for baths today), trainers walk to and from the training track, and veterinarians and farriers visit their clients. It's as if I'm inside a giant beehive.

Linda and I almost collide in the cafeteria entrance.

"Something awful's happened," Linda says as she stops in the doorway.

"Let's go inside."

We huddle in a corner beside the inner entrance to the cafeteria. Linda's been crying.

"I assume it's Rose?"

"No. Not the horses. It's Jaden. Neal and I think Cliff beat him up 'cause he reported the holding back and took that video. He's such a nice guy. He's kind to the horses and he always talks to me. That brute Cliff shouldn't be here." Tears stream down her cheeks. I motion to her to stay where she is and run in on wobbly legs to get some napkins. As I turn to leave the cafeteria, my eyes land on a couple of people sitting at the far end. Thomas Caldermat and Zoey—his hand is resting on hers. She must have signed him in at the security office.

"I hope he's alive," I say as I hand Linda a wadge of napkins. My hands are shaking.

"Neal thinks he is. He's a good guy. It's not fair."

"How did Neal find out?"

"A security guard told him first thing."

"It must have happened last night then."

"Don't know." Her nose is running. She sniffs and then wipes it with the brown napkins that aren't absorbent enough and chucks them into the garbage bin as we leave the building.

"I'll walk with you back to the barn." My meeting with Thomas will have to wait until I find out what's happened to Jaden. And I should be looking for Elsa. And Detective Valeska will be wondering why I haven't found Noah yet. There are too many avenues for me to follow and the priorities are hard to figure out.

"Linda," Neal says, as soon as he meets us in the shedrow, "why don't you go home? Meg and I'll look into this. You need a break anyway, and this business with Jaden has really upset you."

Linda doesn't say anything. She just nods as she wipes fresh tears away from her face with the backs of her hands.

"Meg, let's go into my office."

Neal explains that Jaden was beaten up this morning as trainers, exercise riders, grooms, hotwalkers and jockeys were entering the backstretch. On the mornings that Jaden arrives early, he parks his scooter by the cafeteria and picks up a coffee. It's a routine. But this morning someone heard odd noises coming from the adjacent men's washroom. It's not used much first thing. When they went in, they found Jaden on the floor lying in vomit and couldn't get any response from him. Someone called 911. No one's been allowed in the washroom since the police came.

Just as Neal mentions police, Detective Valeska's face appears on my mobile.

"Sorry, Neal, I have to answer this."

"Meg," Detective Valeska says, "you have another beating at the racetrack. I'd appreciate your cooperation."

"Of course."

"I'm disappointed that you failed to inform me that Noah Pestel visited you and stayed at William's office. I could have you charged with obstruction. So far, you've done little to assist Vannersville Police Services and more to interfere."

Am I under surveillance? "I assure you that's not my intent," I say.

"From now on, I'd appreciate your full cooperation at all times."

"I'll get back to you as soon as I find out more about either or both of the beatings." It's almost as if she thinks I'm one of her officers.

"Good." She ends the call.

"That didn't sound like a friendly call," Neal says, as he grabs a couple of bottles of water out of his tiny fridge.

"Is Jaden in hospital? I need to talk to him as soon as possible."

"I don't know where he is, but I guess so."

"Linda told me you both think Cliff beat him up. It can be dangerous to jump to conclusions."

"But it's obvious. Who else would want to hurt someone like Jaden?"

"I admit I can't think of anyone, but I don't know him well. He could have enemies."

"Meg, that's bullshit. He's a nice guy. Everyone knows that. Who would leave him for dead in the washroom for Pete's sake?"

"He was left for dead? How do you know that?"

"I don't know for sure, but that's what's going around. Can't you do your sleuthing stuff and get this guy Cliff out of our lives?" Neal rarely raises his voice or loses his temper, and I imagine he's usually much more unlikely to lose his cool with an owner—a client like me.

"I'll do my best to find out the truth." With that, I leave his office. I pay a quick visit to each of my five horses on the way to the administration building.

The temperature has dropped again and there's a thin layer of slushy sludge on the ground, except for the roads. The sleet continues its relentless attack, aided and abetted by the wind, as I walk towards Bill Price's office.

Bill leans back in his chair and clasps his hands over his stomach. He's wearing a smart crisp shirt that looks as if it's just come out of its wrapping.

"Nice win you had with Alusio," he says.

"That race is one of the things I wanted to ask you about. You must know that Jaden was beaten up this morning."

"I was sorry to hear that. Dreadful." He keeps his eyes fixed on me. I sense a slight hostility, but that could be my imagination.

"You must have seen the video Jaden took with his Jockey Cam when Hector, I mean Ginger Victor, raced. And you must have reviewed Alusio's race—Jaden was convinced that Cliff Ryman held his horse back."

"Mm," he says, without moving. "First, I must point out that penalties are not awarded lightly. We must be sure of our facts. We're talking of livelihoods here. Elsa was suspended because we had proof she used an electrical device. Roxi Quentin supplied the evidence. But the video Jaden took did not prove that Cliff used such a device. And what's more, I have no ability to determine whether or not the video is fake. But I'm inclined to believe it is. As you know, the one of Roxi Quentin was revealed to be fake. And the replay of Alusio's race does not show, beyond reasonable doubt, that Cliff held his horse back. I'm sure you understand our position, especially since you're an investigator."

"How do you explain Jaden getting beaten up?"

"It's not my business to know. I don't have to explain that. I'm sorry he's dead, but it's nothing to do with this office."

"What makes you think he's dead? Have you been advised of his death? As far as I know, he's recovering in hospital."

His left eye twitches. "That's good news, then. Sorry, Mrs. Sheppard, I have a lot of work to do. I hope you understand. I wish I could have been of more help." He stands and offers his hand. I'm being dismissed. His cold and clammy handshake makes me feel as if I'm waving a wet fish around.

It's good to be outside in the sleet away from Bill. There's an unsettled feeling in my stomach and I'm a little confused. Something about that meeting isn't sitting well with me, yet Bill is a well-respected racing official. He and Frank got on well. Perhaps Bill's reticence to be more open with me is because he's not at liberty to divulge details and a hearing is scheduled for Cliff. But, if so, why couldn't he tell me that?

* * *

Dr. Milton is my go-to guy at the hospital, and he returns my call promptly. He tells me I should keep confidential the information he's about to give me about Jaden. But I remind him that I'll have to tell Detective Valeska.

Jaden is alive but in a coma. He has an intracranial hematoma which Dr. Milton says is between the brain and the dura mater—which are the membrane layers that cover the brain. Some blood vessels have ruptured, and blood is accumulating and putting pressure on the brain. This is life-threatening and requires emergency surgery. Jaden is on his way to the operating theatre at this very moment, Dr. Milton says. The surgeon plans to drain the blood and relieve the pressure. There are no guarantees.

"The rumour at the track is that he was left for dead," I say.

"It would be reasonable for a lay person to think he was dead if he was unconscious."

"But someone heard him throwing up."

"That can happen."

"So, he must have been conscious when he vomited?"

"No. He probably wasn't if the rumour is true—that he was left for dead, I mean. You can vomit while unconscious. It's dangerous though, because you can choke. Vomiting while unconscious can be a symptom of head trauma."

Detective Valeska is my next call and I give her a synopsis of what Dr. Milton told me. She tells me that police officers found a blood-smear on one of the urinals, so it's assumed that the attacker smacked Jaden's head against the top corner of the urinal and that was enough to do the damage. Cliff Ryman is wanted for questioning.

"What about Roxi's beating?" I ask.

"We remain interested in questioning Elsa. I'm looking forward to hearing from you the whereabouts of Noah and Elsa. We have no leads at the present." I don't respond because I have nothing to report. I plan to go home but Neal calls me as I'm about to start the engine. Kelly and Jake sit up. We all want to be back at the farm.

"Meg, Cliff has turned up at the track."

"Do you know where he is?"

"I don't."

"I need to talk with him." Before I can end the call, my truck door is yanked open by a short, slight man with beady eyes and thin lips. In the split second before he punches me in the face, I realize that it's Cliff even though he has a hoodie pulled down to his eyebrows. Kelly's claws dig into my thighs as she squeezes past me, barking. Jake follows. It's tougher for him to get between me and the steering wheel, but it's as if he lunges at Cliff. His growly barks almost deafen me. As the shock wears off and my vision clears, I tumble out of the pickup. The dogs bark, growl, snap, and snarl at Cliff as he kicks out at them using language I would rather forget.

"Leave them alone. What the hell's wrong with you, Cliff?" I yell as I walk towards him.

"Mind your own effing business and you won't get hurt or worse," he tries to grab Jake, but he darts to one side and snarls. "This has just been a warning. Count yourself lucky. Hear me?" He kicks at Kelly, but she jumps back. Jake's hackles are up as he springs forwards and growls. Cliff makes a hand gesture that I don't want to describe and turns. Before I reach him, he runs off. I tell the dogs to stay. Too late to be of any help, a security guard lumbers over from the nearby office.

"What's going on?"

"Cliff Ryman assaulted me," I say in a mumbled voice. The left side of my face throbs and my teeth are on edge. The metallic taste of blood makes me wonder what the damage is.

"Are you sure it was Cliff?" he asks as he looks towards the barns.
"Yes."

"I didn't see what happened or who it was."

"You're saying it's my word against his. Come on dogs, we're going home."

*   *   *

A bag of frozen peas is all I can find to put on my face. I've taken a couple of ibuprofen capsules and hope I don't look too much like I've been in a fight. Gabriel will be home soon, and I don't want to frighten him. He's been through too much.

The dogs are sprawled out side by side on the kitchen floor. I gave them extra cuddles and treats as soon as we got home but bending over made me dizzy.

I hear a car door slam, so I hastily put the peas back in the freezer and sit with my undamaged side facing the door.

"Hello, Gabriel. Did you have a good day?" I ask.

"No." He runs up the stairs. I needn't have been concerned about him noticing anything. But I'm worried about him being upset about his day.

"William, what's wrong with Gabriel?"

"The teacher came out with him and talked to me. She said she asked him to stand in front of the class and read out a story he wrote. She'd given it a gold star. But he couldn't speak, and he cried. He was so upset that even the surrogate grandmother couldn't console him. The teacher apologized and said she'd made a mistake—he wasn't ready to present to the class. He needs more time. But she's very pleased with his work. Elizabeth must have done a reasonable job of home-schooling."

"That's all very well," I say, doing my best not to mumble. The side of my face feels as if it's been pulled taut. "But there's more

154

to growing up than academics. Don't they call it socio-emotional intelligence?"

"He's not stupid."

"I don't mean that, William. You know I don't. I just mean he hasn't had the opportunity to develop his interpersonal skills and to grow his confidence in a social setting."

"Have you been to the dentist or something? Your voice sounds mumbled."

Melissa crashes through the door with three grocery bags and kicks it shut.

"Meg, what's happened to your face?" Nothing gets past Melissa.

"I was hoping no one would notice."

"Don't tell me you walked into a lamppost because I won't believe you," she says as she dumps the bags on the kitchen counter.

"Thanks for getting groceries again, Melissa."

"Don't avoid the issue. What happened?"

"Cliff Ryman punched me."

"What?" William sits down next to me. "He assaulted you?"

"Are the dogs okay?" Melissa asks.

"You can see they are."

"But you're not," William says. "It's already swollen and red. What about ice? Should you see a doctor? What if something's broken?"

"I'll be fine. I put a bag of frozen peas on it and that helped, and I've taken some ibuprofen."

"You called the police I hope," William says.

"There's no point. As a security guard made clear, it's my word against Cliff's. But I will tell Detective Valeska. I should keep her in the loop."

"I assume he threatened you with worse if you continue with your investigation. So, that means he's involved in what, exactly, do you think?"

"I don't know for sure."

Melissa is rummaging around in the freezer compartment of the fridge.

"Here we are," she says, as she pulls out an icepack. "I knew it was in here somewhere." She wraps it in a tea towel and hands it to me.

"What about Gabriel?" I ask, as I hold the icepack against my face.

"We're going to have a movie night," William says. "Gabriel has heard about a couple of movies from his school mates. We could all do with a break."

"I'm in," Melissa says. "I'll make something to eat. But we need popcorn."

"I'll get some," William says. "I'm sure Gabriel will be okay, Meg. He just needs time."

"How about asking Gabriel if he'll let you record him reading his story?" asks Melissa, as she turns from the sink to look at William. "Then the teacher can share it with the class, and he'll feel better about himself."

"That's brilliant," I say.

*   *   *

My face is swollen and bruised but I convinced William and Melissa that I'm okay and did my barn chores. I'm quite pleased with the cover-up job I've done with make-up I found hiding at the back of a bathroom drawer.

The fate of the horses in Roxi's barn is the first thing that demands my attention after my shower.

Thomas is hard to get hold of. My last attempt is a voicemail telling him I'll call in at the Branderton Town offices later this morning. Perhaps I shouldn't have told him—assuming he's avoiding me. So, I text Zoey and Olivia in case they know where he is. Olivia calls me.

"Can you come to the house?" she asks. "Like, now?"

"I suppose I can do that."

"Thanks."

That didn't sound like the Olivia I know—the tough, serious woman who said she doesn't enjoy her job, but likely thrives on the challenges and confrontations.

The dogs come with me because no one's at home and I don't want to leave them to their own devices. We park in the driveway and before I have the truck door open, Olivia has opened the door. Her auburn hair is brushed off her face, she has no make-up on, and her jeans look too big for her. She appears diminished in stature and in presence.

She opens the door wide for me to enter. There's no sign of wine, just the smell of toast.

"Thanks for coming so quickly," she says. "What's wrong with your face?"

"It's nothing. I'm fine."

I follow her into the kitchen. We sit at the counter. She grabs two bottles of water from the fridge and hands one to me.

"So, what's this about?" I ask. The kitchen counters have several dirty dishes and open packets scattered about. A pile of large cardboard boxes leans precariously in the corner. "Are you moving out?"

"I'm being evicted." She slams her fist down on the cream granite counter and although it doesn't make much noise, the action startles me.

"Evicted? By Zoey?"

"She promised me I could stay. I know she gets the house, but she told me right from the beginning that I wouldn't have to leave. And I've lost my job. Yes, I get severance, but I've got to find something else, and it won't be easy. It could take a long time. Getting a management job can be tough, especially when I want something in health care administration. Perhaps I'll have to leave Vannersville."

"You may have to get out of this house, anyway. It could be necessary to sell it because of Barnaby's debts."

"I guessed that. But that's not why I'm so upset about Zoey evicting me. It's because of what it means."

"What does it mean? I don't understand."

"I'm almost too scared to tell you."

"What is there for you to be scared of?" I suck in a little air, and she notices.

"You've got an idea, haven't you?"

"I think I'm catching on. You and Zoey were a team."

"We were. And now I think she'll betray me. She could make me the scapegoat so she can be with her lover."

"Don't tell me. Thomas, right?"

"I thought we'd got away with it. When we heard Barnaby was already dead before we stabbed him, we laughed. That sealed it. It was funny, really. He must have committed suicide. He must have taken the barbiturate with his morning whisky. We thought we'd killed him. But we didn't." She's talking at a fast pace, but she stops to pour some water into her mouth from the plastic bottle which crackles as she squeezes it. "And now Zoey wants to pin the stabbing onto me. She's found out we could be facing jail time—even though Barnaby was already dead."

"So, you and Zoey stabbed Barnaby? What made you do that?"

"He was the most despicable person on the face of this earth. Well, I suppose that's an exaggeration." She giggles, but it's a nervous, agitated cackle rather than anything close to laughter. This behaviour doesn't fit with the Olivia I first met.

"I get the picture. But what did he do to you and Zoey to make you want to take such extreme action?"

"He was an abuser. He hit Zoey. That was the worst of it. But he also wanted her to cheat with his racehorses. Zoey said he bought them without professional advice and made a lot of mistakes, but then he expected her to perform miracles. I don't know what he demanded be done. You'd have to ask Zoey."

"How did Zoey get out of the relationship?"

"It's best to ask her."

"Fair enough. What about you?"

"He wanted to control everything I did. I couldn't go anywhere without his okay. I was in a trap of work and home. He wouldn't let me see friends or join anything or go to conferences. I had to make excuses. He would come with me when I did the shopping. I couldn't talk to anyone."

"How did you and Zoey get together then?"

"Zoey came to the house a couple of times to get stuff when he wasn't here. There must have been a lawyer's letter or something legal that gave her permission. I don't think she'd have dared to do it otherwise. He had a raging temper." She shudders, crushes the bottle and puts the top back on. "I was here but I didn't know how to react to what she said the first time she came. At that point, I hadn't had much trouble with Barnaby. She warned me. She told me to move out. But I wondered if she was jealous and didn't want Barnaby to have another woman in his life. But things quickly deteriorated with Barnaby and when she came the next time, I told her about it. We talked and I told her I couldn't leave because he'd told me he'd come and find me, and it would be more than my life was worth to walk out. By then I was frightened of him. We didn't get many opportunities to meet but she'd come to the hospital sometimes for a cup of coffee in the afternoon on her way home from the track. I enjoyed those times." She looks down at the crumpled bottle. "My insides feel crushed just like this bottle. I've lost my confidence. I'm sure that's why I lost my way at work. I lashed out at the wrong people over the wrong things at the wrong times."

"I can see how that could happen, under the circumstances."

"I won't have the chance to redeem myself because, even though Barnaby was dead when we stabbed him, we could be in prison for several years."

"You need a lawyer. I'm sure she or he will advise you to talk to the police. In my inexpert opinion I'd expect you to get a reduced sentence that way. Do you have proof that he was abusive to you?"

"I have some photos on my phone of bruising when he got physical, which wasn't often. But how can I prove it was him?"

"It would be a lot better for you if Zoey was on your side."

"She was, but I think that obnoxious man Thomas has her under his spell. He can be a charmer like Barnaby, and just as dangerous."

"Oh, that's interesting. Do you need the name of a lawyer? I can get one for you."

"That's probably a good idea."

13

Gone

A drying wind has picked up and little spirals of dirt pop up near the barns in the backstretch. Pieces of straw and hay whirl around me as I walk from the truck. Grit hits my face and I'm glad to get into the shedrow. The horses are unsettled by the rattling of loose siding and roofing as the wind whistles through crevices.

Roxi hobbles towards me. Her usually pale face is flushed and she's waving her good arm about. I look behind me but can't see anything. She must be signalling me for some reason.

"Meg, thank god you're here."

"What on earth is going on?"

"The shipper has come to load the horses to go to that auction place in Quebec. I can't bear it. I just can't stand it. I could murder that goddam Thomas."

"Don't say that Roxi. Let me deal with the shipper."

"You won't get anywhere."

"We'll see. Where is he?"

"In the large parking lot by the admin building."

I phone Thomas as I jog over to the large, shiny, horse trailer. The horses won't like being loaded in a howling gale. No answer from Thomas. I text him saying that I'll pay $500 per horse, which is a fair price. Just as I reach the enormous horse trailer, I text Thomas again to say I'll call him at work and have him paged if he doesn't answer my phone call or my text.

The shipper tells me there are two more trucks coming because there are thirty horses.

"I hate going there," he says as he lowers the ramp. "It's a killing pen. And sometimes the horses stay in tiny pens for days, could even be weeks. It should be shut down."

"Why do you do this job, then?"

"You got me. I suppose I'm no different from the guys who run those places. I need the work. I need the pay. I wish I didn't."

"This trailer is huge." My mobile rings and Thomas' name comes up.

"Meg, what's the problem? I don't like being interrupted at work."

"I assume you accept my offer of $500 per horse?"

"No. I don't. I won't take any less that $800 per horse. They've got good weight on them. And you'll have to pay the shippers. I want cash by tomorrow noon. Same café as before. That's the way it is. Take it or leave it. I don't care about those useless animals. All they've done is deplete Barnaby's pathetic estate." Not as charming as I thought. Olivia is right.

"I'll get back to you by text in five." I turn to the truck driver. "Can you give me five minutes. I want to talk to someone before I make a final decision."

"Must be good to have that kind of money. I'd save them if I had that sort of dough."

162

"You're right. I do have the money. Thanks for making me realize I must do this, I want to do this."

The other two trucks show up and I ask them to bill me what they think is fair. They chat amongst themselves and then tell me if I pay for the diesel to get to the track and return to their base, that would be fine. They want to do a little something to help the horses and wish they could do more. They won't charge for their time or lost business.

After thanking them and handing them one of my business cards each, I tell them I'll be sending the horses to Four Rs and I'll connect with them for shipping when I've set it up.

"That's great," the first truck driver says. "Ain't it guys?" The other two nod their heads. "They'll get good homes. Made my day!" He shakes my hand and moves towards the ramp to raise it as the others return to their rumbling trucks.

"Meg, Meg!" Roxi yells as soon as I appear in the doorway of the barn. "That was your truck, right? The dark blue one with the big shiny front grill?"

"What do you mean 'was'?"

"It's gone. I hope it wasn't yours."

I look out of the door into the small parking lot by the barn and see a vacant spot where I left the truck. She's right. It's gone.

"Oh, no! Kelly and Jake are in there. Someone must have stolen it. When?" I punch in 911.

"I don't know. I just noticed it gone. I thought it might be yours."

My mouth's dry. Anxiety has taken hold. It's hard to give coherent information. I'm assured, in a voice that's too calm, that the police are alerted.

"I risked bringing it into the backstretch because Jake's learned how to keep down behind the front seats like Kelly. That was a terrible mistake. I didn't lock it and I should know better. Bad things have happened before." I need to stop talking and think.

"Who would do this? It must be someone with access to the backstretch."

"Kelly and Jake will be okay."

"I know you're trying to help me feel better, but you can't say that. You've no idea what's happening to them."

"No, I don't."

"You know something. Tell me! They're both lovely dogs and you like Kelly a lot."

"I do. Oh hell."

"Tell me!" My voice is almost a scream. My hands are visibly shaking.

"Shit." Roxi grinds her teeth as if she's in pain.

"Let me guess. Elsa. You saw Elsa here."

She doesn't say anything. I get my act together and phone Melissa.

"Hi, I'm," she says. I cut her off.

"Melissa, my truck's been stolen from the backstretch with Kelly and Jake inside. I'm frantic. I must look for them. I need your car."

"Oh no, no! That's the worst. Poor dogs. Oh no!"

"Melissa, help me."

"Just give me a sec."

"Are the horses going?" Roxi asks with a small voice, giving the impression she'd like to vanish into thin air.

"No. I'll tell you later." Roxi takes a couple of tottering steps backwards. I must have snapped at her. "Look after them for a couple more days," I say in a softer voice.

"Meg," Melissa says. "Edwin and I are coming. Where are you?"

"Roxi's. I'll wait by the road."

I leave Roxi's barn without uttering another word. Sirens grow louder as vehicles travel on the main road outside the track. I call William and tell him what's happened in as few words as possible.

"I'm driving Gabriel home," he says, with a slight tremble in his voice. He doesn't want to upset the boy. I get it.

"Don't worry. See you soon," I say. I wish I hadn't called him. I forgot this is picking-up time at school.

Edwin and Melissa are taking too long, and I can't stand still. It's hard to watch out for them—my eyes want to shut against the wind and airborne grit, and the gusts are doing their best to push me sideways. I shield my eyes with my hands cupped around them as I peer down the road, wishing Edwin and Melissa to appear.

At last, Edwin's silver SUV creeps towards me. I know he's considerate of the horses, but this is ridiculous. It's as if everything's in slow motion. I run towards them, wrench the door open, and dive onto the back seat. But I can't think where to go.

"Where to?" asks Edwin. He turns around and smiles. "What happened to your face?"

"Never mind that. I don't mean to be rude, but I'm terrified something awful's going to happen to Kelly and Jake. I don't know where to go. I suppose we start by driving along the main road towards the city centre. Roxi didn't deny it was Elsa—she could be going to her flat or perhaps Cliff's place."

"They're at opposite ends of the city," Edwin says. "I happen to know because,"

"Let's try Cliff's place first."

"We need to turn left at the lights, then." His calm demeanour makes me more agitated. I haven't put my seatbelt on and I'm twitching as if I'm being tortured by electric prods. Melissa isn't doing much better than I am. She's peering out of the windshield and then out of the side window and back again as she writhes in her seat.

My mobile rings. It's William.

"Meg. The police have just been called to an accident at the intersection of Northern Dancer Avenue and Queen's Plate Drive. It's near the racetrack."

"I know where it is. We'll check it out. We're pretty close. Thanks a lot."

"Good luck."

Edwin has to turn the vehicle around, so he steers into a side street and does a U-turn, and it takes forever. As we near the main road, a person is waving at the traffic. Something black is tearing along the edge of the road towards oncoming vehicles.

"Jake! Edwin, stop!"

Edwin brakes as the SUV pokes its nose into the intersection. Melissa and I jump out while it's still moving. We both scream Jake's name and run. Several cars stop. A few drivers put their feet down and zoom past, scaring the bejeebies out of me. Jake must be terrified. He keeps running.

We tear after him. We're both pretty fit, but we can't keep up with him. A large semi rumbles towards Jake, stirring up clouds of dust at the edge of the road. My heart's thumping and I think it's going to burst. The looming truck startles him and he leaps into the ditch, loses his footing and rolls. We can see his sides heaving and his tongue lolling out as he lies sprawled on the bank of the ditch. He scrambles to get up and makes it onto his front legs, but then flops back down.

We yell out his name. He hears us over the roar of the traffic. He lifts his head, but only for a second. He's exhausted and he may be seriously hurt from the accident and his tumble. And where's Kelly? Why aren't they together?

"Melissa, you look after Jake." I cough. The dust irritates my throat. Strands of hair stick in my mouth. I want to cry but I mustn't use up energy I need for running. "I'm going to look for Kelly."

"Be careful, Meg. You sound exhausted." Melissa is crouched down. "I'm texting Edwin. He'll help me get Jake to the vet pronto."

"Does he seem okay?"

"I can't tell. Can you call William to meet you? You need a vehicle."

"Don't worry. I'll figure something out. I must go."

I decide to run back the way we've come, retracing the route Jake likely took—it's on the way to the intersection of Northern Dancer Avenue and Queen's Plate Drive. I'm guessing it's my truck that's involved in the accident and the dogs were probably thrown when it crashed.

The short breather I had with Jake and Melissa has helped me to recoup a little, but my heart is still racing, and I can't maintain a fast pace. No sign of Kelly as I jog along the side of the road towards Northern Dancer Avenue. I'm not sure how much longer I can keep going. I'm flagging. Sweat is dripping down my nose and my eyes are stinging. The wind is against me—making it harder to breathe.

A siren approaches behind me and a police vehicle, a large SUV, pulls up in front. The last thing I want is to be held up.

A burly police officer gets out and holds his hand up as if he's stopping the traffic.

"My truck's been stolen with my two dogs inside," I yell at him, but in spurts because I can't catch my breath. "We've found one dog running along this road, but I can't find my border collie." Oh no, I'm crying. I lean over with my hands on my thighs and try to catch my breath.

"What's the licence plate number?"

I tell him, all the while counting the seconds being lost.

"That's the accident that was called in. Get in." So, Jake must have been thrown from the pickup, as I suspected. He opens the front passenger door. I'm not sure he's permitted to transport me in the front, but I'm grateful.

I've not been inside a police vehicle with the siren going, and it's quite something to watch cars pull over and stop as we charge past. He's not going at an alarming speed, but fast enough. I keep my eyes wide open as I peer out of the side window. He says he's watching out for her as well, and he doesn't want to go faster just in case she darts across the road.

He tells me he's an animal lover and has a shepherd-cross at home. I don't hear most of what he's saying because my brain is focused on Kelly and all my memories of our time together and my heart aches at the possibility that I've lost her. Anger simmers inside me. What would possess Elsa to steal my truck? Does she have no compassion for animals? She's an electric jockey and she's just smashed my truck with my beloved dogs inside. But I suppose I shouldn't assume it was her. Just because Roxi didn't deny she was around her barn doesn't mean it was Elsa. I take in a deep breath and wipe by forehead with my sleeve. My dry lips are peeling, and I have a raging thirst.

"Do you know who stole my truck?"

"It's being investigated. It's just ahead."

We've turned onto Northern Dancer Avenue and Queen's Park Drive isn't far away. The front of my blue truck is crunched up and attached to a concrete lamppost. The doors are all open. I jump down from the police vehicle, but my legs buckle underneath me. They're sore and stiff and won't work properly. The police officer comes to my aid and gives me an arm.

"Did they find my dog inside the truck?"

"Stay here. I'll find out what I can." My legs shake and feel unreliable as supports.

The police officer takes long strides towards the two officers at the scene. He turns and shakes his head. That's an enormous relief. I dreaded the thought of finding her dead inside the truck. Perhaps she was thrown out and got injured. I shuffle towards the truck.

"No further, please miss."

"Were the doors all open like this when your arrived?" I ask the officers.

"No. Just the two front doors."

I try to think like Kelly. She's so smart. I don't think she would take off like Jake did. She'd wait. She'd depend on me finding her and rescuing her. She trusts me to protect her. We have such a strong bond.

"Kelly, Kelly, it's me." I take a deep breath and try to call louder. "Kelly, Kelly. Come!" I stand on the sidewalk as close to the truck as I'm permitted to be. The older homes have verdant front gardens with lush shrubs bursting with buds and forsythia in full yellow bloom. The wind carries my voice away. I go to the other side of the pickup and try calling again. I turn around on the spot and call in every direction. I'm dizzy and nauseated.

"Kelly, it's me. Kelly!" I'm near collapse. I sit down on the uneven, cold curb, and hold my head in my hands. I don't want to believe I've lost my beloved dog. Kelly is so precious to me. I gasp as if I'm choking on my tears.

There's a curious sensation on my cheek. A cool, wet nose that I know so well.

"Kelly, oh Kelly. Thank goodness. Are you okay?" I'm in a full flood of tears as I envelop her in my trembling arms. I hoped she'd be smart and wait, but I was afraid of what could have happened.

"That your dog?" the officer asks.

"Yes." I sob.

"She's beautiful. I'll give you both a lift home. Your vehicle is about to be towed and we'll be checking it out. Here, let me help you up. Have you got a leash?"

"Kelly doesn't need one. She's a very intelligent and wonderful dog."

"I can see that. You get in the back seat with Kelly. Good dog." He pats her and she wags her tail slowly and then gets into the SUV. As far as I can tell, she's fine. I can't wait to get home. I text William and Melissa.

Now to find out how Jake is.

I can't let go of Kelly's neck and she presses against me. Tears still run down my flushed cheeks.

When we finally arrive at the farm, the officer asks me why my face is swollen and bruised. I tell him someone hit me at the race-track, but I don't want to press charges.

"If you change your mind, you know where to find us."

I thank him for everything and ask for his name and badge number. I'll be letting Detective Valeska know how helpful and supportive he's been.

Gabriel's peering out of the kitchen door and before I can stop him, he's running towards the police vehicle, past me and Kelly.

"Well, hello there, young man," the officer says. "Would you like to see inside?"

"Thank goodness you're here, William," I say, as he steps out of the backdoor.

"Didn't you expect me?" He has a twinkle in his eye, but then he notices how exhausted and filthy I am. Dust swirls around my feet. The wind is relentless. I point to the police vehicle and William walks over. Kelly trots ahead of me as we enter the house, but it's as if I'm dragging my body about. I use the rail to heave myself upstairs, and turn the bath taps on, pouring in cupfuls of lavender-scented Epsom salts.

14

On the Run

Just as I'm beginning to fear the worst about Jake, I receive a text from Melissa. She, Edwin, and Jake are on their way here and Jake's okay. She doesn't say 'fine', but he must be alive. William insisted earlier that I lie back in a recliner in the family room. He and Gabriel are playing cards on the floor at my feet. Kelly is stretched out fast asleep. Cooper is weaving between William and Gabriel and making a nuisance of himself, but neither of the humans seems to mind. Gabriel's still not talking much, but he's making progress. He's grown closer to William and Melissa than to me. I'm struggling with how to reach out to him.

The backdoor opens but I don't hear the patter of Jake's paws. Kelly lifts her head but puts it down again when she hears Melissa's voice. The accident must have taken its toll on Kelly even though she didn't run away.

Edwin comes into the family room carrying Jake.

"He's okay. We took him to a friend of mine who's a small animal vet—the best. He checked him out thoroughly. The only injury he could find was a minor sprain in his back leg. Ted's assessment pointed to exhaustion and dehydration being the primary diagnoses. He administered intravenous fluids and Jake's shown improvement already. He's on pain meds and should be kept quiet to help the healing process."

Gabriel gets up and strokes Jake's head gently.

"I'll lay him down now," Edwin tells Gabriel. Melissa places one of the dog blankets near the bookshelves and fetches a bowl of water. Kelly doesn't pay any attention to the kerfuffle.

"Thanks very much for taking care of him," I tell Edwin.

"My pleasure."

"We're about to eat," William says. "I hope you'll join us?"

"Edwin and I are getting takeout and then going to the clinic," Melissa says.

"Perhaps another time, then?" suggests William.

"Love to," Edwin says.

"What about your car, Melissa?" I ask.

"We're going to pick it up now," she says. "Well, after I have a quick shower. I can't go anywhere in this state." She trots out of the room. William offers Edwin a drink, but he says he's fine.

"What do you know about Bill Price?" I ask.

"You've heard the rumours, I suppose. The backstretch has the longest grapevine on the planet. I try to ignore it but find it impossible. Everyone likes to talk while I'm treating their horses."

"I haven't heard the rumours. It's just that the meeting I had with Bill recently left me with questions. I wasn't happy with how it went or with his demeanor. Usually, he's open and friendly and cooperative. He was a big supporter of Frank's attempts to improve racehorse welfare."

"He's changed. Ever since his wife died a year ago, actually. He should retire, but he's not about to. The rumours are not pleasant, and I shouldn't be helping to spread them, but sometimes these things are based on a grain of truth. And I know you'll not take them at face value."

"So, what is this rumour?"

"There's no proof that I'm aware of, but I've been told that Bill Price, Barnaby Caldermat, and Cliff Ryman were running an illegal gambling business. Since Barnaby's out of the picture it seems that another member of the Caldermat family, I don't know his name, has joined this circle. But he could have been involved before Barnaby's death. Anyway, the gossip is that the business continues, the major surprise being the conjecture that Bill's involved. No shock to hear Cliff could be part of it."

"That would explain Cliff's use of the electrical device in Hector's race, and him holding back his horse in Rose's race. You must know that Jaden was beaten up and left for dead?"

"Of course. There are rumours about that as well."

"Which are?"

"That he reported Cliff to the stewards, so he had it coming, as they say. It's very disturbing. Virtually all of us working every day with the horses want a fair, level playing field. And I know that's why you do investigative work, to catch the bad guys and get them out of the picture and let the rest of us good guys carry on in peace."

"That would be nice. By far the majority of us want horse racing to have—and to be perceived to have—integrity, and to put the welfare of the horse first. Few as they are, we still have a long way to go to get rid of the cheats."

"Other sports do too, I can assure you. There's corruption everywhere. But that doesn't mean we should just give up. I don't hesitate to report people when I have evidence. For example, I've just submitted a formal complaint to the College of Veterinarians of Ontario about Dr. Berzinski."

"Roxi mentioned his name to me. She has concerns about him."

"That's interesting. I'm aware his name has been bandied around in the context of PEDs. I'm a member of the death review committee, as you know. A horse died unexpectedly, and I recommended a necropsy. The results revealed banned substances. When the trainer was questioned, he said Dr. Berzinski had sold him supplements that were purported to improve cardiovascular function. He showed us the bottles but there were no labels."

"He could have used Dr. Berzinski's name in a ploy to transfer suspicion to him," William says.

"Right. And I don't have evidence to back up the trainer's claim. However, this incident combined with the stories I've heard in the backstretch have raised my concern. This may not be sufficient for the College, but I hope they nevertheless investigate him. It's abhorrent to me that a veterinarian would harm horses for personal financial gain. In what context did Roxi mention his name?"

"She found Elsa holding a syringe while she was in one of the stalls and was concerned that Elsa could have given PEDs to one or more of her horses. That's when she mentioned Dr. Berzinski."

"She could be mistaken. It's well known that Elsa's a diabetic. It has caused controversy and some jockeys believe she's a liability on the track. And, while I don't know her, what I've heard is that she's far from cruel. It strikes me unlikely she administered PEDs."

"Meg, we should tone it down," William says, as he nods towards Gabriel.

"Edwin," I say. "We can talk some other time. Thanks for this, though. I appreciate it."

Melissa appears in the doorway smelling of citrus, wearing a sky-blue top, perhaps made of cashmere. I hope she puts overalls on when she helps out in the clinic.

Edwin digs his wallet out of his pocket and gives Gabriel a five-dollar bill. He whispers to me, "it'll take his mind off what he's heard."

Melissa and Edwin give Jake and Kelly a few pats and leave.

My stomach fluttered and I'm sure my heart missed a beat when I saw Edwin's wallet. It reminded me that my bag containing my money purse and card holder was in the pickup. The police would have given it to me if they'd found it. Elsa or whoever stole the truck must have it. I blurt it all out to William who says the three of us need to eat first and then he'll be happy to help, if I need it. It seems daunting. I keep all my cards in the same wallet: credit and debit cards, as well as my driver's licence and health card. I send off a note to Detective Valeska and she responds almost at once that she'll forward my message. She asks me to call her in about fifteen minutes.

Although William has made a delicious-smelling pasta dish which Gabriel tucks into, I play around with my fork and eat hardly any of it.

"You need to eat something, Meg. Gabriel's doing a fine job."

"I'm sorry. It's delicious but my stomach's not right."

Gabriel looks at me as if I'm about to vomit.

"Don't worry, Gabriel, I'm just feeling queasy, that's all. I'll be fine by tomorrow morning."

William asks if I'll read a story to Gabriel once he's ready for bed, but Gabriel turns to William and makes it clear that he's the preferred reader. The way I feel at the moment, that's fine by me. And I must call Detective Valeska.

While William gets Gabriel ready for bed, I clear up and then start work on my missing cards. Most of it can be done online. I'm put on hold by the bank after answering too many questions and punching in so many numbers that I have a headache. The music is irritating and repetitive but eventually I get through to a live person who I can understand, and she deals with everything efficiently and courteously.

William enters the kitchen with a smile on his face.

"You should read to Gabriel some time. He can read himself of course, but he really enjoys being read to, especially if you can voice the parts and bring it all to life."

"I didn't realize you have that talent. I must call Detective Valeska. I'm late. I'll put you on speaker."

"Okay. Drink?"

"Do we have some wine open?"

"We can finish this bottle of white that's been open in the fridge for a few days."

"Sounds good. Let's go into the family room." It doesn't take William long to pour the wine and join me.

"Meg, thanks for calling," Detective Valeska says. I tell her about the police officer who was so helpful and thoughtful today and add that William is with me on speaker phone.

"I'm pleased to hear that the officer did his job with professionalism and grace. Thanks for letting me know. I've made a note to follow up. Do you have any idea who stole your truck?"

"I don't know for sure, but I was told that Elsa Lorenza was in the area just before it disappeared."

"My officers reported a witness saw a man of small stature running from the scene. Fingerprints on the vehicle do not match any in our database."

"If the witness is correct, then it's possible that it was Cliff Ryman."

"No. We have his fingerprints on file."

"That's weird. Those are the only two I can think of."

"What about Noah?" asks William. "Is he small?"

"Not as small as a jockey," I say. "And he has distinctive red hair."

There's a loud knock on the back door. Kelly and I are startled. She barks and runs into the kitchen. Jake growls but doesn't stir from his blanket. I tell him to stay, and William says he and Kelly will check things out.

"Someone's at the door. Can I call you back?" I ask the Detective.

"There've been some other developments and we need to be sure we're on the same page. But I've had a long day and you sound exhausted. I'll call you tomorrow."

"I suppose I am. I'll watch for your call."

There are agitated voices in the kitchen. I pull the recliner upright and walk towards them less stiffly than I expected.

"Noah? Is that you?" I ask. The person in front of me looks as if he's been living in a ditch for a couple of months.

"I'm not a criminal. I didn't steal your truck. Here's your bag."

"Come and sit down," I say. "No, on second thoughts, you need a shower and clean clothes. Have you got any?"

"I guess I smell bad. I've probably got used to it. What can I say? I have nothing."

"I'm larger than you," William says, "but I'll find something. Follow me."

"Thanks, William," I say. "Have you eaten anything recently, Noah?"

"I had a sandwich from someone in a van," he says, as he stumbles up the stairs.

"When?"

"I can't remember."

There's a desperation about him that makes me believe he's telling the truth when he says he's not a criminal. Kelly seems to have warmed to him too, so maybe she's changed her mind about him. We can get the wrong first impression about people, so I suppose dogs can too, although she's usually right. But how come he had my bag? Nothing seems to have been touched, although it does smell of bonfire smoke.

William comes down clutching Noah's clothes in a ball at arm's length. If he had a third hand, I'm sure he'd be holding his nose.

"I'll look after those, although I'm tempted to put them in the garbage as opposed to the wash."

"He's a physical and emotional wreck."

"Perhaps you should hang around upstairs. He wouldn't be suicidal, would he?"

"I've no idea. But he's not improved since he turned up at the barn, except for his hand."

"I'm going to heat up this leftover pasta. And perhaps some hot chocolate would be good."

"I'll go upstairs. You've got me concerned."

Something makes me text Detective Valeska after I've put the clothes into the washing machine and washed my hands thoroughly. The smells of stagnant water and stale sweat hang around. I spray some air freshener, but it makes me sneeze.

My mobile rings. I hurry into the office to take the call.

"Is Noah facing charges?" I ask. "Sorry, I haven't got much time to talk with you."

"I'm soaking in a bath and trying to relax, so I don't want this to be a prolonged call either. The short answer is no. But I should let you know Olivia Matterson turned herself in this evening and gave a full statement with her lawyer present. My officers are paying a visit to Zoey Caldermat as we speak. It seems we have you to thank for these developments. I would have told you this earlier but, let me guess, Noah showed up."

"Yes. He's in a terrible state. We're concerned."

"Assuming Olivia is telling the truth, Noah didn't stab Barnaby. We still don't know who's responsible for his death. But an astute officer found a syringe tossed into a hedge when he was assisting with the neighbourhood door-to-door. I suspect that the person who chucked it there reckoned anyone who found it would just assume it was thrown there by a drug user. The syringe has a partial fingerprint that's going to be difficult to work with, apparently, and traces of a barbiturate. The fact is we don't have enough evidence to arrest Noah."

"Can I tell him that?"

"Yes. Remember to keep me in the loop."

The three of us convene at the kitchen table. I give Noah the news from Detective Valeska that he's not about to be arrested. He doesn't say anything and tucks into the pasta with gusto. He smells of William's aftershave which reminds me of nutmeg and cedarwood. We let him eat.

Kelly's lying under the table, but Jake's still on his blanket in the family room. After Noah has finished his meal and we've cleared the dishes away, we join Jake.

"Noah," I say, once we're all seated, "how come you had my bag?"

"Elsa stole your truck. It was a mad thing to do. She wanted to give it to Roxi. Pure insanity."

"I don't disagree. And the irony is, it was a rental."

"Anyway, she texted me, in a panic. Since Cliff won't have anything to do with her anymore, she turned to me for help, and I agreed to meet her in the park. She was hysterical. She told me she didn't know the dogs were in your truck and when they suddenly both barked, she was startled and crashed the truck. I'm glad they're here. Elsa says she ran off and she couldn't tell me what happened to Kelly and Jake. She gave me your purse and pleaded with me to give it back to you. She didn't have the guts. So, that's Elsa's latest crazy stunt."

"Well, I guess I should thank you for returning my purse. But let's start at the beginning again. How did you meet Barnaby?"

"I told you, through a mate who I play poker with. I'm a gambler. Well, I used to be."

"Were you a professional poker player?"

"I suppose I was, yes. I don't know how my mate knew Barnaby, but he said he'd made a lot of money. I told you this before. When we didn't hear from him for a month, and we'd given him a lot of cash with no return, I said I'd go after him for the statistical formula.

I'd met with Barnaby in his house, and he'd shown me graphs and tables on his laptop—not for long enough for me to see details, but my greed had taken over by then. What can I say? It was like a kind of guaranteed gamble. I know that's an oxymoron."

"So, what did you do? Truth this time."

"I didn't set up a meeting like I told you. I sat alone in my car in the street and waited for an opportunity to break in. There were three cars in the driveway when I got there. Two Mercedes and a large SUV, not sure what make. Olivia came out of the house with another woman. I don't know who she was, and they seemed flustered and in a hurry to get out of there. Olivia dropped her purse, and the other woman slammed her door and reversed out of the driveway so fast I thought she'd lose control. No sign of Barnaby. I was going to leave, but I was that angry and upset, I couldn't. I thought he must be in there but there may be a chance he wasn't. I'm a gambler. What can I say? I reckoned the odds were in favour of him being out."

"You planned to break in?"

"I had no plan. I'm not cut out to be a criminal. I rang the bell. No answer. I rang it again and listened. Silence. I went around to the back of the house. The patio doors were open. I called Barnaby's name. I shouted. Not a sound. I went into his office, took his laptop and then tripped over his body on the way out. So, I reckon Olivia and that woman murdered him. But how can I tell the police that? They won't believe it."

"Actually, they might." Both he and William listen without saying a word as I give them a synopsis of what Detective Valeska told me.

"But I bet they think I tossed that syringe wherever you said they found it," Noah says as he gets down on the floor with Jake. He touches Jake's shoulder lightly, as if he's afraid of what he might feel, or how Jake will react. The dog merely raises his head, sighs, and puts it down again. "They'll try to convict me on circumstantial evidence, won't they?"

"Help me here," I say. "Have you any idea who would want Barnaby dead?"

"Did you meet anyone else who was caught up in Barnaby's scheme?" asks William.

"Don't think I haven't been trying to think of someone."

"What about at the races?" I ask. "Did you go at any time? Did you see Barnaby there with someone?"

"I don't know. I'm not sure."

"What about?" I ask.

"Who I saw Barnaby with."

"When and where?"

"I didn't go to the races, but I got to like watching them. My mate and I, we'd put a few bets on in this bar. One afternoon we were watching a race and we'd put money on the long shot just for fun. Barnaby's name wasn't listed as one of the owners, and he wasn't in the Winner's Circle, but we saw him walk up to the jockey after the photos were taken and shake his hand. The winner had long odds, just so you know."

"What was the jockey's name?"

"I'm trying to remember. A name that began with C, I think. We thought it was odd because we've noticed each jockey shakes hands with the owners, if there, of the horse they've just ridden, but not with other owners—it wouldn't make sense. So, if Barnaby was the owner of the winner, why wasn't he in the Winner's Circle? And if he wasn't the owner, why did he shake the jockey's hand and pat him on the back? We lost, by the way. Our horse came last."

"What was the date?" asks William. He's fetched his laptop and opens it on his lap.

After a few minutes, William finds the race and, sure enough, the jockey is Cliff Ryman and we see Barnaby shaking his hand and patting him on the back, as Noah described.

"My guess is that Cliff was handing over an electrical device to Barnaby," I say. "Noah, there never was any statistical formula. It was Cliff either using an electrical device to stimulate the horse, or him holding his horse back. Barnaby was running an illegal gambling ring. Cliff was on his payroll and other jockeys must have been as well. And it could be continuing without Barnaby."

"So, he used our money to bet on the horses and Cliff rigged the races by using a shock thing? It sounds horrible. I honestly thought I was taking advantage of something harmless, just a way of predicting winners, and that he kept a percentage of the take."

"Ah," William says.

"And you had no record of what was bet on what. You trusted him?" I ask Noah.

"You think I'm an idiot. Yeah, I did a stupid thing. My greed blinded me, and Barnaby was really convincing. What can I say? He easily got me and my mate on side."

"Your clothes are dry." I get up and fetch them. They smell of lavender, but they don't look much better. He's obviously been wearing them day and night.

"What are your plans?" William asks.

"Don't have any."

"Before we get into next steps," I say as I sit down in the recliner again, "where does Elsa fit into all this?"

Since Jake is fast asleep and snoring, Noah gets up, stretches and sits in an armchair.

"It's nice in here," he says. "I wish I didn't have to talk about Elsa. It's so complicated."

"We need to know," I say. "She's mixed up in this and my feeling is that she's her own worst enemy." Cooper jumps up onto my lap and I wonder if Gabriel is okay. Cooper usually stays with him. William must be reading my mind. He sprints upstairs to check.

"That's a good way of putting it." Noah sighs and stretches his legs out. William's khaki pants are too long and baggy on him and make him look as if he belongs in a comedy sketch. "Elsa's messed up. I don't mean that in a nasty way. She has mental health issues—I think that's the politically correct way to describe it. The trouble is, I have feelings for her. Note the present tense."

"Explain what's happened between you and her."

"Oh, where to start." He runs a hand through his shiny red hair. It needs cutting, but the shampoo has restored its lustre.

William returns and gives me a 'thumbs up' signal as Cooper decides against my lap and curls up with Jake.

"I met Elsa at a charity event. You won't want the details. Anyway, we saw each other quite often and then she moved into my condo. But she started acting strange. When I asked her what was going on, all she'd say was her granny was in trouble and needed her help."

"That would be Roxi."

"Yeah, her. I'm too tired to give you the whole story. I'll try to pick out the important bits."

"We'll ask questions if we need more," I say.

"Sure. Elsa thought I was loaded. She asked if I could help Roxi out, like give her an interest-free loan. She didn't ask me to give her money outright. But I said I couldn't. Elsa got really down. So, I thought I should tell her why I couldn't just hand over money, that I'd lost a lot and I told her Barnaby's name. She acted funny."

"What do you mean by 'funny'?"

"I don't know. Just odd, like she knew him or something about him. Anyway, that's when she started to drift away from me and when I did see her, I could sense her anxiety and stress. One day she sort of lost it and I asked her what the hell was the matter, or words like that. She told me Roxi had betrayed her and she'd probably be suspended when she hadn't done anything wrong. Then Elsa mentioned a video which Roxi accused her of making to get revenge. I couldn't understand any of it. She was acting like a raving lunatic at that point. She told me I was next to useless because I wouldn't give her money, and other stuff I won't repeat."

"How did your hand get hurt?"

"I was worried about her, and went to her flat. She let me in. When I hung up my jacket, I noticed what looked like another guy's jacket. She saw me looking at it and told me it was none of my business whose it was, and I didn't own her. I tried to calm her down, but she just got more and more angry. She said her licence was suspended and yelled that if I'd given her some money to help Roxi none of this would have happened. She was blaming me for everything. I wanted to make her feel better, to get her to cool off, but as I approached her, she was waving a knife about. My reaction was to put up my hand. I didn't see how it happened, but she cut me with the knife and then pushed me away. I tripped over the rug and fell. I'd had enough. I just left. I didn't know what to do. She didn't seem to realize she'd cut me. I was as miserable as hell. I suppose I care about her a lot even though she sometimes loses her grip on things. I should have done something." He rubs his knees and looks at me. But I can't fix their relationship.

"It's getting late," I say. "We'll talk some more tomorrow."

"Where are you going to stay tonight?" asks William. "We can't offer you a room here."

"Are you completely broke?" I ask.

"I've sold the condo, but I won't get the funds until the closing date which is in a couple of months. I feel like I'm in limbo between my old life and the new life I'm going to have to create. I need to get my act together. The direct answer to your question is that I'm not broke, just a lot worse off. I wasn't stupid enough to gamble all my inheritance away."

"What about the other farm?" asks William as he looks at me.

"That's a great idea. Noah, I bought a place further down the road called Milkweed Farm. The people, Joanna and Ewert, have moved out and I haven't got around to finding new tenants yet. You can stay there without payment, but with some conditions."

"Wow, that's amazing. Thanks."

"There won't be any supplies," William says. "Where's your car?"

"Still in the condo garage."

"And you can't stay in your condo?"

"I don't feel safe there. Everyone thinks I'm a murderer."

"I'll take you to the farm now," William says. "I'll give you some basic supplies, then tomorrow I'll drop you off at your condo so you can pick up some belongings, including your car."

"What are you doing with your furniture?" I ask.

"I haven't even thought about that."

15

Pushed

Yesterday was a long day and I have a feeling this day isn't going to seem any shorter or easier. At least the dogs are fine. Even Jake's leg has made a miraculous recovery. I can't detect a limp. He's a stoic and faithful companion. But I won't be able to leave them alone in the truck until some considerable time has passed. None of us could cope with the anxiety.

So, one of the conditions I've laid down for Noah is that he'll dog-sit now and then, even though Kelly isn't a fan. And this is one of those occasions. I must meet Thomas at the café in Branderton and give him $800 per horse in cash, as we agreed. Roxi confirmed that there are thirty, so that's $24,000. It won't be a quick and easy process to get my hands on this amount of cash, but I've already put the wheels in motion. I'm apprehensive about having that much money on my person—I'm sure it'll be written all over my face and I'll be a mugging waiting to happen.

As soon as I've paid Thomas, I'll call the shippers and set up their move to Four Rs. I plan to follow the horses' progress and look forward to their successful adoptions into new forever homes.

*   *   *

The café is busy, but I find a table for two where I can see the new metallic blue rental truck I picked up this morning gleaming in the sunshine. I'm confident it won't stay clean and shiny for long. The rental company staff appear to find amusement in my record of truck fatalities. I suppose they benefit from my misadventures, since I've been turning up at their counter fairly regularly in recent years.

I've been sitting at this small round table for over half an hour. I check my mobile for messages yet again and just as I'm about to drop it back into my bag, I see Detective Valeska's name pop up.

A text message tells me Vannersville Police Services have taken Zoey Caldermat in for questioning. Perhaps there's a connection with Thomas' absence.

He isn't coming. No message and no sign of him. I pick up my bag and take my sparkling truck to the Branderton Town offices. I take a chance and tell reception that I have a meeting with Thomas Caldermat and they give me directions to his office.

The office is a disappointment. He's in a cubicle constructed out of grey fabric dividers. It's much smaller than a horse stall which, for some odd reason, gives me a sense of satisfaction. I simply say hello and when he sees me standing just outside his space his face flushes pink, his lips purse and he thumps his fists on the desk.

"How dare you come here," he says, through clenched teeth.

"You failed to show up, so I thought I'd seek you out. I have the money you asked for, in cash."

"Keep your voice down. Follow me."

"Need help, Tommy?" A squeaky voice drifts over one of the partitions.

"No, thanks. Everything's fine. Be back in a tick."

Thomas leads me to a door that opens onto a stairway. As we walk down, he swings clenched fists by his sides, and the noise of his heavy footsteps bounces off the grey concrete walls. He stops when we reach a dimly lit landing half-way between two floors and turns to face me. I stand as far away from him as the space allows but he edges closer. I can smell stale coffee. His grey eyes look icy cold—without a fleck of colour.

"I don't understand what the issue is," I say. "I have the cash you asked for."

"The problem is you. You're an interfering bitch."

"I don't know what you're talking about."

"Oh, don't give me that shit. You know exactly what this is about."

I stare at him with unblinking eyes. He moves closer. I go around him and realize my mistake. I've ended up too near to the edge of the landing and to the next flight going down, and he's furious and vengeful. There's a flicker of a smile as he thrusts his two fists into my shoulders. They feel like hammers.

"That's for Zoey, you piece of garbage," he says through gritted teeth and with narrowed, steely eyes peering at me.

He doesn't hang around to watch me fall.

As I stumble, I wonder if I'll end up in a body cast. It terrifies me that I may not be able to stop my tumble down the hard, unforgiving stairs that descend to the floor below.

My right hip hits the edge of a stair and the top of my head brushes against the rough breezeblock. As my body twists, I kick out my right leg hoping to hook into the metal railing. I could risk breaking my leg, but I must stop this plunge, so I take the chance.

My leg finds a gap in the railing, and I use all the strength I can summon to protect it while I strain to stop my fall. I grab the edge of a stair and brace my arm against the wall. I'm lying diagonally with my head lower than my right foot. But I've halted my descent and let out a gasp. I must have been holding my breath. Sweat trickles into my left ear. My jacket has slipped off my shoulders, but my keys and mobile are still safely zipped in the pockets. I lie in this awkward position for a few seconds to catch my breath and to figure out how to get myself upright without any more damage. It's tough and painful to unravel my body but I'm alive and there are no broken bones as far as I can tell. I sit on the stairs for a few minutes to give my heart a chance to stop thumping, and to regain some strength.

Glad to be up on my feet at last, I hobble away from the building. The fresh air and warm sunshine revive me a little.

As soon as I get my battered and bruised body into the truck, I call Roxi.

"Meg. I'm sure glad you called. The shippers are taking the horses this afternoon to that awful place. You know, the killing pen. What happened? I thought you were going to save them." She coughs and sobs at the same time.

"I will. I'll be there in about an hour."

I sound more confident than I am. My plan is like the slime Gabriel likes to play with. There's no structure to it and it changes shape every time I think about it. But there's enough substance for me to get started. I call Melissa and she leaps into action with Edwin's help, which is a first step.

The next step involves picking up the dogs. I promised William and Melissa I wouldn't put the dogs in danger again, but they're all I've got. They're my trusty back-up team. So, I drive to Milkweed Farm where Noah's staying.

My body is so stiff that I walk sluggishly back to the truck from the farmhouse. Jake runs backwards and forwards in front of me, showing no signs of his sprain, but Kelly stays at my side. I can almost see a question-mark hanging over her head when she looks up at me.

"It's okay, Kelly."

Fortunately, Noah didn't seem to notice any difference in me. I suppose he's got too many of his own worries.

I'm thankful I have a new pickup that no one at the track is familiar with. I park in the lot where the shippers will position their trucks ready for loading and tell Kelly and Jake to lie down behind the seats. The windows of this vehicle look almost black from the outside which helps to keep the dogs out of view, but I can't help worrying about leaving them. I promised myself I wouldn't. Roxi's barn is a one minute brisk walk away.

"Meg, I just can't bear this. I can't take any more."

"It's going to be alright. When the horses are safely loaded, you and I are going to follow the trucks."

"What then?"

"I have a vague plan. Do you have their microchip numbers and copies of their registration papers?"

"It's all here." Roxi hands me a crumpled brown envelope thick with documents. She's trembling.

"I'll take a headshot of each horse, with your help."

She grabs a leather lead-rein that's hungry for nourishment and follows me. She still has her arm in a splint but has adapted well. It doesn't take us long since most of the horses can sense something's up and are conveniently hanging their heads over their stall doors. It's as if they're trying to figure out why Roxi is tottering about at a faster pace than usual.

"Meg, I have it," Melissa says as she jogs into the barn. "I'm sorry. It took longer than I thought it would. Someone was using it." She holds out the microchip reader.

"The trucks are coming, I can hear them," Roxi says. "This is the end for me and these beautiful horses." She chews her bottom lip as if to stop it from trembling. She's holding back tears.

"Not if I can help it," I say with as much confidence as I can muster.

"I'm sure Meg has a plan," Melissa says as she puts an arm around Roxi's shoulders. Melissa looks at me and I cross my fingers.

The truck drivers are the same three who turned up last time. I suppose there aren't many shippers with trailers that can hold ten horses.

"I'm Zach. Don't think I told you my name last time. You lost the battle, then."

"The battle, but I hope we haven't lost the war," I say. I hand Zach the crumpled envelope with the registration papers they need.

He and the other two drivers prepare their trailers for loading. They let the ramps down to reveal rubber matting, fresh wood-shavings and net bags of green grassy hay. This time I can't stop the horses from leaving.

Roxi refuses to help which is a good decision. Some of the horses don't want to get on the ramp even though they've been shipped several times in their lives. They've probably missed training for a couple of days and have a lot of pent up energy.

A few rear, several back up, and others plant their feet solidly on the ground, and it takes three strong men to get them into the trailers: one leading and two either side of the horse's rear with locked hands held near the top of the back legs. It seems as if they lift a couple of the horses up the ramp.

Roxi watches three or four of them being loaded but it's agonizing for her. She looks older and frailer as Melissa holds her arm and guides her back to her office to sit down. Melissa probably thinks she's near to collapse.

I explain to Zach, as he starts preparations for leaving, that I haven't given up on rescuing the horses even though my deal to purchase them has fallen through. He gives me a sideways glance. He's sceptical.

"The horse meat business is strong," he says. "There's quick money in it."

"Can you tell me where these horses are going and what will happen to them?"

"Sure. We're to take them to a place near the Quebec border, called Penchesterton Farms. There's a big set-up with hundreds of pens. It stinks. If a horse is lucky, he gets a pen to himself but can't turn around. He might get a bucket with some water in it."

"Don't some of them die?"

"Yeah, I guess. But I reckon they don't stay there for long, but I've seen some in poor shape. I know horses need food in their bellies. They should be out grazing in some nice field."

"What happens to them?"

"Penchesterton prefers to buy the horses outright and then post them on-line. The Penchesterton operators are smart. They appeal to animal lovers saying that they need their help to save the horses from slaughter. They post an amount, like bail I guess, that will save them from the meat packers. People fall for it. But there are nasty rumours about what happens to the horses people paid bail for but can't take home themselves. Penchesterton promises the horses will get TLC but sometimes they're posted online again. And other times—well."

"I can guess what happens to those horses and to the ones no one bails out."

"Slaughter."

"So, the ones that were supposedly bailed out, but the people can't take care of, they go to slaughter anyway? That means the operators get double their money."

"That's what they say. I've heard that the operators get a guaranteed price per pound from the slaughterhouse in Quebec."

"They probably have a contract."

"Yeah, something like that. I hate to add to this, but there are so-called animal lovers who take them but have no idea how to look after a horse. That's another issue."

"It seems like it's lose-lose for the horses whichever way you look at it."

"That's what I reckon."

"So, to rescue Roxi's horses I need to approach the Penchesterton operators with an offer that beats what they'd get for meat or from bail."

"You'll have to offer more 'cause they can get both in some cases. And you'll be supporting their rotten business."

"Mm."

"We're almost ready to leave."

"I don't want to hold you up. It's not fair on the horses. Some sound restless in there."

Zach resumes his inspection of the trucks. He makes sure the open windows are secure and the side door is latched. There's just one ramp to lift and fasten.

"Thanks a lot for the info," I say. "I'm going to follow your trucks and see what I can do at Penchesterton."

"Fine. By the way, I thought you might want a quick way to identify them, so I've put a sticker on each horse's rump like the ones they use in the sale, and I've pencilled the number on the registration papers."

"That'll be a huge help." Although, I'm hoping that I'll be able to work some magic and they'll stay on the trucks until we get to Four Rs.

"Thanks. Be warned—there'll be a lot of sad looking horses there."

"I know. I can't save them all. It'll be tough but I'll focus on these thirty."

"We're off, then." He lifts the ramp of the truck he'll be driving and bolts it into place. "Hope to see you at Penchesterton and good luck."

"Thanks."

Roxi, Melissa and I scramble into my pickup. Melissa sits on the back seat and keeps the dogs company.

The journey is tedious and our conversation sporadic and minimal. Melissa attempts to raise a topic now and then, but no one picks up the thread and it's left dangling among us. Roxi leans her head against the passenger window and closes her eyes, although she's not asleep. She fidgets and fiddles with her splint as if it's irritating her.

The sun is on its way down to the horizon as our part of the world turns away from it. I would rather have daylight when we arrive at Penchesterton. The wind has picked up again and little dust devils skim across the highway in front of us. Even my truck wobbles with each gust. I clench the steering wheel and grind my teeth as my insides quiver with doubt. I have a horrible feeling my vague plan won't work. It probably would be better to wait for the horses to be posted on-line and then bail each one out. But from what Zach says, that wouldn't be without risk.

"What are we going to do when we get there?" asks Melissa.

"I'm going to play it by ear," I say.

Roxi sits up and turns to look at me, although I don't take my eyes off the road. "You said you had a plan."

"I do, sort of. It's nebulous and subject to change at any moment."

"That's not a goddam plan. Don't say we're travelling all this way just to see them go to slaughter." She drops her head, clasps her forehead with her free hand, and lets out a shuddery sigh.

"I learned a lot of useful information from Zach, one of the drivers. I'm planning to put that helpful info to good use."

"Perhaps we should just give up," Roxi says. She sounds defeated and exhausted.

"No!" Melissa yells from the back.

"We have to try," I say.

The truck ahead of us signals left to leave the main highway. It's not an easy corner to maneuver a large articulated truck and trailer around, but Zach does it without lurching into the ditch, and the other two drivers follow suit. The road is narrow and undulating, but it's paved. Further ahead, a sea of silvery meal roofs appears on our left in the fading daylight. A spotlight illuminates a sign that announces Penchesterton Farms, but the paint is peeling off and a chunk of the top right corner is missing—as if a large rabbit has taken a bite out of it.

Although the roofs are visible from the road, horses are not. The pens are shielded from view by a sprawling barn. The three trucks enter the premises through a wide gateway and the gates close behind us. The paved driveway is expansive and ends at a brightly-lit spacious area sufficient for large vehicles to turn around. Three small horse trailers are parked along the eastern edge.

Zach jumps down from the truck and greets a burly man in a red-and-black-checkered flannel shirt which hangs over baggy, low-slung jeans. I want to sprint over to them, but my body is stiff and sore. It won't move quickly. Zach must be alerting the man to my presence.

"Hello, Miss. I'm Ralph. You must be the one wanting to bail out all these here horses," Ralph says as he nods his head towards the trailers. He puts his hands in his pockets as if he's waiting for me to make a move. "Hang on, lads. We're not unloading yet. We're having a business meeting here." He winks at me.

"Thanks for being willing to talk to me about this," I say. I return his wink with a half-hearted smile.

"Well, get on with it," Ralph says. "If this is a business meeting, let's get down to brass tacks." He stands with his legs apart and keeps his eyes fixed on me. I'm not sure what I'm supposed to read into his body language.

"What do you want for the horses?" I ask.

"Direct. That's good. We won't waste time. I haven't looked at them, but I can guess. Straight off the track, probably not a lot of meat on them, but in good condition, well cared for. Make me an offer I can't refuse."

"I have cash."

"We're getting somewhere. How much?"

"$600 per horse."

"I think more than that. I heard you offered $800 a head."

Something sinks to the bottom of my stomach. It feels like a rock.

"You've talked to Thomas Caldermat."

"Of course I have. He's the one I bought these here horses off. I paid him big bucks."

"Thomas Caldermat is the cousin of the murdered man, Barnaby."

"Murdered, eh?" His eyes leave mine. He stares at his boots for a couple of seconds.

"Thomas agreed to accept $800 per horse in cash and I was to pay the shippers. But then his girlfriend was taken in for questioning by the police for the role she allegedly played. Thomas blames me for her being detained and pushed me down a concrete and steel stairway when I went to his office to ask him about the horses. He doesn't care about these useless animals, as he put it. He said all they've done is deplete Barnaby's pathetic estate. So, that's the true story, in a nutshell."

"Ha! Ha! That Thomas sounds like my kind o' guy, from a business point of view. But I don't like dealing with people who push young ladies down the stairs. I thought you'd fallen off your horse the way you're walking, and you've got some bump on the side of your head."

I didn't realize I have a noticeable lump on my head. My hand reaches up and finds a sore bump about the size of a walnut.

"I moved a bunch of horses out when I got the call this lot were coming," Ralph says. "I've put myself out. It's cost me. I have to make a buck."

"$800 each is the limit of my offer."

"You've got cash?" Ralph asks.

"Yes."

"$800 per horse. That's $24,000. A lot of dough to be carrying around."

Ralph hasn't made me feel the least bit nervous until he said that. I'm not sure if the truck drivers would help me out if things got nasty, but I'm certain my body can't take another battering.

I turn and signal to Melissa who's in the pickup. She understands and lets the dogs out of the truck. They come trotting over and sit either side of me. It's as if they're impeccably trained and they lift my spirits—as they never fail to do. Their eyes fix on Ralph.

"No need to set these vicious dogs on me," Ralph says. He chuckles and bends down to reach his hand out to Jake. Jake curls his top lip revealing pearly white teeth and emits a low, grumbling growl. Ralph takes a backwards step.

"What's it going to be?" I ask. "You won't get $800 if you post them. I've checked out your website and it's usually about $400. And you certainly wouldn't get more than that for meat. I've checked out those prices too. You'd be lucky to get $350 and you'd have to pay shipping. And I'm sure $800 is much more than you paid Thomas Caldermat for them. He's anxious to stop further drains on his cousin's estate."

"I want to see the cash," Ralph says. He moves closer to me. The dogs stand. Jake has his hackles up and Kelly snarls. Melissa and Roxi are behind me, almost touching my back. I can hear Roxi breathing.

"I can vouch for the money," Zach says. He's been leaning against his trailer trying not to appear impatient, although he's been tapping his foot now and then. He hasn't seen the cash, but I don't blame him for stretching the truth.

A gust of wind is so powerful it rattles the metal roofs of the pens and unsettles the horses. Their hooves pound on the floors, making the trailers bob as if they're out at sea.

"Let's get on with this," Zach says. "Sorry, Ralph, but time is money for us."

"Well, Miss, looks like you've got yourself a deal." Ralph winks at me again.

"I need a receipt and the registration papers."

"No receipt, but you can have the horses and all these here documents. And you can feel good Thomas whatshisname didn't get $800. I have to be compensated for all my time and inconvenience, after all." He winks. If he winks at me one more time, I'm likely to slug him. But he probably wouldn't even notice since he's such a big heavy-set man.

I snatch the battered envelope out of his hand and fetch the cash from the truck with the dogs beside me. I'm thankful that Zach is a witness, as well as Roxi and Melissa. Ralph checks the wad of notes. He must have a lot of experience with cash. He doesn't count it but seems satisfied that it's all there.

"What will you tell Thomas Caldermat?" I ask.

"Our business is done, but if he asks, they were bailed out by a humane society. That's close enough not to be a lie. Just a white one, eh?" He smiles. His yellow teeth clash with his red and black shirt. "Nice doing business with you Miss."

"Goodbye," I say. It could have gone a lot worse.

"Follow us," Zach says as we all turn our backs on Ralph. I have a creepy sensation that his eyes are following every move I make. I'll be relieved when we're out of here. "We'll regroup at the truck stop back about five miles."

"Fine."

Melissa helps Roxi get back into the truck as the dogs jump in behind the front seats. It seems that we're all wanting out of

Penchesterton Farms like yesterday. Melissa encourages the dogs to sit next to her.

"Why did you need the microchip reader?" asks Melissa as we sit and wait for the trucks to turn around.

"I'm glad we didn't. The plan was to follow the trucks, but we could have got separated for some reason and the horses unloaded before we got here. I was expecting to see lots of horses and I'm not sure how Ralph keeps track. I wanted to be sure to rescue the right thirty horses."

"Good idea," Roxi says. "But why did you need the photos as well?"

"I don't know how much they would have helped because not all of them had distinctive face markings, as you know. But I thought it might speed things up—identifying them, I mean." I can't tell Roxi it was a way to keep her occupied as we waited for the dreaded trucks. She was about to self-destruct.

"I know each one like the back of my hand."

"You may not have come with us. In fact, I could have been entirely on my own. I'm glad I wasn't. It really helped to have you both here."

"And Kelly and Jake," Melissa says as she gives them each an ear rub. "They were brilliant."

"They always are," I say. "The trucks are on their way out. Time to leave."

"Meg, I'm sorry I was short with you," Roxi says.

"Don't be sorry. I didn't have a definite plan."

"And I can't pay you the $24,000—not now, anyway. Perhaps later."

"I don't want to hear any more about that. I did it for the horses."

16

Unwelcome Visitor

The truck stop has an enormous parking lot with huge semis lined up, side by side, as if they're ready to charge out of there en masse. My pickup is like an ant next to these monsters. I park close to the building. Zach and the two other drivers walk towards us.

"The next stop for these horses is Four Rs, right?" Zach asks.

"Yes."

"You're in luck. We haven't driven up to the fourteen-hour limit. Some days we're close. But the horses should have water and we should restock the hay. It's a long drive to that place."

"So, how do we do that?"

"First, we'll have a break. The horses aren't the only ones who need food and drink. We won't be long. Then we'll regroup at the pit stop for horses down the road. I've used them before. I've already called ahead and they'll be ready for us. But it'll be quicker if all hands are on deck."

"Sounds good," I say. All three of us nod. We're still sitting in the pickup. "We'll have a break too, then. Will we be able to get water for the dogs at that pit stop as you call it?"

"For sure."

We get out of the pickup. My left leg feels as if it's swollen as well as bruised and my back is stiffer than it was at Penchesterton Farms. But I'm in one piece. It just takes me longer to get moving. Roxi accepts Melissa's offer of an arm. I guess her splint isn't the only thing bothering her, and the wind's gusts make you want to hold onto something. The horses won't like the trailers being buffeted so I hope it won't be long before we resume our journey.

"Your mobile has been beeping," Melissa says as we sit down with our drinks and snacks. I have two oatmeal raisin cookies in a bag for the heroes left in the pickup.

"I hadn't noticed," I say as I retrieve it from my bag. There are three texts from Noah. I let out a long sigh.

"What's the matter?" asks Melissa.

"Noah says Thomas Caldermat has been around. I'd better call him."

"He's been at our farm?"

"Hi, Noah?"

"Meg. I've got a swollen lip from that guy, and a bloody nose."

"He hit you?"

"He sure did. He thinks I know where you are, and he tried to beat it out of me. He said you're to blame for Zoey being charged with doing something to a dead body. I don't know what he's talking about. And then he said you'd stolen horses. I think he's gone mental."

"How did he know where to find you?"

"He must have access to Barnaby's list of contacts and found my address. And I went back to my condo at the wrong time. I had to meet with the auctioneers who're getting rid of my stuff. I'd left your business card on the coffee table. He waved it at me as I walked through the door. No apologies for breaking in. Just red rage on his face."

"Do you know why he was at your condo?"

"He'd trashed the place. You can't see the floor for stuff. He accused me of stealing from Barnaby. I laughed and he hit me again. He asked me where I'd hidden the laptop and said he knew the police had me in for questioning because it's been on social media. I yelled at him that Barnaby stole from me, not the other way around. He's nuts and mad as hell. But he did finally leave without killing me. Saved by the auction guys, I guess."

"When was this?"

"About two hours ago. Not long after you picked up the dogs. I'd forgotten about the auctioneers, but they texted me to say they were on their way. So, I scrambled to get there. He's a psycho, that Thomas."

"I'm sorry you've been hurt."

"And shaken up. I'm like a cocktail inside. My lip's the cherry on top."

"Put some ice on it."

"I'm not worried about that. It'll heal soon enough. I'm concerned this psycho's after your blood."

"What about your condo?"

"The auction guys I'd finally got hold of took one look at the mess and turned around. I guess I'll have to find another company after I've got someone in to clear up."

"Where are you now?"

"Back at your rental place. I brought my airbed and some other stuff I couldn't pick up earlier. I hope you don't mind. I feel safe here."

"That's fine. We won't evict you until this is all settled. Ha, ha."

"Wow. That's really good of you. I'll dog-sit for you for sure since I don't mind your dogs. And I'll do some chores if you like."

Zach signals to us that we need to get moving. I grab my cup and the bag of oatmeal raisin cookies and ask Melissa if she'll drive so I can use my mobile. It takes the three of us to push the service station door open as the wind does its best to keep it shut.

Melissa drives over to the trailers, and we tag along for the journey to the pitstop.

I text Detective Valeska to let her know what Noah told me about Thomas. She replies almost instantly that they have just brought Thomas in for questioning—she doesn't say why—and thanks me for the information about his visit to Noah's condo.

* * *

"The sentence can be up to five years for interfering with a dead body," William says as we relax in the family room. Melissa went out for dinner again, but she's not revealed who she's seeing so regularly. I don't know how she's able to cope with the long hours, especially today when we were on the road for what felt like an eternity. We didn't follow the trucks to Four Rs though. Four Rs said they had enough volunteers to help unload and put them in stalls. It was dark by the time we left the pitstop, so I hope they have some outside lighting.

I'd given them a heads-up as soon as I'd concocted my vague plan. And I made a large donation that should cover most of the cost of retraining and rehoming all thirty horses. It's a pleasant feeling to be able to help them get second careers. And I've signed a petition that demands the slaughter of horses in Canada be made illegal.

"What were you saying?" I ask William.

"You must be exhausted. I said that Zoey could get up to five years for interfering with a dead body. If it can be proven that she and Olivia didn't know he was dead, it may be longer. It depends on what the charges are."

"I wonder how Jaden is, you know, the jockey who took the video."

"That's one of a couple of things I want to tell you. I heard that he's much improved. Dr. Milton called on our landline and told me that Jaden is conscious, has responded well to the surgery and is able to talk. I heard from a contact in police services that they've already had a chat with him. He's confused about the attack, but he repeated to them that he thought the person was bigger than a jockey. He was pushed from behind."

"Now, who could that be? I have an idea."

"Good. The other thing is that it's a PD Day tomorrow. I asked Melissa, but she has to work. I'm in court all day."

"What's a PD Day?"

"Professional development time for teachers."

"You're asking me to look after Gabriel all day?"

"Yes. I realize it's inconvenient, but it may help the two of you to develop more of a bond."

"Mm. I suppose I have to keep out of trouble, then."

*   *   *

Gabriel and I sit at the kitchen table. When I went out to the barn earlier, I wrote a note on a large piece of paper and left it just outside Gabriel's bedroom door. He didn't come looking for me but brushed his teeth and got dressed and was walking down the stairs when the dogs and I got back.

Now, what do I do?

"Gabriel, what do you like for breakfast?"

"I don't want anything."

"I have an idea. Why don't we eat at McDonald's?"

"Can we take Kelly and Jake?"

"Sure. We'll get a treat for them too."

That's one challenge dealt with, but I need to do something drastic about my lack of meal preparation skills. A young boy needs good nutrition, but I've done nothing about it. Melissa and William are at least putting in an effort.

When we return to the farm the gate is open. It was padlocked shut when we left. Perhaps William or Melissa came home but neither of their vehicles are in the usual places.

"What's wrong?" asks Gabriel, as I hesitate at the bottom of the driveway.

"I'm not sure." There's a large SUV parked by the barn. Three names come to mind: Thomas, Olivia, and Zoey. The most likely one is Thomas, especially since bolt cutters aren't easy to use—the gate was locked with a heavy-duty padlock.

And Thomas is furious with me. I wish Vannersville Police Services still had hold of him—he couldn't have been there for long.

Gabriel's on his booster seat behind me, and the dogs are sitting next to him. They aren't usually allowed up on the seat, but they know something's not right. I see all three faces in the rear-view mirror and my insides quiver.

I can't approach Thomas. But what if he hurts the horses? Or Cooper? Or the barn cats? Or all of the above? Why did he park by the barn? I text Detective Valeska. I don't want to alarm Gabriel by talking to her. She doesn't respond.

"Gabriel, I just have to make an important call. It's private, so I'm going to get out of the truck, but I'm right here." He frowns and grabs Kelly around the neck.

I call 911.

I call Noah.

"Can you keep an eye on Gabriel? Thomas Caldermat is at the farm. Keep out of his sight. Run up here and take Gabriel back with you. Don't bring your car."

"Be right there."

I want to minimize our movements because we could draw Thomas' attention. And I want to keep the driveway blocked. I hold Gabriel's hand as he climbs off his booster seat, and we crouch down behind the pickup. Gabriel looks puzzled, especially when I tell him Noah is coming and he'll be going with him to Milkweed Farm.

"I can't go with strange people."

"You're right. But Uncle William and I know Noah. He's a friend and he lives at Milkweed Farm. That's our other farm. He'll show you around."

"Can Kelly and Jake come?"

"No, I'm sorry. I need them here. But we'll all come down to fetch you in a bit."

"I don't want to go."

"Gabriel, I've just set up my tv," Noah says, as he bends down. He's out of breath from his run to the farm. "Do you want to watch a movie?"

"Do you have Ice Age?"

"I'm sure I do. And I have ice cream sandwiches. They could be too big for you though."

"Okay." He draws out the word, making it sound mournful.

I give Gabriel a hug which he doesn't reciprocate. It's as if I'm abandoning him.

"Hold hands guys," I say. "See you soon."

I get back in the truck with the dogs. I'm playing it safe. I don't want to have a confrontation with Thomas—if I can help it—but I need to know what he's up to. My pickup crawls up the driveway with barely a sound except for crunching gravel, thanks to a gasoline-powered engine rather than a diesel one.

I'm right. It's Thomas. He jumps up from behind his truck brandishing what looks like a handgun. What sort of man in Canada has a handgun? He waves it at me, motioning me to get out of the truck. I can't think what he wants from me. I don't let the dogs out even though they're barking. They don't deserve to be shot. But I have no choice but to get out myself. I leave the door open, hoping it'll provide some protection.

There's something tugging at my jeans, from behind.

"Gabriel!"

"I don't like that man. I don't like this man either."

Frantic, with my body shaking beyond my control, I lift Gabriel onto the front seat and close the door. Somehow, the dogs have got out. Nobody's staying where I want them, including Thomas who's approaching. I don't have the protection of the open pickup door anymore. The dogs sit either side of me growling, hackles up. I'm sure they can sense my stress but rather than their presence reassuring me, it increases my anxiety.

But I don't know what Thomas would achieve by killing us all.

"You tell me where Noah is, right now." Thomas stands erect about twenty feet in front of us. Jake barks. "Shut that goddam dog up or I'll shoot."

"Why do you want Noah?"

"He's stolen money from Barnaby. It's my money. He's got the laptop. I'm going to use this if you don't tell me." He waves the handgun.

"He didn't steal from Barnaby. Barnaby stole from Noah."

"I'm warning you. I won't hesitate to shoot your stupid dogs. It's because of you that Zoey's in trouble. Tell me where Noah is. That money's mine and Noah's stolen it."

"Thomas, you know that's not true."

The pickup starts to move. I hadn't cut out the engine and Gabriel must have been playing with the levers. The indicators are going and now the horn. The four-way signals flash. Since it was pointing straight up the driveway, it's keeping to the gravel, albeit at a slow pace. The dark tinted windows are not giving Gabriel away, thank goodness, but my heart's thumping is reverberating throughout my whole body.

"What's going on with your truck?"

"I've been having issues with the transmission."

"I asked you a question. Where's Noah?"

"I don't know. But I do know he's broke and selling his condo."

"You're lying. He was in it just yesterday. I was there. But my meeting was cut short. Next time, I'm getting answers."

He's now close enough that I can see sweat on his forehead and the handgun in his clenched hand.

The dogs are edgy. They're standing now and snarling. I don't know if Kelly copies Jake or Jake copies Kelly, but they're a team.

"Call those dogs off. I don't like the look of them. I'll shoot." He waves the handgun around. I'm afraid he's going to pull the trigger accidentally which could be worse. I tell the dogs to sit, but they don't stop growling. "I'll take you hostage, then. That lawyer you live with will tell me where Noah is if he knows you're going to die if he doesn't."

"You'll face charges of abduction. You can't get away with this. Is money worth going to prison for?" I hope my shaking body isn't reflected in my voice.

"It's gotta be a lot of money. Zoey and I plan to be off to some exotic place. We've been planning this for some time."

His delusional thinking almost makes me feel sorry for him.

The pickup is honking again.

"There must be someone in there. I bet it's Noah." He steps towards me and thrusts the gun under my chin. It's painful. A searing ache travels down from my throat to my stomach. He reaches for the pickup door, but it lurches away. Gabriel has found the accelerator, but it must have scared him because the pickup reverts back to a crawl almost immediately. The movement draws Thomas' attention away from me and he turns so he can grab the vehicle's door handle. I seize the opportunity to kick him behind the knee and yell at the dogs to stay. But Kelly doesn't obey me. I forgive her because I know this rare show of disobedience is driven by her overwhelming desire to protect me, and perhaps Gabriel as well.

My kick has some effect. Thomas collapses on one side and loses his balance. Kelly jumps up and lands her front paws on his side. It's as if she's trying to topple him. She would make an amazing agility dog. Jake wants to help but doesn't know what to do, so he barks and then settles for a grumbling growl.

Thomas still has the handgun. I'm frantic with worry about the dogs' safety. My mouth is so dry it's as if it's lined with sandpaper, and my heart's pounding is resounding in my ears. But there's no time to dwell on these things. I must act. I'd much rather I was the one to be shot if Thomas pulls the trigger.

Kelly has almost knocked Thomas over with her courageous lunge. He has one hand on the gravel driveway, but the other hand waves the gun around. Before he has a chance to right himself, I kick the arm he's using to get his balance. A deafening explosion of noise makes my ears ring. It's enough to terrify the dogs and I'm relieved beyond words as they scamper towards the house. Is Gabriel okay? The truck door is opening very slowly. I lean against it wondering what's trickling down my arm. I don't know how to get out of this.

Sirens.

They send Thomas scurrying back to his SUV. I open the truck door and Gabriel scrambles off the floor and onto the front passenger seat. I put the truck into reverse and plan to block the driveway but I'm too late. Thomas veers past me, throwing up chunks of our front lawn behind him. He makes it out of the driveway, gravel flying as he turns sharply to the left just as police vehicles appear over the hill from the opposite direction. They don't give chase. I'm not sure why.

I whistle for Kelly and Jake and entice them into the truck. I want to be sure they're safe.

The police officers don't stay long. Gabriel gets to sit in one of their vehicles as I give a brief statement. The officer tells me

Detective Valeska wants me to follow up with her as soon as possible. He also points at my arm and says I should have it checked by a doctor. Did I need an ambulance? No. I look at my arm. The sleeve of my green, spring jacket is ripped and there's a small dark patch. No pain. I'll clean it up myself. But looking at it shakes me up a little. I turn my attention to Gabriel who's reluctant to leave the police vehicle. But I tell him Kelly and Jake are waiting in the truck and I won't let them out until the officers have left.

"He's a bright young lad," the officer says.

"I want to be a police," Gabriel says.

"That's great," I say.

"Here's some Vannersville Police Services stickers," the officer says.

"Thanks." Gabriel smiles.

"I'll shut the gate," the officer says, "but I don't think he'll be back."

I don't know what makes him think that, but I don't say anything. Gabriel and I wave goodbye as we get into the pickup again. We drive to the usual parking spot. All four of us get out. The dogs rush to their water bowl in the kitchen and I get Gabriel some chocolate milk and put the kettle on. Tea is called for. We've been through more than enough for one day and it's not even lunchtime.

I text William and ask him to bring two strong padlocks home. I call the security company yet again (I've had to do this several times in the past).

Noah's number comes up.

"Meg, are you and Gabriel alright? I heard a shot and sirens. I've been worried sick."

"We're all fine. I'm shaken up, but otherwise okay. Do you know the back way to our place, across the fields and through the neighbour's property?"

"No." I describe it to him in detail. "I'd say we'll meet you half-way but we've had more than enough adventure for one day."

"I'll find it."

"Gabriel, are you okay?'

"I'm good."

"I know you're good, but are you feeling okay?"

"I'm hungry."

I order pizza from a new place that has a delivery service. The dogs and I collect it at the end of the driveway.

Gabriel giggles when I give Kelly and Jake some crusts. I take a deep breath and am grateful that we're all relatively unscathed. This morning could have been an utter disaster.

And I clean up my graze after taking a couple of photos for Detective Valeska.

*　　*　　*

The kitchen door slams, and I'm jolted awake. Gabriel and Noah are playing with Lego on the floor as strange, urgent music accompanies them. The dogs are stretched out on their sides. The door slamming might have caused them to raise their heads, but I didn't notice. William walks into the room. Before I can stop him, Gabriel rushes over to William and says "Guess what!"

"What?" William asks as he hugs Gabriel.

"There was a man here with a gun, then the police people came and there were sirens. I got to drive the truck and I got to sit in the police car. It was awesome. I had the best time."

Tears pour down my cheeks. I think they must be tears of relief that Gabriel has apparently not been traumatized while under my care. And he's spoken more words in one utterance than I've heard before.

"We had McDonald's for breakfast and pizza for lunch." Gabriel smiles.

"Meg, we need to talk about this later. Are you okay?" He's just noticed I'm wiping away tears and that I have a large Band-aid on my upper arm.

"Just relieved, and this is nothing." I point to my arm. "I'll tell you later."

"I have a feeling that my day was a lot more boring than yours. Noah, how are you doing?" William asks.

"I like him now," Gabriel says.

"That's good," William says with some hesitation in his voice. He looks at Gabriel who's brandishing a gun made of Lego, then at me as I dab my eyes with a tissue, and then back to Noah who's started pacing. William appears bewildered but he doesn't probe deeper into today's events. I'm sure that will come later.

"I got dinner," he says, "and there's enough to feed an army, so stay if you like, Noah."

17

Dead

Gabriel couldn't stop talking during the meal. So, there's a silver lining to all this. But both William and Noah's eyebrows were raised now and then as Gabriel described what happened from his point of view. He didn't like the man with the gun, he said, but it was as if he thought he was in a movie and didn't perceive the real danger we were in. William opened his mouth a couple of times but thought twice about challenging Gabriel's version of events. We all held back our comments.

"My god, Meg, what were you thinking?" asks William once Gabriel's in bed. We three adults sit at the kitchen table, holding the stems of three glasses of wine, each staring at the red liquid as if mesmerized.

Noah breaks the taut silence.

"It's my fault. Gabriel slipped away from me. Meg asked me to take him back to Milkweed Farm, but it was obvious he was scared. He didn't know me and has never been to that farm."

"I'm just relieved," I say. "That's all I can say about it. As far as I can tell, he's not been traumatized, far from it. I'm more traumatized than he is. And he loved being in the police vehicle. And, I have to say that Gabriel playing around with my truck probably saved us getting hurt and bought me a little time."

"Besides the fact that he wasn't adequately supervised or protected..."

I interrupt William. "I don't need to be told that. Fortunately, I'd got him into the truck, and he was entertained by levers and horns and so on, so he wasn't paying much attention."

"It's not only the lack of protection, I'm also having trouble coming to terms with Gabriel's reaction to the events. Shouldn't he have been scared? He was too frightened to go with Noah, but not all that bothered about a strange man waving a gun around. I'm concerned about him."

"I don't know anything about kids," Noah says. "But my guess is that he felt safe with Meg and the dogs. He thought he was protected. He didn't know me and didn't trust that I'd protect him."

"I suspect he has more confidence in the dogs than in Meg."

"I don't want to talk about it anymore," I say, as I take a sip of the fruity red wine. I suppose I deserve William's comment, but I'd rather not dwell on what happened. It's not helpful. "Noah, do you know why Thomas would have it in his head that you have Barnaby's money?"

"I have no idea. Really, I don't. Barnaby took my money, not the other way round."

"Somehow, he's sure that you have lots of money. How did he come to that conclusion?" I swirl the wine around in my glass, gazing at the shimmering liquid. "I have a thought."

"Well, share it then," William says.

"I bet Thomas thinks you killed Barnaby, Noah. You killed him so you could steal his laptop, and Thomas probably reckons you accessed Barnaby's bank account and took out the funds. He should be able to check that out, but perhaps he thinks there was a bank account he wasn't aware of under a different name. And you're lying low because you're guilty of murdering Barnaby."

"That's crazy," Noah says. He folds his arms and leans back. "But it would explain his obsession with finding me. He probably had the gun to threaten me, so I'd tell him what he thinks I know. I wonder where he got the gun?"

"It's an interesting theory Meg," William says, as he stands up. "Let's go into the family room. I need to relax in a recliner."

"Good idea," I say. As I get up from the chair, I do my best to hide my stiffness.

The dogs follow us, but Cooper is on Gabriel's bed. It's a relief to lean back and put my feet up. I'm wearier than I realized. My chin still hurts from when Thomas rammed his gun there and my arm is stinging from being grazed by the bullet. It hurts more now than it did earlier. I pull a throw over me. I'm chilly.

"I don't know what to say about that theory," Noah says. He sits on the floor and starts to pick up the Lego that's scattered in a large circle around him. "That means you think Thomas didn't murder Barnaby. Then who did?"

"Motive is all important," William says. "I'm not usually one for conjecture, but I wouldn't be surprised if Dr. Berzinski was involved in the Caldermat Gambling Circle. That would give him a motive."

"He was, as far as I know," I say. "And he would have access to barbiturate and a syringe. But Olivia detested Barnaby and could have got drugs from the hospital somehow. I'm still working on it." My eyes close and all I can hear is Jake's snores and the clacking of Lego pieces. Noah's taking his time to clear up.

"Noah, you have something on your mind," I say. He lets out a barely audible groan, or perhaps it was a sigh.

217

"I feel awkward about raising it," Noah says. He throws the last of the Lego into the bin and sits in a chair. "I'll have to explain things first."

"You have our attention," William says. He finishes his wine and puts the glass onto the coffee table. I've drunk only half of mine, and don't feel like any more. I shiver.

"It's about Elsa."

"Oh," I say. But I'm not surprised.

"I know she's messed up. Actually, she's messed up as a person and she's messed up things in her life. She's all-round messed up."

"We understand that," William says. He puts his recliner in the upright position as if to convey impatience.

"Meg, I've told her she should talk to you. She wanted me to explain everything, but I said she should tell you directly. If okay with you, she's agreed to come to Milkweed Farm tomorrow. She doesn't want us to come here. She thinks too many people know where you live, and anyone could show up. She's right too. That was proved today by Thomas. Anyway, she knows she's in a bad place. She wants to turn things around."

"I'll meet with her. But I must go to bed now. Go back the way you came, Noah. Elsa's right, you both need to be careful. That reminds me, I meant to tell you that there'll be a security guard at each of the farms by 6am tomorrow."

"Good," William says. "I was going to suggest that."

* * *

Noah texted me while I was in the shower to let me know Elsa arrived and a security guard showed up. I instructed the security guard who arrived here that the gate at the end of the driveway must be kept padlocked.

My day has been unfurling at a snail's pace so far, hindered by

218

my unwilling body. It took me longer than usual to do the barn chores, and my tea and toast stared back at me for some time as I attempted to organize my scattered thoughts. William and Gabriel left before I finished my work in the barn. I haven't seen much of Melissa recently, and no sign of her this morning.

Kelly, Jake, and I take the route across the fields to Milkweed Farm about an hour after I receive Noah's text. The dogs run ahead and come dashing back to me several times as we follow the unbeaten path to the farm. They seem to have put yesterday's events behind them and to be enjoying the present moment.

Just as we arrive at the backdoor of the farmhouse, my mobile rings. I ignore it, and knock. Noah opens the door almost before I take my hand away. The dogs sniff around the doorstep, interested in an animal that visited early this morning I expect.

My mobile rings again.

"Hi," Noah says. "Come in. Dogs, I have water for you."

As if they understand and want to be polite, they go to the plastic mixing bowl and lap at the water with gusto as if they've not had a drink all morning.

My mobile rings again.

"You might want to take that," Noah says. "We'll be in the front room."

"Thanks." It's William. My heart skips a beat as I remember he planned to take Gabriel to the zoo for the morning. He wanted me to go with them, but I said I wasn't feeling great. I'm still not up to par. Usually I bounce back quickly from incidents like our confrontation with Thomas, but I haven't recuperated well this time. Now I'm worried that something has happened to Gabriel. Maybe he fell into an enclosure or something.

"William, are you and Gabriel okay?"

"We're fine. Just want you to call Detective Valeska. I can't talk right now."

That sounds ominous. I get through to Detective Valeska without a hitch.

"William told me I should call you?"

"You're lucky to catch me. I tried calling you earlier. I thought you'd want to know right away, but I don't have time to give you details. In any case, we have little to go on at this point. Thomas Caldermat was found dead in Barnaby Caldermat's garage by Olivia Matterson early this morning. We are treating it as a homicide even though there's a note. The scene, in our opinion, has been staged to look like a suicide case. Carbon monoxide. Fancy large SUV."

"Wow, that's unexpected. By the way, has Zoey been charged? I heard you had her in for questioning."

"We haven't sufficient evidence to lay charges at this point in our investigation and, by the way, we don't think she had anything to do with Thomas' death. As far as we know, they were an item. Must go. Give me a call later if you have any information that could help."

"Of course. Thanks for telling me."

Jake is sitting beside Noah, and Kelly is lying at Elsa's feet. Kelly must have forgiven Elsa for what she did to her, but I'm having a tough time with it. Dogs are paragons of unconditional love. Nevertheless, both Noah and Elsa look tense.

Noah has brought a few items of furniture which look out of place in the old farmhouse even though it's been restored thanks to Joanne and Ewert (the previous tenants). He's perched on the edge of a chair which is upholstered in white linen and Elsa is sitting on the corner of a glass coffee table with black metal legs. The wooden floor with its wide pine planks and semi-gloss finish needs an area rug.

"Hello, Elsa," I say.

"Hi."

"Would you like something to drink?" Noah asks. "I have coffee."

"No, I'm fine, thanks. I should tell you the news I just received. Thomas Caldermat, you know, Barnaby's cousin, was found dead this morning."

"What? How did it happen?" Noah asks. Elsa looks at me with wide eyes and raised eyebrows.

"I don't have details," I say, as I sit down on a black leather chair.

"That's scary," Elsa says. She stands and paces up and down the room. Her short, black hair still sticks out in all directions. It must always be like that. As though to confirm this, she ruffles it as if to make sure of its chaos.

"We'll just have to park this for the moment," I say, wishing Elsa would sit down. Her agitation makes me feel unsettled.

"Not for long, I hope," Noah says. He moves even further forward on the chair. I hope it's solid enough not to tip. "The cops will come after me. I'll be a suspect."

"Why?" asks Elsa. She stares at him as if he's said something utterly preposterous.

"I don't know exactly. I just feel like a victim in all this."

"Let's not go there," I say. "Elsa, Noah told me you want to talk."

Kelly comes to me and sits by the chair and Jake joins her. I don't think they're happy here. Perhaps they haven't enjoyed their brief stays when I've left them with Noah. I shake off the guilt and glance at Elsa's wan face as she paces past me.

"Yeah, I do. I do. But I don't know. It's such a muddle. It doesn't make sense, a lot of it, and I suppose I don't either."

"I'm not here to judge you. And I expect if you tell me your story, you'll feel better, and I may even be able to help you. Why don't you sit down?"

"My legs won't stay still."

"Well, whatever works for you."

"I don't know where to start," she turns to face me and stops pacing for a second. "Yeah, the beginning. Ha!"

"Why don't you tell me a bit about yourself, your family, perhaps."

"I'm the only one who survived the car crash. My mom and dad and baby brother were all killed. I was injured. No-one will tell me what caused it, so I guess it was my dad's fault. Granny Roxi looked after me. I never met the other grandparents. There are lots of secrets in my family and Roxi won't tell. She probably doesn't know. We've both got issues which makes it good sometimes and bad others." Her words spill out in rapid succession as if a dam has been burst inside her mind.

"What do you mean by issues?"

"Roxi has been diagnosed bi-polar, the mild kind. She can be a bit manic for a few weeks and then depressed for the next few weeks. It's a cycle. I don't think I have the same thing, but I feel bad sometimes. We both have anger issues, that's a cert. I thought we understood one another, but I don't know anything anymore." She sits on the glass coffee table again and rests her head in her hands. Noah looks at me and shakes his head slightly.

"You wanted to help Roxi. Tell me about that, from the beginning of course."

"Oh. Where is the beginning?" She lifts her head and stares into space, her eyes sparkling with tears. "It's not difficult to work out some of it. She taught me just about all I know about horses. We lived on her horse farm then, the one she's had to rent out. I loved riding and used to exercise some of the racehorses before the racing season began. Some people could say it's boring going around in circles, but I mixed it up with trotting poles and other stuff. Those were the good days. Roxi took me to the backstretch and to the races, and I soon discovered what I wanted to be. Yeah, a jockey. Roxi was pretty proud of me when I got my first win. It felt so good."

"Everything was going well. But this didn't last, right?"

"It's complicated. It wasn't one thing. But what I think was the worst is Zoey Caldermat bamboozled Roxi into taking her hubby's horses."

"You think Zoey tricked Roxi into taking Barnaby's horses?"

"I don't think that. I know."

"How come?"

"It's so complicated. It's all mixed up." She throws her head back as if it's taking too much energy to tell me. Noah says he'll get water for all of us and adds he'll be able to hear us from the kitchen.

"What's mixed up?"

"Everything."

"Meg," Noah says as he comes back into the room with two glasses of water. "I think Elsa needs something to eat. She's diabetic and hasn't eaten this morning, have you Elsa? And she's trying this new insulin pump. She's not good at sticking to a routine and the pump was supposed to help, but I'm not so sure."

"Tell me about it," Elsa says as she flops her head onto her knees. He arms hang down at her side. Noah rushes out to the kitchen and comes back with orange juice. He entices Elsa to sip it.

"Noah," I say. "Roxi obviously knows Elsa's a diabetic. I don't understand why she could think Elsa gave at least one of her horses a performance enhancing drug. She said she saw Elsa with a syringe in one of the stalls."

"I'm going to take Elsa to the clinic. Where's the closest one?"

* * *

Olivia is barely recognizable. Wisps of her dyed auburn hair are stuck to her forehead and cheeks. Her pale lips are dry and scaly. Her hand trembles so much that, as she lifts the glass off the table, water sloshes onto her pajamas.

"What can I do for you?" I ask.

"There's nothing anyone can do."

"Have you seen a doctor? It must have been a terrible shock to find Thomas."

"I don't want anything to do with doctors. They were the bane of my existence at the hospital for god's sake."

"I want to help find out what happened to Thomas."

"So far you haven't found out much of anything about anything." She slams the glass down onto the table and more water escapes.

"You're obviously very upset. And this question'll probably make you angrier. Why are you so distraught?"

"If you'd found out who killed Barnaby I wouldn't be, would I? I don't know what the hell's going on. Thomas sure didn't kill himself. The police have admitted that to me. Barnaby and then Thomas. And what's really got my blood pressure up is that Zoey is very busy framing me for both murders. She gets rid of all three of us and then takes all the money."

"But there isn't any money of any significance, right?"

"Zoey thinks there is and convinced Thomas there is. I don't give a shit. I just want this to stop. I want to feel safe and lead a normal, boring life. Ever since I met Barnaby my life's been full of stress and angst and pain." She pulls her legs up onto the sofa and hugs her knees. "At least I'll be out of here tomorrow."

"You've found somewhere to live?"

She nods her head slightly. "And I've landed a job."

"Congratulations. That was quick."

"They snapped me up. I'm over-qualified. It's a nursing home administrator position with a big private chain. I'm not looking forward to working with smelly old dodderers, but they say there are opportunities coming up in head office."

"I see. I wish you luck." I stand up. "I get that you don't think I've done anything to help, but I'm still investigating and have some ideas. Did you hear Barnaby talk about a gambling business?"

"I told you before we hardly ever talked."

"So, nothing about the racetrack?"

"Zoey told me she trained some horses for him but he'd bought too many for the wrong reasons, and didn't pay his bills, even hers."

"But she managed to get them transferred to Roxi."

"That happened soon after she and Barnaby split up. Zoey isn't a friend anymore, so I don't mind telling you she laughed when she told me Roxi was taking them. She called her a 'silly cow' and a 'dupe' for agreeing to take them on."

"Zoey told me that she had to get financial help from her father as a result of those bills not being paid."

"I don't know about that. I gave her some money. I can't believe I did that."

"A lot?"

"Not in comparison with the amount owing to her, but it was a lot to me. How is this helping? This chitchat?"

"It helps me to understand who had a motive to murder Barnaby and Thomas, although there could be two killers and two motives. That shouldn't be ruled out. Do you know why Thomas was here?"

"That's one of the reasons I'm so shaken up. What was he doing in our garage?"

"Do you have any idea why the murderer would want to make it seem like suicide? You said that Zoey is trying to frame you for both murders, but if she murdered Thomas and wants you to be blamed, she wouldn't have planted a note."

"I think it was an afterthought. I wasn't here and perhaps she thought I was going to be in. But I was moving some of my stuff, not that there's much that's mine, into the flat. I'm taking the rest of it today. So, I reckon her plan didn't unfold the way she intended."

"She can't be trying to frame you then, at least for Thomas' murder."

"She's still trying it on because it's being investigated as a homicide, and she doesn't know where I was. She could be betting I don't have a watertight alibi."

"Do you?"

"Actually, I do. The man in the flat below mine offered to help. He was with me the whole time and the landlady dropped by to check everything was okay. I got a lot done. I'd rented a small van and all of it got unloaded, unpacked, and put where I wanted it. It only took four hours. Just odds and ends to do today. I'll be so bloody glad to get out of this place." She brushes a wisp of hair off her face.

18

Jockeys

Jake doesn't like being left alone in the truck in the hospital parking lot when Kelly and I get out. I don't recall ever hearing him whine before. It's quite a pitiful sound, and his ears look as if they've shrunk into his head. I talk to him to try to reassure him, but we have to go. Kelly has her therapy vest on and perhaps Jake could qualify too. He's come a long way since we adopted him.

Jaden texted me and asked me to visit. I've been wanting to see him and talk to him for quite a while, but understood he wasn't up to chatting with visitors. The surgery was successful, thank goodness, and the prognosis is good, but he won't be riding any racehorses for the rest of this racing season.

"I'm going home soon," he says as Kelly and I amble into his room. He's sitting in a chair with a high back that emphasizes his small stature. The picture looks out of proportion.

"I'm so relieved to hear that." I sit in a smaller, padded chair that faces him.

"I want to talk to you about a couple of things." He pulls the white blanket further up onto his lap. He has little or no body fat, so he must have trouble keeping warm. "Sometimes I get a bit foggy, but I'm pretty good."

"I'm glad you're getting better. It must have been terrifying to endure such a brutal attack."

"Not really. I didn't have much time to think about it. Wham, I was out. I want to talk to you because Neal thinks you're a good amateur sleuth—is that the right word?"

"That'll do. I'm not a licensed investigator."

"Yeah, I know. But if Neal says you're good, that's enough for me." He smiles and pats Kelly's head. "And what's really important is you know what racing is all about."

"I don't think anyone knows what it's all about." I smile.

"You've got that right. Anyhow, most of this I've told the cops, but some I haven't. Do you want to get a coffee or something?"

"I'm fine, but I can get you a drink."

"I'm sticking to water. I'm going to get right to what's bothering me. This is something I did tell the cops. It couldn't have been a jockey who attacked me. The man was too big. I got a glimpse enough to be sure of that. I know everyone thinks it was Cliff, but it wasn't."

"Do you have any idea who?"

"This is where it gets interesting. Do you know about the Caldermat Gambling Circle?"

"I've heard about it."

"I didn't tell the cops 'cause I think the Vannersville Racing Authority should deal with it, at least to start off. They should do the policing at the track."

"You have a point."

"There's this group and they have a gambling business—illegal—and what gives it a real edge is that they fix races."

"Who and how?"

"I knew you'd ask. I got myself nearly killed 'cause I reported it to a steward."

"Bill Price, right?"

"How did you know it was him?"

"I suspected. He's been acting out of character recently."

"If you mean odd, then yeah, he has. But the stewards have always been fair to me and are decent guys, and Bill had a good reputation until now. It's hard to accept he's gone to the dark side."

"I feel the same way."

"I'll tell you, but you have to agree not to use my name. Although, I don't think I'm going to be attacked again."

"Why do you feel safe now?"

"I'll get to that. I really like your dog. She's lifted my spirits."

"Kelly's almost human. She's special."

"I'll say." He reaches for his bottle of water and takes a couple of sips. "Okay, here goes. It still makes me sick to think about all this. You already know Cliff Ryman's an electric jockey—he sometimes uses a device to spur his mount on. I say 'sometimes' because I've also seen him deliberately holding his mount back. But he's not acting on his own. That's what I found out later. He's controlled by the Caldermat Gambling Circle."

"How do you know this?"

"He has weight issues. I don't really—I'm lucky—but I go to the sauna sometimes. He was in there one day recently and in bad shape. He could've been on something. I can't say. He blabbered away to me as if I was a close mate. It was awkward, odd. But what he said stopped me from scarpering. He asked me if he was going to get caught. I was itching to ask him a whole bunch of questions, but my gut told me to keep my trap shut. I just listened."

"What did he say that was so intriguing?"

"I hope he's forgotten because it was more than intriguing, as you put it."

"Go on." I shouldn't feel impatient. He probably gets few people to talk to and I'm not in a rush really. Kelly puts her head on his lap. He strokes her silky head gently.

"Sorry, I lost my train of thought."

"You met Cliff in the sauna, and he told you some interesting stuff, probably related to the Caldermat Gambling Circle you mentioned."

"Yeah, he did. I remember. He rambled on about his weight and said he'd just brought up his lunch and he was tired of the fight to keep his weight down. I'm not quoting him 'cause his language was, you know, not repeatable, especially to someone like you." He looks directly at me with his bright green eyes.

Perhaps he was seeking a reaction.

"He didn't look well. But I need to tell you the important stuff. He couldn't ride his mounts how he wanted to. He was told to use a machine, you know, one of those electric things. I think I already mentioned that. I took a video, right?"

"Yes."

"He said he was to use the machine if the horse had to win. It didn't always work and then he'd get flack something terrible. And then other times he had to hold the horse back. He said there must be other jockeys involved if they want to fix a race that way. No good just him holding his horse back if they needed the longshot to win to make lots of money. And one thing I know for sure is Cliff likes to win. He lords it over us whenever he comes back from the Winner's Circle."

"Did he say who's involved?"

"Yeah, well, I did ask that question. I was afraid he might shut down or pass out, but he answered. He said he dealt with the

Caldermat guys. I've forgotten their names. And there are other people in the circle, a steward and a couple of trainers. They would be in deep, deep shit if they were caught, right?"

"Absolutely. Do the names Barnaby and Thomas Caldermat ring any bells?"

"They sound familiar. I expect that's them. And, yeah, he mentioned Price. He mumbled other names, and I remember thinking they were trainers, but the names didn't stick, except for Zoey's, which is pretty upsetting. But I know she's a Caldermat, so I suppose I shouldn't be surprised, and that must be why I remember her name. It's just that I've ridden for her several times, and I can't imagine her cheating. But now I think of it, she did say she was going through a rough patch. But lots of trainers say that from time to time. You know, no wins, owners upset because their horse was last, you know all about it."

"What else did he say?"

"He didn't say it straight, but he hinted that the Caldermats had some hold over him. But he didn't say what it was."

"Did he mention Elsa Lorenza at all?"

"No."

"What else?"

"I'm thinking." He caresses Kelly's ears. She looks as if she'd like to lie down and have a nap, but she knows she's on duty, so she's being stoic. "I remember what else I want to mention. He said he knew Dr. Berzinski was involved. Cliff spat on the sauna floor and said he was disgusted when he found out they drugged horses. He was shaking by then and I was worried I'd have a corpse on my hands. He looked like a slimy lump of lard. I told him we should leave, but he waved his hand at me as if to tell me to go. So, I left. I think that's it. But it's bad. It's like there are a lot of people involved and they're doing illegal things to fix races and make their money on gambling. And the rules are that trainers and owners cannot bet against their own horse. But I'd say these guys did, when it suited them."

"Barnaby Caldermat's horses were doing very badly."

"I think Zoey was the trainer? It's coming back to me."

"Yes."

"Then I think I know why. I got a couple of rides. She told me the owner wasn't paying his bills and the horses had become a liability. Could be she wasn't getting her cut from the Caldermat Gambling Circle—perhaps she was shafted. Just guessing."

"That would have made her furious, I would have thought."

"Me too."

"If you had to guess, who do you think beat you up? You must have an idea."

"My money's on a Caldermat guy because I reported Cliff to Bill and gave him the video. That would have put a wrinkle in their gambling circle, wouldn't it? Or perhaps not, if Bill was part of the shenanigans."

* * *

Jake gives Kelly and me an exuberant greeting. I escape the face wash, but Kelly has to put up with it. Fortunately, the truck hasn't suffered from Jake being left to his own devices except the front passenger window is decorated with dog nose smears that make its bottom half almost opaque. My mobile shows a text from Neal. He wants me to drop by his office as soon as possible. I tell him I'll be there in about twenty minutes.

Before I can get going, William calls. He told me earlier he'd help with some following-up today. Gabriel must be his priority, but I miss William's support and encouragement. And he has great contacts who trust him enough to give him inside scoops.

"Meg," he says.

"How are things going?"

"I have to pick Gabriel up from school, so I don't have much time. You told me Zoey Caldermat said her father helped her out financially when Barnaby didn't pay his training bills."

"I remember her saying her father came to the rescue. Why?"

"One of my contacts has told me there's been a forensic audit of Zoey's financial records and she did receive a payment from her father, but I would not classify it as a bail-out. It was only $50,000."

"You're right. She told me Barnaby owed her about a quarter of a million. That's important information. Thanks."

"We'll talk more when Gabriel's in bed. I have to go."

"See you later."

* * *

The dogs look disappointed that we've parked at the track rather than at home. I'll do my best to keep this visit short, but I have to give the horses a few mints and say hello to Linda.

As I step into the barn, the tension that must have sneaked up on me peels off in layers. I take a deep breath and walk towards Fay's stall. I'd nearly forgotten that Neal told me a while back that there's the perfect race for her on the turf coming up. He entered her today. It's an optional claiming race, and she must carry a little more weight because she'll not be available for claiming since I don't want to risk losing her, even though she's had some health issues.

But before I reach her, Linda emerges from a different stall.

"Neal wants me to let him know you're here."

"That's odd. Shouldn't I just knock on his door?"

"No. Just wait here. Thanks."

Since I'm close to Fay's stall, I venture on to visit and offer her some treats. She takes the mints, gently brushing my palm with her velvety muzzle. Her large, convex eyes are dark and shiny, trusting

233

and kind. Her ears have lots of inner hairs and I'm glad they haven't been clipped since they provide some protection. She moves her ears more than my other horses—she must be more sensitive to sounds around her. And she hears Linda puffing as she waddles towards me. Neal is close behind.

"Meg," Neal says, "Fay looks good, doesn't she?"

"Thanks to you and Linda."

"There's someone who wants to talk to you. He's in my office." Neal hesitates and bites his bottom lip. I can't make out what's going on. "He asks to have an opportunity to say his piece first. I said I'd ask you if you'd be okay with that."

"Ah. It's Cliff. What the hell does he want? He punched me in the face."

"I didn't know that. I'm sorry."

Linda disappears into Fay's stall. She probably doesn't want anything to do with this.

"Obviously I'm asking a lot," Neal says.

"If you're asking me, then I'll listen to him." I'm already angry before I even see Cliff, so this meeting probably won't go well.

"Thanks."

Neal's office is stuffy even though the door's been open while he came to find me. Cliff jumps to his feet as we enter. Neal perches on the edge of his rickety desk while Cliff and I sit down on two chairs that have rusty legs.

"Thank you, Mrs. Sheppard for giving me this opportunity." Cliff looks at me but hastily gazes down into his lap at his white-knuckled, clasped hands. He seems diminutive, as if a puff of wind would blow him away. But he gave me a hefty punch, so his appearance belies his strength.

I say nothing. I don't trust myself to be civil to him.

"Neal told me about your investigation work and that's a reason I want to talk with you and explain some stuff. But the biggest reason is that I must apologize. And I mean it. I've been out of control—but that's no excuse for hitting you. I'm sorry." He looks at me with wide, childlike eyes as if he's scared of what I might say.

"Go on." My face is taut as I remember the sudden pain of his punch.

He sits more upright in the chair. His small feet barely touch the floor.

"This is tough." He grabs hold of the seat of the chair either side of his lap and takes a deep breath. "But I can't go on like this." He looks at me again, but I don't react. "I don't want to get myself into even more trouble."

"Cliff," Neal says. He wags his finger at him in a non-threatening way. I think he means to encourage him. "Cliff, you were the one who asked for this meeting. I arranged it, Meg has shown up, and now you need to talk."

Cliff looks at the floor. "You guys likely know some of this already."

"Just tell us the whole story," Neal says.

"I was a darn good jockey, usually in the top five in the standings here. But I've always had weight issues and things went badly for a while and I slipped in my earnings."

"What things?" I ask.

"I was taking drugs to help me lose weight and I ended up with a couple of suspensions. I was in a bad place. That's when the Caldermat Gambling Circle approached me."

"Who?" I ask.

"I'll tell you. Just let me get this stuff out." His frown deepens as he purses his colourless lips. I give him a slight nod. "Barnaby Caldermat asked me to be the jockey for his horses. He told me his wife, Zoey, was the trainer. Barnaby wined and dined me. That's not true, he bought me a coffee and told me that if I played the game there'd be good rewards. I fessed up about by weight struggle and he said they'd pay for a nutritionist. It'd all be fine, and I'd make a lot more money than I was at the time. I look back on it now, and it's as if they were vultures looking for vulnerable jockeys and using them up for their gain—because we get caught. They make it sound as if they can protect us. They tell us about Bill Price, the steward, who's in on it, and they say he protects the members of the Circle from, you know, the authorities."

"You say 'us', so you know of other jockeys who are members?" I ask.

"We weren't told who the other jockeys were. They said it's best that way. I don't know if it is. But that's how they worked. I just knew what I was supposed to do. It was either hold back or give a shock."

"How did you make money from this?" Neal asks.

"I was given money when my horse did what they wanted, and the race worked out they way they planned. If it didn't all work out, I didn't get anything from them. But they also put money on for me. It's illegal to bet on other horses, but the Caldermat Gambling Circle told us it was a perk they offered. They'd place bets for us jockeys. So, when we held our horse back and the longshot won, we made some dough."

"It couldn't always have worked, though?" Neal asks.

"No. Sometimes things didn't go as planned. I don't think the Circle had enough jockeys as members, for one thing."

"So, why are you telling us this?" I ask. "And you're talking in the past tense as if the Circle has collapsed?"

"It has."

"After Barnaby died?"

"It was collapsing before that. His cousin, Thomas, got involved. Perhaps he thought he could turn it around. But it kept on dying. Neal, can I have some water?"

Neal opens the door of his fridge which is tucked away in the corner, beside a rusty filing cabinet, and tosses a bottle to Cliff. I tell him I don't need any. We sit in silence as Cliff gulps some water.

"And now the Circle's gone for sure——Barnaby and Thomas aren't around. But I reckon Bill's having second thoughts and could turn on us jockeys. And no one would believe any of us if we said Bill was part of it. He's got us, especially me. I've been suspended a few times because of my problems. It's obvious they won't listen to me, and they'll believe him."

"What about Zoey? What was her role?" I ask.

"I'm not sure. I suppose she must have gambled. I heard there was a fight. I don't know if it's true, but a mate told me she was beaten up so bad she had to go to hospital. Could have been around the time Barnaby's horses moved to Roxi's barn."

"Before we go any further with this discussion," I say, "were you involved in any way with Barnaby's murder, Roxi's beating, my deflated tires, Jaden's near-death experience, the explosion at Roxi's farm, the theft of my truck, Thomas's murder, or Elsa's exploits? I accept your apology for thumping me, but I need to know."

"You're joking, right?"

"No, I'm serious. I want to know if you played a role in any of the above."

"I sure as hell didn't murder anybody." He stands up and moves towards the door, crushing the water bottle when he turns around to face us. I regret putting my question so bluntly, but I don't think he wants to leave.

"I'm not accusing you, Cliff, I'm just asking. Perhaps you know something about those events that will help catch the murderers."

He hovers by the door for several seconds, and Neal buries his face in his hands. I'm too direct with my questions sometimes—especially when I'm frustrated.

Cliff sidles back to the chair and sits on the edge of the seat as if ready to spring up in an instant. He's on tenterhooks. He keeps squashing the bottle, taking the cap off and putting it back on. The crackling sounds reverberate around the small office. He sits back and takes another deep breath. Neal and I stay still and silent.

"I'm not a murderer. I don't have what it takes to kill a person or an animal." He holds his head back for a couple of seconds. "But I have a temper. Yep, I can get pretty mad about some things and yep, I can give a good punch." He looks at me. "When I punched you, I was really losing it. I got caught with the electrical device and Bill didn't do anything to help. And now that I'm getting my health under control, I'm seeing straighter, and I want to be straight. I want to get back to how I used to be in the old days."

"That's going to be tough, Cliff," Neal says. "And you're facing a hearing, aren't you?"

"It's not till next month."

"Is there anything else you can tell me?" I ask.

"You mentioned Elsa's name. She wanted so bad to be in the Circle. She heard about it from someone else, not me. She kept going on about it. Someone told her about the electrical device, and she asked me to get her one. I caved."

"That's why you went to her flat?"

"You know about that, do you? I left my favourite jacket there. I shouldn't have taken it off, but she wanted me to explain exactly how to use the device. She didn't want to hurt the horse, she said."

"Did you go back to the flat to get your jacket?"

"How do you know? There was a copper. I couldn't get in. It was when Elsa had gone missing for a while and I didn't want to get mixed up in that, so I wanted my jacket out of there."

"Any idea where she went?"

"Not a clue."

"Roxi saw her drop the device."

"Yeah, I know all about that. Elsa probably didn't handle it properly. She should have slipped it into her pants, but she fumbled it."

238

"So, Elsa wasn't one of the jockeys in the Circle as far as you know."

"I'm sure she wasn't."

"Thanks for the info."

"There's something else. Jaden's not back yet. No, I didn't have anything to do with what happened to him."

"Good."

"I want to fill in for Jaden when you run Fabulocity."

I look at Neal as I suck in my lips. Neal raises his eyebrows, but I have a feeling he's already talked to Cliff about it.

"I'm a good jockey and she's a nice horse."

"I believe you when you say you want to go straight, but I'm still concerned. Fay deserves a fair shot in this race and Bill Price could cause us trouble if you ride her."

"We'll think about it," Neal says.

19

Innocent Victims

The house is quiet except for the patter of three sets of paws following me around. They miss the rest of the household as much as I do.

William and Gabriel are at the cinema. I have relied on William and his contacts for key information in the past, but William's priority is Gabriel. And, of course, I can't argue with that. But I miss his help and his company. And Melissa is helping Edwin. I hardly ever see her these days. Edwin must have an extremely busy clinic.

We are drifting apart.

Partly to help prevent me from becoming morbid about the emptiness of the house, I've arranged to visit Noah and Elsa later this evening, but not until I've done a bit more research. William would have checked them both out more thoroughly a long time ago. Armed with a mug of tea and my laptop, I settle down at the kitchen table with two dogs lying on the floor either side of my chair and a cat on my lap.

It takes me more than an hour to find anything useful. I'm not able to dig up much about Elsa. What I do find is consistent with what Roxi told me. Elsa is her granddaughter.

I get distracted and follow some leads about the Caldermat family. Just as Thomas told me, Barnaby's father left his mother for another woman when he was five and I've found a couple of articles in the local papers. It caused quite a stir in the community, although I get the impression that it wasn't entirely unexpected.

But what has caught my interest is the obituary of Jeff Pestel. It states that he leaves a wife, Carrie Pestel, nee Caldermat, and a young son, Noah. Jeff was President and CEO of Golden Horizons, a large international gold mining company. So, that's where Noah's money came from. And, even more intriguing: is Noah related to Barnaby and Thomas Caldermat? Perhaps I've been duped, and I should have Noah in the crosshairs as a potential suspect. Detective Valeska's boss is apparently convinced he's their man, and he could be right.

My thoughts are disrupted by a sudden rapping on the kitchen door. The dogs scramble to their feet, barking, and Cooper flies out of the kitchen as if his tail's been lit.

"It's me, Elsa. Let me in." The dogs stop barking and wag their tails. They recognize her voice. I open the door.

"You got past the security guard," I say as she strides in. She doesn't answer but sits on the floor and makes a fuss of the dogs who lick her face. It's as if they're long-lost buddies. Her hair looks as if she's had her finger in a socket. It's even more dishevelled than usual. Her face is flushed, and her eyes are full of tears about to run down her cheeks.

"I'm going to wake the security guard," I say. Something isn't right and I need him to be on guard.

As I suspected, he's snoring in his car. I shake his arm to rouse him and after a couple of grunts he's fully alert and apologizes five times before I can get away.

242

I understand why the security guard sat in his car—a chilling mist is spreading its dampness and sucking up the day's warmth. My ears tingle with the cold. The dogs are waiting just inside the backdoor as I step in. I plug in the kettle. Elsa gets off the floor and sits at the table.

"Elsa, the first priority is to keep you safe. Tell me what's going on."

"I'm in so much trouble."

"I guessed that, but why are you here? I thought I was visiting Milkweed Farm later."

"I'm scared. Hard to admit." She looks down at Kelly who's wagging her tail in slow motion. "Noah's angry because that gambling thing went wrong."

"He lost a lot of money. But how does that affect you?"

"He said he could play them at their own game. So, he told me to get an electrical device, you know, like the one Cliff uses, and to get some winners. He told me to ride longshots and make sure they won."

"Why did you agree to do it?"

"I was infatuated. That's such a crazy word. But I was. I'm not anymore, though. I've had a hard time finding boyfriends because of my issues, including diabetes and helping Roxi."

"So, what happened?" I fill the kettle and switch it on.

"I got one from Cliff. He told me how to use it, but I was never ever to tell anyone where I got it. Both Cliff and Noah were furious when I dropped it on the track. I suppose I should have, like, practised or something. I couldn't slip it into my pants because my hands were shaking so much."

"Noah wouldn't have liked you trying it out on one of Roxi's horses because Barnaby was the majority owner and would have got most of the winnings."

"You won't believe this, but I thought Roxi owned them and that's why she was so broke and desperate. But now I know Barnaby wasn't paying his bills. I thought I'd help Roxi out. But she was mad as hell. So, I actually had three people mad at me. And I'm mad at myself."

"But why are you here?" Very little of this makes any sense, and I recall Noah saying Elsa's a pathological liar.

"Because Noah's insane. He's so angry. He believes Thomas and Barnaby stole his money and he wants it back." She stands up and paces around the room. Watching her could make me dizzy.

"That's not going to happen." I pour boiling water over a couple of teabags in the bottom of a flowery teapot with gold trim.

"He thinks it is. He told me that if Zoey was out of the picture, he'd get his money."

"I see." He must believe he would be the only living relative left if Zoey wasn't around, and he'd inherit what he thinks must be a fortune if Zoey dies. "I must call Detective Valeska."

"Don't!" She stops abruptly and spins around to face me. "That's why I'm scared. I'll be his next victim if he thinks I've said a word about this."

"But what about Zoey?"

"Can't you protect her? And me?"

"No. I can't." I pour the tea. Elsa sits down and stares into her mug as if looking for the magic answer to all her troubles. We sit in silence for a couple of minutes. "We're going to the Vannersville Inn. I'll ask Zoey to meet us there. You should both stay there for the night."

"I suppose that could be a good idea."

"Let's see what Zoey says."

* * *

The dogs and I wait in the pickup as Elsa collects a few things from her flat for a—hopefully short—stay at the Inn. Zoey sounded confused and reluctant to join us when I called her. She has not been officially charged—I'm not sure why. She must know it's just a matter of time before she faces the music for stabbing Barnaby's dead body.

But something is niggling at me. I stare at my phone trying to make up my mind if I should call Noah and nearly hit my head on the roof of the truck when it rings.

"Hi, Meg." It's William.

"Are you okay?"

"Fine. I'm at home and Noah's shown up. Is Elsa with you?"

"She's getting some of her things from her flat. I'm waiting in the truck."

"Good. Be careful. According to Noah, she's mentally unstable right now and could be dangerous."

"Something's been bothering me about her. Do me a huge favour and get a message to Zoey somehow. We were to meet her at Vannersville Inn. I don't think that should happen. Got to go." I hope he has success.

Elsa jumps into the pickup as if she has springs in her running shoes. She thrusts a small backpack onto the floor in front of her legs. It's as if her tiny frame is vibrating with energy. The dogs wag their tails expecting the truck to move. I'd like to buy some time because I'm not sure what's going on.

Elsa can't sit still. Once I get the engine started, I drive at a moderate pace towards Vannersville Inn.

"You're a slow driver," Elsa says. "I thought you'd be heavy on the metal." Her voice is high-pitched, and sounds forced. It's as if she's on adrenalin overload.

"I'm defensive, especially since I've got through a couple of rentals recently. Things happen to the trucks I'm driving." I turn my head towards her to glimpse any reaction because she crashed one of my rentals with the dogs inside. She doesn't flinch but continues to fidget and twitch.

"Are you okay?" I ask.

"Why? I dunno. Sure."

It's almost dark. The cloak of mist around Vannersville Inn disperses the lighting, creating an eerie scene. The inn appears to be on an island. The surrounding buildings are only partially lit and their shapes hard to distinguish.

As we approach the parking lot, William's on my mind. I hope he's safe. Perhaps Noah's the one who's dangerous—and Gabriel's with William without the dogs to help protect them both. I shudder.

"It's chilly, isn't it?" Elsa says, as if it's a good thing.

"My mobile's just vibrated." I park the truck near the entrance to the Inn. "Let me see. A message from Zoey. She can't make it after all."

"What?" Elsa almost screams.

"I suppose she doesn't see Noah as a threat."

"Did you tell her about him?"

"You were with me. You heard what I said."

"What did she say? Didn't she believe you?"

"I can't remember but she sounded confused."

She grabs my mobile. Fortunately, I'd shut it down and it's password protected. She chucks it at my feet with a groan and pulls her bag up onto her lap. She turns away from me and rummages in it, out of my view. I pick up my mobile and thrust it into my pocket.

"Shall we get you a room?" I ask as I open the truck door.

"No. Stay where you are." She brandishes a syringe and waves it in my face. "I must see Zoey, like now."

"But she's not here. Elsa, you're making a big mistake."

"I'm doing this for Noah. If he gets his money, he'll give some to Roxi, to help her. He said so."

"I thought you didn't care for him anymore."

"No way I said that. None of your business anyhow."

"I'm sure he doesn't mean for you to kill her. You'll be in prison for murder."

"No, no, no. That's where you come in. My clever plan is to frame you for Zoey's murder. You'll do what I say, or I'll hurt Kelly."

"I thought you loved animals. Why would you want to harm Kelly? She's innocent. All she's done is lick your face."

"Don't confuse me." Diffused light from the Inn's entrance reveals her pallid face with her wild, dark eyes staring at me. She has a rare moment of stillness but the dogs sense something is wrong. Kelly barks. Jake follows suit with a deep, grumbling roar.

"Shut up!" Elsa yells. The dogs don't pay any attention. "Tell them to be quiet."

"What do you want, Elsa?"

"I want Noah to get what he deserves."

"What do you mean?"

"I try to help people and look where it gets me."

"So, you're trying to help Noah. Why did you come to the farm?"

"I told you. Noah's angry."

"Why's he angry if you're trying to help him?"

"I'm not talking any more. You have to take me to Zoey or Kelly gets hurt. I'm getting in the back seat." She opens the door. My door is already unlatched so I jump down and open the back door in a flash. I don't think I've ever moved this fast—I don't register any of the aches and pains from my misadventures. Kelly and Jake leap off the seat and sit either side of me on the asphalt. Elsa yells at me to get back in and drive to Zoey's place. We stay put. She sidles across the backseat and out of the door. We should make a run for it, but something catches my attention. A slim, black figure stands in front of the truck. It appeared without a sound.

"Who are you?" I ask.

No answer. The dogs catch sight of the dark apparition and growl in unison. Jake's black hackles are up. Whoever it is has a knife. It glints in the headlights of my truck, but the figure itself is out of the range of the beams. The night's mist combined with dark clothes effectively hide the person's identity.

"What do you want?" I ask. I sense sudden movement behind me and turn around. Elsa jumps into the pickup, and the tires squeal as she circles around me. The black figure has to leap to one side, but then walks away as the truck disappears down the road.

Another pickup gone. My first reaction is relief that I didn't leave my mobile or cards in it. I tap my jacket pockets to reassure myself. But this is the second time Elsa's stolen my truck.

I don't try to pursue the mysterious figure. I won't risk getting any one of us stabbed. The body language of the person conveyed confidence and assurance. He or she emitted an eerie, silent calmness. I wish I knew who they were, what they want, and why they were here. The fact that Elsa sped off may have resolved whatever issue brought the black figure here. I have a lot of questions.

If I hadn't been chilly already, I certainly would be now.

Thank goodness the dogs are safe. I pat Jake's head. But where's Kelly? I gasp. Kelly is a black and white mound slumped on the dark, damp asphalt. What has Elsa done and why? The syringe is stuck into Kelly's shoulder and wobbles as I pick her up. I struggle with my precious load towards the door of the Inn. It's as if each step takes five minutes. My legs tremble as I make an extreme effort to get Kelly to the Inn as quickly as possible. Her heart beats against my arm but she lies still in my awkward embrace.

There's a large sign propped outside stating that the inn is temporarily closed due to flooding. My gut ties itself into a knot, but there are lights on, so there's hope. And as I reach the glass doors a man stops and watches us from the lobby. He then wanders towards us.

"Is your dog hurt? What's going on?" His voice is muffled by the glass doors.

"Please let us in. I must call the police." I'm almost screaming so as to be heard and also because I'm getting more frantic about Kelly as each minute passes.

He stands and looks at us. "Why's that dog got a needle in him?"

"A woman did it. Please let us in."

He unlocks the door. The automatic doors seem slow to open. The warm air hits us as I struggle into the Inn. I lay Kelly down gently onto the cool tiles in the foyer and the man has the sense to lock the doors. I take my jacket off and drape it over my beloved dog.

I set up an appointment for Kelly to see our veterinarian. She says she'll return to the clinic. It's after hours. The man tells me he's called 911.

It's a relief that Kelly is more alert now that we're inside, but she's trying to reach the needle with her teeth. I should pull it out but I'd rather the vet did. Now she's scratching at it, even though she's lying on her side, and my jacket isn't stopping her. It's no good, I must get it out. I'm guessing it was insulin in the syringe and wonder how much of it made it into her system. And if it has, did it enter under her skin or into muscle, and does this makes a difference? But Noah said Elsa has an insulin pump now, so the contents could be much more dangerous—barbiturate perhaps. That thought gives me goosebumps.

She's panting, but I can't tell if she's sick or simply stressed.

Swallowing and taking a deep breath, I kneel beside her on the hard floor and talk to her to explain what I'm going to do while doing my best to stop my voice from revealing my jittery nerves. She lays her head down as if to submit to me. I touch the syringe. She flinches. It must hurt. At least she's reacting which gives me hope. I press down on the skin surrounding the site as best I can with my left hand and get hold of the syringe with the other. I clench my teeth and pull. It comes out easier than I expected, and Kelly barely moves. She lifts her head as if to check on what I was doing but puts it down again.

"Do you have a clean plastic bag I can put this in?" I ask the man. I don't know who he is or what he does at the Inn.

"I'll check."

Flashing lights come from two different directions and converge on the parking lot, their colours dispersing into the mist. Elsa has long gone—with my truck.

"Here you go," the man says as he hands me a new plastic bag with a zip. "I'll unlock the doors for the cops." He ambles over to the entrance as if he lets the police in every day.

"I wish I'd taken a photo of Kelly with the syringe in her," I tell the man as he unlocks the doors. "That woman should be charged with animal cruelty."

But I expect she'll be facing more serious charges.

"We have cameras on this building. The cops can check them out."

"That's good." I hope they help. The mist could be an issue.

*   *   *

William hasn't answered my texts so I call Melissa, but she says she's tied up and can't go to the farm. It surprises me that she isn't able, or perhaps willing to help.

I wonder what's going on at home.

Kelly, Jake, and I wait in a cab for the veterinarian. Detective Valeska said I could leave the Inn and get Kelly attended to, but I'm to meet with her tomorrow morning. I try texting William again. It's been too long. I call the security company and am told that they can't get hold of their man. I ask them to call 911.

The vet's blurred headlights enter the parking lot. I lift Kelly off the back seat, and we're engulfed by an even thicker and cooler mist. Jake's beside me with his body pressed against my right leg.

After a quick and rather garbled account of my concern for

William, the vet suggests I leave Kelly with her so Jake and I can go to the farm. She lifts Kelly out of my arms. I hate to leave her, but the vet assures me that Kelly doesn't appear to be in distress and is probably fine.

The cab driver is a bit of a cowboy and breaks speed limits to get us to the farm. The gates are open. I leave a hefty tip and tell him to go since I'm sure the police will be here any minute. The security guard's car door is open and he's hanging out with his head almost touching the gravel. Jake sniffs at him and licks his face. The man groans. I take that as a good sign and run to the backdoor. It's open. William's attached to a chair with duct tape around his body, legs and wrists. And there's tape over his mouth. He's slouched and there's some blood dripping from his nose. My stomach does a nauseating somersault but he's alive. My hands shake so much I take longer than I should to get hold of the scissors that are stuck in the knife block.

Blabbering at him, I cut the tape in a few places, but I'm still wrestling with it when two armed police officers barge in. They lower their guns and, without a word, take over the task of freeing William. I rush upstairs to find Gabriel. His room is empty. In fact, there's virtually no trace of him ever having been here except for the dinosaur-patterned bedding and wallpaper. Surely, they wouldn't have taken him?

Jake dashes down the stairs in front of me and skids to a halt in front of William.

"An ambulance is on its way, Mrs. Sheppard."

"William, can you hear me?" He nods slightly. His eyes are shut. "Where's Gabriel? Did they take him?" He moves his head slowly as if to say 'no'. More blood drips from his nose. I don't know what to think. I kneel beside him and hold his limp, cool hand. I turn to the police officer who's standing next to us. "The security guard should be checked as well."

"He'll be attended to."

More flashing lights dot about on the hall floor and wall. The ambulance has arrived.

20

Suspects

William and I lie back in recliners in the family room in semi-darkness. It's way past my preferred bedtime. His wrists are sore. The duct tape was pulled tight, and he reacted to the glue—it has given him a pimply rash. He looks strange with his blue-striped shirt sleeves rolled up revealing white bandages wrapped around his lower arms. He says his ankles are bothering him as well. Each had been taped to a chair leg. The swelling on the side of his face makes him look lop-sided—almost comical. But I have no inclination to laugh.

The vet drove Kelly to the farm earlier and told us the patient is fine. I was right about the insulin—Kelly's blood sugar was on the low side, but nothing to be concerned about. Kelly ate her biscuit and is lying at my side. She smells vaguely of disinfectant. Jake and Cooper are curled up in the corner of the room. A few moments of welcome silence hover around us until I start to give William an abbreviated version of all that's happened. He insists that he'll give me his news afterwards. I'm on tenterhooks. I can't understand why Gabriel isn't here and why anyone would want to attack William.

"What about the security guard?" I ask.

"He was sound asleep when I got home."

"I think someone drugged him."

"Ah."

"You don't sound surprised."

"Because I'm not."

"Now for the important question: where's Gabriel? You said you were going to the cinema, but all his stuff's gone out of his room."

"My cousin Maddy called."

"I didn't know you have a cousin called Maddy."

"I must have mentioned her. She's the one who's adopting Gabriel."

"What?" I jerk the recliner into an upright position. "I thought we were."

"Oh, goodness. We have our wires crossed."

"William! I can't believe you didn't tell me this."

"I must have told you. Perhaps I wasn't clear."

"You weren't. We've never discussed his stay here as if it was temporary. I believed he was part of our family."

"You did? That surprises me." He turns and stares at me. It's almost as if he's accusing me of lying. My stomach gurgles as if it's as unsettled as my mind.

"You had me sign documents that I understood were adoption papers."

"If you'd read them carefully, you'd have realized they documented an interim arrangement for Gabriel pending the return of my cousin Maddy and her husband from the US. This was what Elizabeth wanted and had arranged with Maddy and me because Elizabeth knew she wouldn't survive long enough—Maddy and her husband were not due to return to Canada until this time next year. In the meantime, Maddy and her husband scrambled to have the date of their return brought forward and I recently heard they'd been successful. They crossed the border last week."

"But you should have told me this."

"You should have asked."

"I don't think you're being fair, William."

"In any event, it was apparent to me you weren't comfortable with your role of stepmother. It's for the best that Gabriel is joining his permanent family. Maddy and her husband have one son who's a little older than Gabriel. They can't have more children for some reason, so they're excited about their son having a little brother. They're warm-hearted, caring people. Gabriel will be fine."

"I'm glad to hear that, of course. Why the sudden leaving? He didn't even say goodbye."

"I thought it would be hard."

"So, you decided for me that it would be hard for me to say goodbye?"

"No, I decided it would be hard for Gabriel. He likes you, the animals, and the farm, a lot. He's going to miss it all. I thought it best to make little of his leaving."

"I think it's wrong of you to make that decision without talking to me. I don't believe in deceiving anyone, including children. Gabriel should have been told."

"Told what?"

"That he wasn't going to be living here, that this wasn't his new home."

"I did tell him."

"But you didn't tell me."

"I'm sure I did. You didn't listen."

I lie back in the recliner with a sigh. I don't have the energy to argue and it's obvious that there's nothing to be gained. But I'm hurt. William is usually sensitive and compassionate towards me, and others.

"Do you know who attacked you?" I ask.

"No. All I know is the person was sleight of build and dressed in black. They even wore a black balaclava."

"Did the person say anything?"

"No. He threatened me with a knife and made me sit. I don't know what happened next. I must have been knocked out. I don't remember being tied up."

"That's odd."

"Noah had just left, so I'm sure it wasn't him. He's even more desperate, by the way. I couldn't make him sit. He wants you to find out who killed Thomas, as you well know. He thinks the police are about to charge him."

"What makes him think that?"

"I'm coming to that. Did you know he's due to inherit Barnaby's assets if Zoey's found guilty of Barnaby's murder? He believes there's a strong likelihood she killed him, which contradicts the evidence that Zoey and Olivia stabbed Barnaby after his death."

"Interesting. I found out only recently he's related to the Caldermats."

"He's right. The police may suspect him of Thomas' murder. And he's also correct about the inheritance. A person who murders another is not allowed to profit as a result of the death. In other words, the murderer is precluded from receiving any inheritance from the deceased's estate or any benefits from the death that they might otherwise have received."

"That makes sense. By the way, I think the same person is responsible for both Barnaby and Thomas' deaths. What's tragic is that these men died for money. It's all about the dough—and that makes it even more tragic, and ironic, because I reckon the accumulated debts will eat up a good chunk of the estate, if not all of it."

"If it's all about the dough, the likely suspects must be Zoey and Noah."

"But perhaps Elsa should also be a suspect."

"Noah did tell me she could be dangerous because her behaviour has been particularly irrational and unpredictable recently. And he said she sees herself as an avenging angel. Nothing new there."

"She seems more like the devil to me. I can't understand her hurting Kelly and stealing my truck for the second time. She does have a motive for Barnaby's murder, and it's based on money—Noah's and Roxi's. I just can't bring myself to rule her out."

"Getting back to the black-attired visitor. I'm sure he didn't expect to find me here. He thought you'd be alone because there was only one vehicle outside. My theory is that he changed his plan and thought he'd hold me hostage until you turned up. He must have had duct tape with him, so it makes me wonder if he planned to abduct you. Something must have gone awry. I don't know why or when he left."

"Who do you think it was?"

"I honestly don't know."

"I have an idea but am not at all sure."

William shifts in his chair. "I've got to get some sleep. I have a lot to do tomorrow."

"Will you be well enough to tackle your day?"

"I have to be."

"So, is Gabriel with Maddy and her family now?"

"Maddy lives in Saskatchewan. She met us at the Vannersville airport. Gabriel didn't want to go with her. After all, she's a stranger. But she had books and a dinosaur Lego set, and those helped."

"Saskatchewan! That's so far away."

"We'll visit. And I told Gabriel he can come here of course. We're his family."

"Absolutely." I should have tried harder to be a caring and doting stepmother. I wonder if William arranged for Maddy and her family to adopt Gabriel after his nephew came here? William will probably never let on if he changed the plans because of me.

* * *

Kelly, Jake, and I are on our way to Roxi's dilapidated home again. She called me and it was as if I could hear the tears pouring down her face. I told her I'd be there as soon as I could, but I had to finish the barn chores first.

She's sitting on the back doorstep with her long white hair hanging in whisps over her shoulders. The dogs and I get out of the truck and walk towards her. She strokes Kelly's head. Jake lies down next to her. Her red-rimmed eyes seem smaller, and her clothes need a wash.

"Roxi, you look like you could do with a coffee or tea.'

"No. I need your help, that's what I need."

"What's this about?" I sit on a wobbly plastic chair that feels as if it could collapse at any moment.

"My farm's up for sale but it'll take a while. I need money now. I haven't got the ongoing costs of looking after those horses anymore, but I've got debts. I owe people."

"I'm sure you're really worried about this, but I don't believe it's what's making you so distraught. The people you owe must know you have the farm on the market. What's really bothering you?"

She sits more upright and fondles Kelly's ears. I'm surprised Jake isn't demanding a share of the attention.

"It's about Elsa, isn't it?" I ask.

She hangs her head and mumbles.

"Elsa been taken in for psychiatric assessment."

"Roxi, I'm sorry, but I can't say I'm surprised. Whenever she's around things seem to escalate, and not in a good way."

She shakes her head making tendrils of hair dance on her grimy forehead. "Oh, what has she done? She's ill, so crazed. I've tried. I've really tried." She kisses Kelly's head and teardrops glisten on Kelly's silky fur, but my beloved dog stays put.

"I know. But you can't change a person's hard wiring. I'm sure all that you've done for her has made a difference, but we don't yet know enough about the human brain to mend all the broken pieces. Please don't be so hard on yourself. Perhaps this time she'll get the professional help she needs to cope with her mental illness."

She sighs. "I sure hope so."

"By the way, who owns this place?"

"The gravel pit. Why?"

"Just wondered. When does your rental agreement expire?"

"It's month by month. It changed when my lease was up. They want me out of here and I want out of here, so that's at least one good thing." She hangs her head down again and Kelly lies down beside Jake, but she has her eyes on Roxi. "Why do you want to know?", she mumbles.

"Just wondering. Anyway, back to Elsa. You haven't told me everything."

She buries her face in her hands. I can't tell if she's paying attention to me or not.

"Tell me about Elsa," I say.

"She's my granddaughter."

"Roxi! This is serious."

"Okay. Okay." She sits more upright and reaches towards Kelly who obediently gets up and nestles her head deep into her lap. Roxi strokes Kelly with slow, gentle movements. "You have the best dog."

"Did you know Elsa harmed Kelly?"

She lifts up her head sharply and gasps, and then holds Kelly's head in her two hands and kisses her again.

"I'm sorry, Kelly." She takes in a deep breath, and I wait for a second. "When Elsa was put in my care, she was a cute five-year-old with dark curly hair and a cheeky smile. She was such a happy child even though her parents and baby brother were gone. I lost my son—her father— but had to keep my anguish to myself. Even today the ache of loss still haunts my heart and threatens to tear me apart."

"I'm so sorry, Roxi."

"Having Elsa forced me to keep on living. We managed quite well for the first ten years, all things considered, and even though she's diabetic. By the time she was fifteen she was helping to condition some of the quieter racehorses. I had some reasonable prospects and we both loved my farm. But it was around then that she started acting strange sometimes." Her chest heaves as she sighs. Kelly lies down again since Roxi has stopped stroking her.

"What do you mean?"

"I'm no shrink but I think the horror of the accident and losing her family bubbled up. She was terrified something was going to happen to me—that she'd lose me too. She became over-anxious and sort of protective. It was an odd kind of role reversal."

"So, when things weren't going well for you with Barnaby's horses, she was worried."

"Worried isn't strong enough. She was freaking livid with him for not paying his bills. I couldn't hide stuff from her. If I could have kept up a charade that everything was cool, I would have, I promise you."

"So, what did she do? I think I know some of this."

"You have to remember she's not well. I mean in her head. She needs help but won't listen to me."

"How did she try to help you?"

"In her mind, that's what she was doing, trying to help. But she made things much worse for me."

"How?"

"I keep asking myself if I could have raised her differently. Where did I go wrong?" She looks at me with tears in her eyes which peer out from under sagging eyelids.

"You said she wanted to help you."

"But it was all wrong. I guess she got in contact with that terrible man, Dr. Berzinksi. I actually caught her giving one of the horses a banned drug. I think it was clenbuterol that time."

"She did that more than one time?"

"Yeah. But she stopped for three reasons. One, I was mad as hell. Two, the horses didn't improve enough. Three, and this was the clincher, it dawned on her that Barnaby got most of the winnings."

"What came next, then?"

"She heard about the Caldermat Gambling Circle from someone. Is that what it's called, or was?"

"Yes."

"She befriended Cliff Ryman who she found out was part of it. It didn't work out though."

"She didn't get into the Circle, is that what you mean?"

"She wanted to get in at first, but she hadn't thought it through—the Caldermats benefited from the race fixing much more than the jockeys did."

"I see."

"She can get muddled as well as angry. It can be a frightening combination."

"You must be concerned about her all the time."

"Worse now she's an adult. I have almost no influence."

"It must be hard for you. So, what happened?"

"She met Noah Pestel at some charity thing. I honestly don't know much about their relationship. She seemed to adore him some days and hate him on others. Go figure. She's volatile. That's a good word for her. Could we go out for a cup of coffee? I'll get washed and changed. I need something to eat, and I still don't have any wheels."

"That's fine, but on the condition that you keep talking." I don't want to lose this opportunity to learn more from Roxi.

261

"I will. I just feel shaky and weak. This is taking the stuffing out of me."

Kelly, Jake, and I wait outside while Roxi gets ready. The dogs fall asleep and I'm likely to follow suit if she doesn't hurry up. The air is heavy with humidity and although the fluffy clouds are blocking the sun at the moment, they're evaporating in its heat and their shapes are shifting. The atmosphere will soon be oppressive. The weather made a sharp turn towards summer with the sunrise this morning. I move the dodgy plastic chair to the shade under a tree. The dogs stir and follow.

Roxi comes out of the house at last. Her thin white hair is tied back and she's wearing clean jeans with a fresh blue top.

"You look nice," I say.

"I didn't want to embarrass you. I look a wreck most of the time these days."

We all get settled in the pickup and head towards a fast-food strip on the outskirts of Vannersville. As we turn the corner at the end of Roxi's road, a car appears in my rear-view mirror. I've seen it before. Noah. I turn again and, sure enough, he stays on my tail.

"Roxi. Here's my mobile. Find Detective Valeska and send her a message saying Noah Pestel is in his car on Sideline 5 and following us. I hope she'll see it."

"I'll try. The road's bumpy. What does he want?"

"He thinks I can save him from the police."

"Did he murder Barnaby?"

"Just send the message."

"I can't keep your phone steady."

"Call her."

"She's picked up."

"Put her on speaker."

"Meg?" asks Detective Valeska.

"I'm in my pickup and Noah is following. We're on Sideline 5 about to turn onto the highway."

"On it."

Roxi ends the call, and we sit in silence as I put my foot down. We're still on the dirt road. The truck stirs up sand and grit into a dust storm behind us, and bounces in and out of pot holes. Jake falls off the back seat. Kelly was on the floor. She sensed it would be the smart place to lie as soon as I hit the gas. The highway is clear when we reach it, so I barely touch the brakes. The pickup handles the corner well despite its long wheelbase, but Noah's car snakes and I imagine he has a tough time keeping his vehicle under control. What are his plans if he catches up with us? I still can't believe he's a murderer and I don't think he's the mysterious person in black, but why is he pursuing us? I don't want anything to do with him right now. Despite all this, I don't feel good about doing what Detective Valeska asked by reporting his appearance.

And William and Melissa convinced me that Noah should be evicted from Milkweed Farm. They made good points about keeping suspects at arm's length, reminding me I always get too involved with people who are part of my investigations. William helped to arrange the eviction for tomorrow. There's no contract and Noah's been there for just a matter of days. So, I'm fully within my rights to demand him to go, especially since I haven't charged him any rent. I understand William and Melissa's point of view, and agree to a point, but I don't relish following through.

"Meg, do we have to go this fast?" Roxi asks as she holds onto the handle above the passenger door.

"Sorry, but I don't want to deal with Noah and his problems at the moment."

"Oh dear. That's stupid."

"What?"

Roxi peers into the side mirror.

"I think Elsa's with him."

"I thought she'd been admitted for psychiatric assessment."

263

"Must be outpatient. That's not good."

As we enter the fast-food strip a police vehicle pulls me over. Noah's car has disappeared.

21

Death Threats

William arranged to work from home today to help the healing process. He must be grieving Gabriel's absence, although he won't talk about it. And he's suffering the effects of the pointless assault on his body. A red rash surrounds his mouth with oddly reminds me of an English letterbox. But the swelling on the side of his face is barely noticeable. He's stoic, like the dogs, and refuses to complain or make a fuss.

The fact that I got a speeding ticket raises a whisper of a chuckle. He can't believe it and is astounded that the police didn't pursue Noah.

"It would be funny if it wasn't so serious," he says.

"Roxi and I made it to the coffee shop eventually. I'll give you a rundown of what she said."

"Good." He's taken the bandages off his wrists. They're sore and pimply, but he says they feel better now he's just putting ointment on. The bandages made his wrists warm and the itching and swelling worsened, apparently. "Before you start, I heard a vehicle drive slowly past our gate early this morning and wondered what it was. I was about to call the neighbour who lives next door when he phoned. He thought thieves were taking your furniture from Milkweed Farm. I told him not to worry and I'd check it out. I took the back route and watched from the neighbour's property, out of sight of course. Both Noah and Elsa were there and loading his few items of furniture into a white van. They've had the sense to move out. So, that's one less aggravation."

"That's a relief. However, we don't know where they went or why they left. Would you like a glass of wine?"

"I'll get it."

"And it's Fay's, or Fabulocity's race tomorrow. The kafuffle around Milkweed Farm could have meant I wouldn't be there. Will you come?"

"I can't. I'm behind on my work and have to be in court. What did Roxi have to say? I hope it was useful and worth the speeding ticket." William places two large glasses of red, full-bodied wine on the kitchen table.

"Detective Valeska told me she won't act to have the ticket voided because it could be perceived as unethical, or something like that. And I didn't ask. After all, I was speeding—there's no doubt about that."

"Roxi?"

I tell him what Roxi said before we finally made it to the coffee shop.

"She's distraught over Elsa."

"Before you go on, do you believe what she told you is the truth?"

"I do. As I said, she's distraught. But she says it's so difficult because Elsa sees herself as some kind of avenger. And she can be manic at times for quite long periods. Roxi blames herself for not being able to persuade Elsa to get help, but Elsa apparently thinks she's mostly fine except for her diabetes which she has trouble controlling."

"I'm sitting comfortably. Tell me everything."

"You asked for it. Most of Roxi and Elsa's serious troubles started when Barnaby Caldermat's horses were transferred to Roxi's barn, as you know. The financial burden and the lack of quality of the horses ruined Roxi. Barnaby was a gambler. It was all about the money, and he thought he could cheat and get away with it."

"Did she tell you who beat her up when they found Elsa's glove?"

"It was Thomas. She discovered Elsa had drugged at least a couple of the horses—which Roxi luckily stopped before any of the affected horses were taken to the test barn—but the Caldermat cousins also pressured Roxi to use performance enhancers. They had plans for Barnaby's horses because they were longshots and if they raced with the help of a dose of cheating now and then, the Caldermat Gambling Circle could make a bundle on betting. But Roxi wouldn't play the game. Thomas was the enforcer in the group, so he was the one who beat her up."

"It didn't gain him anything, did it?"

"From what Roxi told me it made her more determined not to succumb. She's a woman of principle. Despite the hardship she's suffered she refused to cheat. And I believe her. But it increased Elsa's frustration with Roxi as well as her anger with the Caldermat cousins."

"It appears to me the Caldermat cousins were not on the leading edge of intellect."

"Perhaps."

"You mentioned that Elsa sees herself as an avenger. If she wanted to help Roxi, what possessed her to fake that video?"

"I asked Roxi that and she doesn't completely understand Elsa's behaviour. But she reckons Elsa lost her head and was beside herself

with rage because she'd risked her jockey licence to help Roxi, and
what does Roxi do? She reports Elsa for using an electrical device.
Roxi thinks Elsa became manic about helping Roxi and believed
she could turn things around for her."

"Where does Noah fit into the picture?"

"Roxi says Elsa met Noah at a charity event. They must have got
talking and realized they both wanted revenge against the Caldermat
cousins. Noah had lost a lot of money which the cousins funnelled
into their failing gambling business. And I'm guessing Elsa wanted
Thomas to pay for beating Roxi up and trying to frame her by leaving one of her gloves behind. And she wanted Barnaby to pay for
ruining Roxi. And there could be more reasons for Elsa and Noah's
relationship developing."

"I wonder why the Caldermat cousins weren't able to make the
gambling business a success, even with the cheating?"

"They couldn't control everything all of the time. There would
only be very few jockeys who'd be willing to risk their careers through
cheating. And some of those would have split loyalties, having good
relationships with certain trainers. And I still can't help but believe
Bill Price, you know, the steward, would have been a reluctant player.
I think the whole thing was doomed to eventual failure."

"More wine?"

"No thanks. But you go ahead."

"No, I won't. I need to have a clear head tomorrow."

"Roxi is a frightened and beaten woman."

"Why's she frightened?"

"She's afraid that Elsa could be a murderer. She doesn't really
believe it, but she's afraid there's some possibility."

"Tell me more."

"As you know, Elsa's a diabetic and is very familiar with the
use of a needle and syringe. She thinks Elsa connected with Dr.
Berzinski and the word on the backstretch is that he'll get you

anything—at a price. So, when Roxi heard Barnaby had likely been injected with a barbiturate, it made her sick. She told me she literally threw up."

"But you don't believe she did it. Am I right?"

"I think the same person murdered both Barnaby and Thomas. The person who staged Thomas' murder to look like suicide with a complicated set-up of a hose connected to the exhaust made some mistakes, according to Detective Valeska. She said it was amateurish and probably done in a hurry. The stuff that was used to plug the gaps around the hose leading into the car through the window was rammed in there from the outside of the car. And Dr. Valeska says she's been told that evidence points to Thomas having been knocked unconscious and shoved into the car beforehand. A crowbar found on the garage floor is being analysed. A petite woman like Elsa wouldn't be capable of doing this."

"She could have assisted."

"I don't think she did. I don't have proof though. And I know she's lost. She wanted to help Roxi but got burned. Then she wanted to help Noah because she thought they were on the same page, but that hasn't worked out either."

"They were in the same car today, you said earlier."

"I know. But I wouldn't be surprised if that relationship ends badly. Both Roxi and I agree on that."

"I must get some sleep, but there are so many questions. What about the tires on your truck and the bomb? That bomb could have killed someone."

"Roxi and I reckon it was Thomas since he was the heavy for the group. They saw my digging around as a threat to their illicit gambling business. The fact that I was in regular contact with Roxi didn't help. Thomas chose the farm for his attacks because it's pretty remote. He'd be less likely to be seen or to be expected."

"What do you think Noah's up to now?"

"He's been under the illusion from the beginning that I could get the police off his back. He thinks I hold amazing sway with the police. I don't know where he got that from."

"I do. Detective Valeska mentioned you in the press conference about the case involving a RCMP officer called Dan. Noah may have concluded that you have considerable influence."

"That's funny. Anyway, Noah's been hounding me. His behaviour is bordering on obsessive. It feels like harassment at times."

"Don't you think he's been attempting to garner sympathy?"

"Living on the streets and letting his hand get infected?"

"He's a desperate man."

* * *

Melissa shows up in the kitchen as the dogs and I stumble through the backdoor. All three of us try to get into the house at the same time. The rain is splashing back up from the ground with such ferocity it's as if we were jogging through an upside-down waterfall. The dogs sit on the mat but not before they've had a good shake and shed water in all directions. I pull off my boots and grab three old towels out of a cupboard and all three of us get a rub-down. I'm about to go upstairs for a shower, but Melissa has her head on the table. Her blond hair is tangled and dull.

"What's wrong, Melissa? Is it about Gabriel?" Melissa is particularly fond of Gabriel, and they developed a bond even though Melissa wasn't around much.

"No. Well, I am upset about Gabriel. I blame you."

"We'll talk about Gabriel some other time. Tell me why you're crying." I put an arm around her shoulders, but she shrugs it off.

"Edwin."

"You care about him a lot. What's happened?"

"He's received death threats. He knows they're from Dr. Berzinski. It's because he reported that slime-bag to the College."

"Has Edwin contacted the police?"

"He won't."

"Because he's afraid?"

Melissa snaps up her head and glares at me. "Well, wouldn't you be?"

"Okay."

"It's not okay. It's definitely not okay."

"So, what's Edwin doing about it?"

"He's leaving. Why does this always happen to me?"

"Where's he going?"

"He doesn't know yet, but he's already found another vet to fill in for him at the track. It's so awful." She bangs her head onto the table and her arms dangle down at her sides. Kelly licks her hand, but Melissa doesn't acknowledge her love.

"Melissa, there must be something we can do. We'll ask William."

"I doubt it."

"I wonder if Bill Price could help."

"Haven't you heard?" She sits up and pulls strands of hair out from around her wet eyes.

"Heard what?"

"Bill committed suicide. It's been on the news and Twitter."

I stare at her with my mouth open. "That's so sad and terrible. But I guess that clinches his guilt."

"What do you mean?'

"He's suspected of being part of the Caldermat Gambling Circle."

"You've mentioned that illegal gambling business, but I didn't know Bill Price was involved. I suppose it makes sense to have a steward on your side."

"You haven't heard anything about him recently?"

"I didn't know him. But when we heard the news, Edwin said Bill was okay until his wife died. Oh, Edwin." Her red eyes stare at me. "I don't think I have any tears left."

"You're shivering. I'll make you a hot chocolate. William isn't going to be home until the evening. Fay is racing this afternoon and he said he can't be there. But I'll text him just in case he gets a break and has a chance to advise us."

"I don't want Edwin to go."

"Why don't you go with him?"

"I want to, but he hasn't asked."

"You need to talk about it then. Also, I have an offer. If he isn't thinking of going to the Caymans or something, he could stay at Milkweed Farm. There's no-one there. We could lend him some basic furniture. He should rent a car to avoid detection. It may not be as far away as he would like, but it would buy a little time. I was thinking of offering it to Roxi, but family comes first."

Melissa gets up and gives me a trembly hug.

"Thanks, Meg. It's so nice to have a sister. I'll call him now. I don't know what he'll say, but you're right, we need to talk about it, and I'll mention Milkweed Farm, just in case."

"Here's the hot chocolate. I'm going to have a shower which won't take me long."

*   *   *

There are stalls back-to-back in the centre of the saddling-up area, and all the horses in Fay's race are being led around them.

Fay's coat is dappled, her eyes are bright and she's on her toes. Linda works hard to keep pace with my stunning racehorse. Neal beckons Linda to lead Fay into the number 5 stall since Fay is in post position 5. Neal puts the tack on with the assistance of the jockey valet. I approve of Neal's attention to detail and Linda's kindness to Fay.

The horse can't stand still and shakes her head to show her impatience. Fay knows she's about to run.

The race has been pulled off the turf because it's too soft due to the rain. We think Fay prefers grass, but she'll be running on the all-weather track. It's not dirt. It's made up of all sorts of mysterious—at least to me—materials.

It's lonely standing outside the barrier, but I don't want to enter the saddling-up area to be with Neal. I'm jittery and Fay would pick up on my uneasiness. Frank would always join the trainer in the paddock if he could. He liked to check on the instructions the trainer planned to issue to the jockey. I've no idea what Neal will tell Cliff, but I know Cliff has studied Fay's works and past racing performance.

"Hi. Sorry, I didn't mean to make you jump."

"Jaden! How wonderful to see you. How are you doing?"

"Good. I had to be here for Fay's race. I've had a chat with Cliff, and I think he's alright. He just went through some tough times. He really wants to do well for you. He's getting his shit, I mean act, together. I'm still foggy now and then, so I'm not ready to get back in the saddle yet, but soon."

"I'm glad to hear it."

"They've just called 'riders up'. It's a blow that it's been pulled off the turf."

"Let's watch them leaving the paddock."

It's as if Fay is dancing on her way out to the track. We walk over to the escalator in the grandstand. Neal has a box in the outside viewing area, and he meets us there. Linda's standing at the rail below us. The rain has stopped but it's left us with high humidity.

"She looks good, Neal," I say.

"She's ready, but there's some tough competition."

"Hoping for a fair trip," Jaden says as he leans forward in his seat. "Hope she doesn't mind the soggy air."

After what seems like an eternity to me, the announcer says "they're off".

"She got bumped just after leaving the gate," Neal says. He has powerful binoculars. I didn't catch it happening. Fay is third from last. There are nine horses, so there are six ahead of her. The race is 6 ½ furlongs in distance.

"Cliff needs to urge her to move on now," Jaden says as they enter the turn.

"May be too soon," Neal says.

The horses are in a tight pack, and I'm concerned Fay will be boxed in and not able to make a move.

They enter the final turn and start coming down the home stretch.

"And Fabulocity is making a move to the outside," the announcer says.

We're all standing and yelling her name. She moves up to third. Jaden grips the rail and I hop from one foot to the other. My hands are clammy, and I could lose my voice as I scream out her name. The leader rapidly fades but the number two horse is gaining ground. She must be a good finisher. Sometimes Fay can put on a last-minute spurt, but it depends—on what, I'm not sure.

My throat is sore. She's level with the front-runner. We're jumping up and down now and shouting out ridiculous things to the horse that she more than likely can't hear and wouldn't understand.

"Photo finish," the announcer says. He's good at calling it usually, but this time it must be too close.

We walk down to the rail. Linda is all smiles.

"She did great, didn't she?" she says.

"She sure did. If she's second, that's fine with me," I say. My voice is so raspy I don't recognize it. We walk onto the track to meet Fay.

The photo finally comes up and the announcer says it's a dead heat, which is rare. Fay and Cliff come trotting over to us. Cliff's smile couldn't be any bigger. His eyes sparkle. He looks like a different person.

We each shake his hand and pat the horse. We get our photo snapped in the Winner's Circle and then Linda leads Fay back towards the barns.

*   *   *

Melissa looks no better. She's lying on the family room floor with the dogs who barely stir when I walk in. I'm convinced they know Melissa's distraught and are doing what they can to comfort her. Kelly has her head on Melissa's outstretched arm and is gazing into the red-rimmed eyes.

"How did Fay do?"

"Dead heat."

"That's great." But her voice is flat and monotonal.

"Has anything happened? I haven't heard from William."

"I have. He's gone to the backstretch to find Dr. Berzinski."

"On his own?"

"I suppose so. He told me Edwin must report the threats to the police. He explained that uttering threats is a crime and can bring up to five years in prison."

"But,"

"I know. In the meantime, Edwin could be killed by that ogre."

"Did William say anything else?"

"He asked Ramona to do some digging and that guy has made death threats before. He was charged but he only got fined. And the College didn't take any action. They responded to questions by saying that it wasn't relevant to his veterinary practice. Ramona has been very helpful."

"That's good. Sometimes I wonder about her."

"Jealousy. That's all it is."

"What on earth do you mean?"

"She's crazy about William. Didn't you know?"

"No, I didn't. And I'd rather not know."

"What's Edwin going to do?"

"I don't know. Are you going to the backstretch? I'm worried about William as well as Edwin."

"I'm going now. Can you stay and look after the dogs?"

"I've nothing else to do."

"Isn't the replacement vet going to take you on?"

"I'm not interested. I think he has his own staff anyway."

"Oh."

"Go!"

* * *

The security guard on the gate says he remembers William entering. He was driving an old Jag and didn't seem to know the backstretch well even though he has an owner's licence. That was him.

My first thought is to go to the veterinarians' trailers lined up near the cafeteria. Dr. Berzinski's trailer is the smallest and the shabbiest of the lot. Its appearance belies the belief that he makes a lot of money from illegal drug sales. I've heard that he drives a Mercedes SUV, and I can guess where that came from—the Caldermat Mercedes-Benz dealership.

There's only one vehicle parked near his trailer. It's small and rusty, but perhaps its driver can tell me where Dr. Berzinski is.

"Hello," I say as I enter the trailer.

"Hi," says a voice coming from behind a partition. "Be with you in a moment."

"It's rather urgent."

"Call the Doc then."

"No, I need to see him. Where is he?"

"No idea."

I leave the trailer having not seen the body that goes with the voice. That was a waste of valuable time. I go down the rickety wooden steps and get into the pickup. Dr. Berzinski must be treating a horse that raced this afternoon. It's not likely that he'd be at the track otherwise. William must have known he'd be here.

After about ten minutes—which seems more like ten hours—I find William's Jag parked behind a black Mercedes SUV.

Dark grey clouds billow and a few raindrops splatter onto my windshield. I park my truck in front of the Mercedes and reverse, stopping within a foot of the black SUV, but I don't think this will block Dr. Berzinski because William has left at least three feet in front of his car.

William stands in a doorway with his arms folded as he watches Dr. Berzinski scope a horse. The vet has put a long tube, with a tiny camera on its end, into the horse's trachea to determine if there's any blood in the airways. The trainer must have been disappointed with the horse's performance in the race and is searching for reasons—such as burst blood capillaries due to the stress of the run—but often there aren't any to be found. Dr. Berzinski studies the small screen and chats with the trainer. I can't hear what he's saying.

I stand beside William, but we don't talk. Dr. Berzinski glances our way a couple of times. As he's packing up the scope, he looks behind him down the shedrow to the back entrance. Neal stands there, also with his arms folded. Linda is at his side. The trainer senses something's up and surely knows Dr. Berzinski's reputation. He disappears into the stall with the horse.

"What the hell do you want?" Dr. Berzinski stares at William and me with small eyes deep-set above pronounced cheekbones. He must be about fifty, but I can't see any laughter lines in his grey face, just a deep frown.

"I'm William Porter, legal counsel. I'm here on behalf of Dr. Edwin Dinkum."

Neal and Linda walk slowly towards us.

"Oh, that louse. Are you here to threaten me? Ha!"

"I'm here to remind you that uttering death threats is a criminal offence."

"What's that got to do with me?" He stomps over to William and stops about two feet from us, with his hands on his hips. I can smell his sour breath. I guess he had a drink or two not long ago.

"Due to the fact that you've faced a charge of uttering death threats in your recent past, you could face up to five years in prison."

"Lying bastard. I've not spoken to him. His word against mine. Won't stand up."

"The phone records show otherwise," I say. William doesn't flinch, but he knows I've not had the opportunity to look at them.

"Ha! You're too late. He's dead. Nothing to do with me. But luck's on my side, I reckon. What do you say to that, fancy lawyer? Ha!" He picks up the case with the scope in it and pushes past Neal and Linda.

"He's lying," I say. But my insides are quivering.

"Let's hope so," William says.

"He stunk of booze," Linda says. "He breathed in my face. It was gross."

"We need to find Edwin," I say.

"We should call the police," William says.

"Let's do two things first. Neal and Linda, you check Edwin's trailer. You may have to get security to let you in."

"Sure, we can do that," Neal says.

"William and I will go to his home. He lives above his clinic."

"So, that's why Melissa keeps going to Edwin's clinic," William says.

Neal strides out of the barn at a brisk pace and Linda does her best to keep up.

"I thought Edwin was in hiding," William says.

"It's just a hunch. He'd want to make sure everything was in order at his clinic. He's a diligent and caring veterinarian. He wouldn't just up and leave. And Berzinski would know that."

"In my opinion, Dr. Berzinski isn't well."

"I don't care. We need to get going. Follow me."

I text Melissa and ask her to meet us at the clinic asap and bring the dogs. They could be helpful. I ignore her questions.

22

Cold

The clinic is a low square building. It's in darkness. A dull streetlight is reflected in a large puddle near the entrance to the carpark. There's one vehicle, a silver SUV. My stomach lurches. This isn't a good sign. William's Jag appears, splashes through the puddle, and parks next to my pickup. Melissa's little car is right behind him, and it lurches to a stop beside me. The dogs scramble out.

"I've got a key. Do you think he's dead?" Melissa drops the key. I grab it. "Which door?" I ask.

"Th-the b-back."

"Sit in the car," William says. "Keep a look out and let us know if you see anything."

Melissa is shaking and must be near to collapse. She eases herself back into her car with William's help. "Go, go!" she screeches.

The dogs, William, and I, trot to the back of the building. Darkness. Raindrops cascade down upon us with a vengeance. The clouds are dumping their contents all over us. My feet are wet. We pass a garage door that must be the access to the horse stalls, and next to it is the door we're looking for. The key turns and the light switch works. We all dash up the stairs. Nothing.

"Dogs, to the clinic," I say. "There must be direct access from this flat."

"Here's a likely door. Come on."

William opens the door and, sure enough, stairs lead down to darkness and smells of ointments, disinfectant, and horse manure. There are whinnies. Uh oh, I wonder if they need feed or medicines or both. The strip lighting comes on and a couple of the horses blink. The dogs trot around sniffing the clean, rubber floor.

"Dogs, I'm counting on you to find Edwin. Where's Edwin?" Jake gives me a blank look and wags his tail. Kelly may have got the message. She sniffs under each stall door as William and I peer inside. Nobody. We enter the operating area. No sign of Edwin. Kelly and Jake are in the front of the building, near the reception desk. They both have their noses down. I follow them and switch the lights on. But they get confused in an adjacent area. They go around in circles, but are most interested in a large, heavy door.

"William! Help me open this. I think it's a freezer. I bet he put him in here."

"I hope not."

"It's a fridge. Call an ambulance." Edwin's curled up on the concrete floor in the middle of the fridge. The walls are lined with shelves packed with bottles, boxes, packets, and other miscellaneous items. "I wonder how long he's been here? At least it's not a freezer. He's alive but his pulse is awfully weak, and he feels so cold. Help me move him out of here."

"Just calling the ambulance."

"There's some blood by his head. He's injured. Oh no!"

"It's on its way."

"We need to move him, now."

"Yes, but we must take photos for the police."

As William takes pictures, I lay my damp jacket on Edwin. William yanks his off to add to mine. The dogs keep circling us, so I tell them to lie down on the mat by the door.

William and I are reasonably fit and strong, but it surprises me how difficult it is to lift Edwin and put him on the reception area floor, and we could do with underfloor heating. I slam the fridge door to stop the cold air from swooping down and around Edwin.

"We need blankets. We must stop him losing more heat," I say.

"I'll text Melissa."

"No, just search for some. While you're doing that, I'll lie next to him."

"I can lie next to him. My body's larger and gives off more heat. You search for blankets."

"Good idea. Kelly and Jake, lie down and stay. Entice them to you, William. You may be able to get them to lie with you and Edwin. Is he still breathing?"

"Yes, but it seems slow and shallow to me."

"Be back soon. Dogs, stay!"

I run into the stable area and find a room full of equipment including lead-reins, halters, buckets, bandages, spray bottles, and miscellany. At the far end of the large room are hooks with an array of clean blankets. I roll up the two thickest ones and run back to the reception area with their straps dangling beside me.

"The ambulance is taking a long time," I say. "I'm not sure if we should lift him again. We don't know anything about his injuries. I was planning on putting him on one of the blankets but perhaps we should just lay them on top of him. Any improvement?"

"I don't think so. But I've noticed something curious. There are a few blades of grass and some soil stuck in his hair where the wound is. Can you see?""

Melissa crashes through the door into the reception area and screams at the sight of Edwin on the floor. The dogs stay put—which is amazing.

"Melissa, he's alive. He has hypothermia. We are warming him up gradually. You can help by lying next to him with the dogs and talking to him. But you must be calm."

She sobs and wretches. I put my arm around her quaking shoulders.

"Melissa, never mind. I can hear the sirens. He'll be fine. Sit down on one of the chairs. The ambulance is almost here, and the paramedics will know what to do."

She doesn't move towards the chairs but kneels next to Edwin and strokes his hair as if he was Kelly. Tears drop onto the blankets.

"He mumbled something!" she says as she turns her head towards me.

"Melissa, can you help me look after the horses? I don't know if they need feed, or medicine, or dressings changed, or what. Edwin wouldn't want the horses under his care to be neglected. Can you do that while William goes with Edwin to the hospital? We'll follow as soon as the horses have been taken care of."

She nods and sniffles. I grab a couple of tissues from the reception desk. "Thanks," she says. "Edwin arranged for a locum vet for the track and another for his clinic, but they don't start until tomorrow." She kisses Edwin's forehead. I hope, with all my heart, that Edwin feels the same way about Melissa.

The paramedics work quickly. They do an efficient assessment and wheel Edwin out to the ambulance within a few minutes. William dashes after them. Melissa slumps in a chair and weeps. The dogs sit at my feet and watch all the commotion.

"Melissa, we have work to do. I can't do it without you. I don't know the horses or where to find everything."

Kelly and Jake sit either side of her and gaze into her face. Kelly puts a paw on her lap which is definitely not allowed, but it works miracles. Melissa smiles and strokes both dogs.

"You are such special dogs," Melissa's tears keep coming. "Give me one minute, Meg. I'm sorry. I seem to have fallen apart."

"We understand, don't we, dogs?"

Melissa stands up, takes my arm, and we all four of us walk into the stable area together.

Melissa vows to stay by Edwin's side for the whole night. Dr. Milton explained to me that hypothermia can be dangerous and even fatal, but Edwin is recovering well and should be back home tomorrow. Meanwhile, I've been in contact with Detective Valeska, and she says Dr. Berzinski has disappeared. She assures me they'll eventually track him down. They have some leads. Meanwhile, Melissa doesn't want Edwin to go back to his flat over the clinic.

William and I leave the hospital and walk to our separate vehicles. The dogs are pleased to see me but we're all tired. They settle down behind the front seats and stay quiet and still until I park by the house. The security guard trots towards me as we three get out of the pickup.

"What's up?" I ask.

"You've got two visitors." Rain drips off the peak of his cap and I'm getting wet. My jacket has given up trying to keep the rain from seeping through. "They won't leave and they're both crying. They're sitting on the back step. I'm sorry. I couldn't throw them out. They came by taxi and climbed over the fence. I know I should've done something." He's gasping.

"It's okay. I can guess who they are. Thanks for keeping an eye on them."

"That's good, then." He's obviously relieved that I'm not about to report him. It must be tough to be a security guard with a heart.

As I guessed, Roxi and Elsa are the uninvited guests. They form a vignette under the glow of the overhead light diffused by the mist, with darkness surrounding them. They're making a fuss of the dogs and getting licks on their faces in return.

"No licking!" I say, but not in a firm voice so it has no effect. Roxi and Elsa both look up with faint smiles. It's amazing what these dogs can do.

"Come in. I'll make some hot chocolate."

"Thanks," Roxi says. Elsa offers her an arm to help her up. Roxi moves slowly as if she's stiff, perhaps from clambering over the fence.

"You want to tell me something?"

"Well, yeah, I suppose that's what we're here for," Elsa says as she glances at Roxi.

"William will be here soon. He's right behind me and I would like him to be with us. Let me take your wet jackets and hang them up to dry." It's fortunate that there's a small roof over the back entrance, otherwise they would have got soaked. The rain clouds refuse to move on to give the farm a chance to dry out.

Roxi and Elsa settle at the kitchen table. Kelly sits next to Roxi and Jake by Elsa. Cooper enters the room with his tail held so high it looks like it's being pulled up by an invisible piece of string.

"What a lovely cat. What's his name?" Elsa asks. She has more colour to her cheeks than I've seen before, but perhaps that's because she's been crying.

"Cooper."

She scoops him up and he smiles at her, as only cats can, and she strokes his head.

William almost jumps into the kitchen out of the rain which has increased its intensity and is lashing down. He blinks when he sees Roxi and Elsa

Cooper jumps out of Elsa's arms and trots over to William.

"We've been waiting for you. I've made you hot chocolate."

"That'll hit the spot." He smiles. He peels off his soaked jacket and hangs it up in the laundry room.

There are only a few preliminaries. We're all eager to get to the crux of why Roxi and Elsa are here.

"Who wants to start?" I ask.

"It's sort of overwhelming," Elsa says. "Because there's so much."

"And people are covering for other people and making it complicated," Roxi says.

"I know," I say, and they both look at me with slight frowns. There's a likeness in their features I hadn't noticed before. Elsa is sitting almost still, which I thought she wasn't capable of. Her hair is standing on end, as usual, but that could be a fashion statement I'm not clued into.

"We've come because we need to talk to someone and we're not ready to go to the cops," Elsa says.

"We don't have any authority. You are aware of that?" William asks.

"Yeah, we know," Roxi says. She stares at the mug of hot chocolate as if its alien to her. Elsa runs her fingers up and down the handle of her mug with eyes cast downwards.

"Someone needs to say something then," I say. "Perhaps I'll start, and you can pick it up from there." Silence. "I know there's a lot of history between you two, but things really went awry after Elsa dropped an electrical device on the racetrack. Elsa, tell us about that." Elsa looks at me as if I've asked her to get airborne around the kitchen. "I know you love each other but there've been misunderstandings and hurt, right?"

"Elsa was trying to help me," Roxi says. She picks up her mug and takes a sip at last.

"I know."

"It all started with those horses Zoey couldn't wait to get rid of. You know, Barnaby's."

"I know about that."

"I made mistakes. It wasn't just Barnaby's fault." She lets the mug drop back onto the table with a clunk and its contents are slow to follow but make it without any loss. "I wasn't in good shape."

"Roxi and I both have bouts of depression. We can't help it," Elsa says, as her nose dips closer to her mug.

"I understand."

"You can't really understand."

"Elsa, I'm sure Meg gets the idea. I made mistakes. I didn't do a good job. To have over thirty horses and have none of them do well is against the odds."

"But the horses were terrible, Granny."

"They weren't the best, but I didn't help them. I entered some into the wrong races, I even forgot to enter now and then, and didn't work a few when I should have, and I only got one claimed. It was bad. If it wasn't for my barn help, they would have lost weight and god knows what else."

"But you were sick," Elsa says as she reaches out and touches Roxi's arm.

"The stress I was under spun me in a vicious circle. I got sicker and the horses did worse and so it continued."

"You said Barnaby showed no interest in the horses," I say.

"He knew nothing about racing, as I've told you before. Money. That's all he cared about. When the horses failed to do anything, he demanded we cheat. I was in a very low place when he talked to me about that."

"She asked me what she should do," Elsa says. "I said if we cheated maybe we could get some of them claimed and earn a bit of money to dig ourselves out. We'd almost lost hope."

"While money isn't everything to me," Roxi says. "I have to pay the rent. I was behind by two months. I couldn't pay the feed mill. They were good, they let me have credit. But I was in a bad place."

"I wasn't doing well," Elsa says. "I wasn't getting rides. I lost my confidence after a couple of spills."

"They were two-year-olds though. Babies," Roxi says.

"I wasn't earning much. I could just afford my flat because I did a lot of exercise riding, but I couldn't get races. My agent isn't all that great, either."

"He sure isn't."

"Tell me about the cheating," I say.

"That's why we don't want to talk to the cops," Roxi says.

"You will probably have to do so eventually," William says in his soft, marbly voice.

Roxi looks at him and frowns. "I guess."

"We didn't kill anyone, just in case you're wondering," Elsa says, also looking at William.

"We know that," I say.

"Cliff told me about the electrical device," Elsa says. "We had a brief thing going on. But he was as sick as I was. He had weight issues and would throw up after he ate. And I'm sure he was on something. I was trying to get into a better place. I thought having a relationship would help. But it was worse. Anyway, he told me about the device and gave me one, and tips on how to use it."

"But you didn't drop it on the track after the race you won?" I ask.

"That whole thing was my fault," Roxi says. "Cliff dropped it after an earlier race that afternoon. I thought Elsa had. I didn't believe her, because she'd just won on a horse I least expected to do anything and there was that thing on the track beside the horse. What was I supposed to think? We'd just chatted about cheating."

"But I didn't use the electrical device. Ever. I was too afraid. I thought the horse would spook and I'd be on the ground. I never even took it to the track. It's still in my drawer in the flat."

"Anyway, you went back to Cliff," I say. I wonder if I'm being told another pack of lies. These two can make me dizzy.

"I was so upset and hurt by you reporting me to the stewards 'cause of the device. I was so angry." Elsa stares at Roxi, with tears pooling in her eyes.

"We both have tempers."

"I was raging. You didn't believe me. That was the worst. So, I faked that video."

"Yeah, I made a terrible mistake. I've said I'm sorry."

"Well, I shouldn't have done it."

"So," I say, "where does Noah fit into all this?"

"He doesn't," Elsa says. She rubs her eyes. "I met him after Cliff and I split up, not that we'd been all that serious. I'm not good at relationships."

"Me neither," Roxi says.

"I either get infatuated or I go off them fast. I sort of went stupid over Noah. He seemed like a real nice guy. He made out he had lots of money, but later told me he'd lost a pile on gambling. He kept asking me to become a jockey with the Caldermat Gambling Circle, but I couldn't do it. He thought he could set up his own illegal gambling gig, but that didn't get off the ground. There's much more to this, but we haven't got a couple of days to tell you all of it."

"Did he mention anything about his relationship with Barnaby and Thomas?"

"He loathed them, but I don't think he killed them. He was angry. He thought Barnaby had stolen his money and wanted revenge. But he still believed Barnaby had a secret formula for betting the horses and wanted to steal it. He's addicted to gambling and he's lost his shirt. That's where things are at for him."

"Was it him who attacked me and the dogs at the Inn?"

"No. I'm sure it wasn't. I thought you'd ask why I didn't help you."

"I want to know why you hurt Kelly."

"I was sick. I took something and it made me crazy."

"Your behaviour was bizarre, even dangerous."

"I've promised not to take it anymore. I can't tolerate it. I don't remember what I did, but whatever it was it would have been because, in my mixed-up mind, I was helping Noah."

"Noah has asked me right from the beginning to get the police off his back because he's a suspect in Barnaby's murder. What makes you so sure he didn't kill Barnaby?"

"'Cause I was with him when it happened."

"You mean, when Barnaby was murdered?"

"He told me, and I believe him. Honestly, I do."

I don't respond but she fixes her eyes on me as if to dare me to challenge her. "Go on."

"He was in the back garden. He planned to steal Barnaby's laptop. He said it was a stupid plan. He hadn't thought it out. He was terrified when he saw Olivia and Zoey stab Barnaby several times."

"Barnaby was dead before they attacked him. There was no blood."

"Oh, wow. I didn't know."

"And why didn't he go to the police?"

"I asked him that. He said he couldn't because he'd stolen the laptop."

"Noah told me he'd tripped over Barnaby's body on the floor."

"Oh, he didn't tell me that. He just said he got the laptop. How was he killed then?"

"He was injected with a barbiturate according to the post-mortem report."

"The only person I know who has every drug you could dream up and then some," Elsa says, "is Dr. Berzinski."

"But why?" asks Roxi.

"That's what I plan to find out," I say.

How much of this is true? Am I getting warmer or being thrown off track?

23

The Will

A security guard is stationed at Edwin's clinic because I've a hunch that Dr. Berzinski hasn't finished his tirade against the people he sees as his enemies, and Melissa is working there all day. Detective Valeska says she's on it, but her officers are no longer at the scene of the attempted murder of Edwin.

Noah has gone underground again and does himself no good by hiding from the police. He continues to dig a deeper hole to bury himself in.

The people who could give me the information I'm seeking are all dead—Barnaby, Thomas, and Bill Price. There's one other person who could help, but he's the least likely to give me information.

* * *

The dogs and I wait in the pickup by a small roadside café out of town called 'Papa's Kitchen'. The parking area at the side of the low, brown, wooden-sided building is unpaved and potholed. The open sign flashes relentlessly in the mist that's dissolving fast in the early morning's emergent sunshine.

Kelly and Jake are restless. They sense I'm waiting for something to happen. Dr. Berzinski replied to my text. I was only a little surprised. He suggested we meet at this place and said there are picnic tables behind the building.

A taxi pulls in and the square shape of Dr. Berzinski appears. His face looks grey and his small eyes are sunken and bloodshot.

"I'm getting a coffee," he says, as I roll down my window.

"I've got a drink."

He nods. It's more like a twitch. "There's somewhere to sit behind the building."

The dogs and I walk over to the damp picnic-tables. Kelly settles down underneath the one I sit on, and Jake lies down behind me. They don't react to Dr. Berzinski when he sits opposite me with his large black coffee. Its steam curls up into his face as he sips.

"I'm not the bad person you think I am." His stare is close to being a glare.

"You don't know what I think."

He grunts and leans back, but his grey face looks less strained.

"Let me guess. You think I'm a murderer."

"No, I don't, actually."

"Uh. You must be the only person who doesn't."

"Perhaps. I want to find out who is, and I think you can help. I believe the same person murdered both Barnaby and Thomas Caldermat. But I'd also like to know what went on between you and Dr. Edwin Dinkum. Let's start with the Caldermat cousins. You were a member of the Caldermat Gambling Circle, right?" Damp seeps through my jeans from the wet picnic table seat, but I'm only partially aware of the cool sensation.

"To my regret. Yes."

"How come you got involved?"

"It's not simple. A few years ago, I had a crush on Roxi—before she went down a rabbit hole and emerged a changed person several years later."

"What do you mean?"

"You must know."

"I don't think I do, unless you're referring to her taking on Barnaby's horses."

"She and Elsa aren't the noble people you think they are."

"Oh?" I sip my tea which is still steaming hot, and my tongue tingles in protest.

"You probably think you keep an open mind, but my assessment is that Roxi's been taking you for a ride."

"I see."

"Elsa asked me to help her get Roxi's horses into the Winner's Circle."

"With PEDs?"

"She said Cliff Ryman told her that the Caldermat Gambling Circle use PEDs and that I supplied them."

"Is that true?"

"No, but that's how Barnaby and Thomas kept me in their loop. They said they and Zoey would claim that I supplied drugs if I didn't play along. Of course, I'd lose everything I've worked for if that happened."

"I don't understand." A breeze shakes droplets off the tree's leaves which splatter down onto us. Jake gets up and shakes. He joins Kelly under the table.

"The mistake I made was to link the Caldermats to a company that makes and distributes PEDs for racehorses. It's in the States but ships to anywhere as far as I can gather. Stupid of me."

"Why did you tell them about that company then?"

"Several years ago, I gave an injection, doesn't matter what, to the wrong horse that was to run the same day. Nothing dangerous. It was a medication I'd prescribed for another horse in the barn. It was a case of mistaken identity. I was careless. The injected horse had to be scratched from its race. It was a medication that was not permitted to be administered to a horse within seventy-two hours of it running. It would have been detected if the horse was tested."

"I'm surprised that would be enough to result in you losing your licence."

"I've assumed it would be."

"Whose horse was it?"

"One of Barnaby's that Zoey was training at the time. They used this to pressure me into joining their ridiculous gambling circle. I had to contribute funds. They used these to help pay the jockeys that held back horses. The ones that were on doped horses or used electrical devices—I'm sure you know about those—got a payout from the illegal gambling winnings."

"You must have got money from those winnings too?"

"No. I wanted no part of it. And I paid as little as possible into that racket."

"It didn't do well."

"Badly managed. Barnaby didn't know anything about horse racing. He was a gambler and owned a car dealership. Nasty man. And Thomas was a thug. He beat up jockeys who made mistakes or didn't play along. Jaden was hurt the worst. The Circle was collapsing at that point, and Thomas was in a rage."

"So, Barnaby and Thomas worked together?"

"Yes, of course. They were the movers and shakers in the Circle."

"Getting back to Roxi and Elsa. You gave Elsa the same contact information so she could get hold of PEDs?"

"No, I refused."

"You must know more about Roxi and Elsa?"

"Roxi and Elsa are each good at playing the victim. They can make people feel sorry for them."

"I can see that."

"They're made of tough stuff, but I don't know if they had anything to do with the murders of the Caldermat cousins."

"I don't either." We peer at each other over the rims of our cups.

"Why did you attack Edwin Dinkum?"

"Is he okay?"

"He says you saw him coming out of his trailer and you pushed him. He fell back and hit his head."

"Oh, god. I hope I didn't. I suppose I could have. I don't remember attacking him."

So far, Dr. Berzinski hasn't been all that helpful. I'm not sure that this meeting's worth the damp chill that's crawling up my spine.

"But I was furious with him for reporting me to the College. He has no evidence. But it would mean a hearing, and the mistake I made with that injection could come up. I thought I'd managed to sidestep it. I admit that was on my mind."

"You didn't go to his clinic?"

"Never been there, although I've sent horses to him for ops."

"You uttered death threats."

"You lied about the phone records because I haven't phoned him for weeks. I checked. I admit you had me worried. If I said anything, and I admit I could have, it would have been to his face."

"Edwin has your written notes."

He slams both of his palms down onto the rough wooden table top and looks as if he wants to launch himself into space.

"Edwin knows they came from you," I say.

"I have no recollection of writing them." He stares at me and neither of us blinks for about two seconds. "But I have to believe you." He picks up his coffee cup and turns it around in his hands.

"Why did you tell us Edwin was dead?"

"I do remember saying that. I was in a rage. I'd been drinking as usual. I was so despondent. I feel trapped, all because of one mistake. Worst of all, someone wants me to take the rap for the murders."

"So, you think there's an attempt to frame you? By whom?"

"Well, that's the million-dollar question, isn't it?"

* * *

Money and revenge can each, or both, be motives for murder. I sit at the kitchen table with three animals curled up underneath, making it hard to find somewhere to put my feet. My tea is much more pleasant than the one I had earlier in a Styrofoam cup outside Papa's Kitchen.

The money. That's what I need to focus on. William sent me a copy of Barnaby's will earlier this morning, but meeting Dr. Berzinski prevented me from looking at it until now. I was itching to read it as soon as I got home, but I had the second hot shower of the day because I felt chilled to the bone. I wouldn't be surprised if the dogs feel cool and that's why they're curled up with the cat. Wafts of damp dog odour rises up from under the table. I'm surprised Cooper tolerates it.

I've always assumed that Barnaby had little money and he was in poor shape financially. Certainly, the gambling circle was not a success. He had a valuable house and a Mercedes-Benz dealership, but by all accounts, he was carrying substantial debt.

William performed another miracle this morning and found out how much Barnaby had in investments—almost zero.

The will is straightforward. Barnaby names his cousin, Thomas Caldermat, as the executor. There are other provisions if Thomas was to predecease him, but I skip that part. The Mercedes-Benz dealership goes to Thomas, the house to Zoey, and the remainder, which I guess is zero, to Olivia. Obviously, the first two would benefit from Barnaby's death, but who would be willing to murder for it? And especially with the debts that must be paid out of the assets. There is no mention of Noah. He would stand to gain if Zoey either murdered Barnaby and/or Thomas, or she died. That assumes there are no other living relatives, and I haven't heard there are any. It seems to me that Thomas was in a conflict of interest as executor, and I wonder if this means Thomas should be a suspect or he at least played some part in Barnaby's death?

Despite digging, I can't calculate how much the dealership is worth, but my guess is it's a lot. On Thomas' death presumably the dealership would go to Zoey since she's Barnaby's widow. As far as I know, there's no legal separation agreement, and they were legally married at the time of Barnaby's murder.

Perhaps Zoey was outraged that Barnaby left the dealership to Thomas especially since Barnaby didn't even pay Zoey's training bills for his racehorses. He left her with almost nothing, it seems.

Zoey was beaten and abused by Barnaby. So, both money and revenge could be in play here. But she confused things by having a relationship with Thomas. Perhaps that was deliberate, to put us off the scent. But did she murder him so she could inherit the dealership? That's too simple. But sometimes it is simple. According to Olivia, Zoey has tried to frame her for both murders. And Zoey wouldn't allow her to continue living in the house, although she'd agreed to that at first.

I suspect the murders have nothing to do with the Caldermat Gambling Circle except, perhaps, that it was a failure and lost money. Maybe Zoey knew Barnaby was eroding the value of his assets and perhaps he'd already used the dealership as collateral for loans. I text a question to William.

The gambling circle has had me going around in a downward spiral. And Roxi, Elsa and Noah have been making me dizzy. It's time I got this straight.

"Come on dogs, we have to visit someone." They get up, stretch and yawn, almost in unison, and wait for me to put a jacket on. The temperature has taken a sudden plunge and it's unseasonably cool, but the rain has stopped. Moisture hangs in the air—it's as if it's chased away some of the oxygen.

I tell the security guard I'll be out for a couple of hours. I hope I won't need to continue with this service for much longer.

As I pull into the driveway in Blackloch Estates, Detective Valeska texts me to say that the partial fingerprint they lifted off the syringe found near Barnaby's house isn't a match for Noah. I almost tell her whose I think it is but decide against it. I park behind a SUV that I remember is Olivia's. The sight of it sends a shiver down my spine. Zoey is the person who'd I arranged to meet and she suggested the house. And I assumed Olivia wouldn't be around since animosity has infiltrated the air between them.

As if to validate my assumption, raised voices penetrate the front door. Jake stands on the flagstone doorstep and twists his head as if he's trying to make out what's being said. Kelly sits and looks up at me as it to ask what's the plan. I don't have a plan, but we walk around the house to the back deck. I tell the dogs to sit and stay on the grass as I edge along the rough brick wall and peer into the kitchen through the patio doors.

"This house is mine!" Zoey screams at Olivia.

"You're disgusting. To think I was under the delusion we were friends."

"Friends? Never."

"How can you say that? We spent so much time together."

"Ugh."

"I can't believe you told them I murdered Barnaby."

"I bet they can trace the syringe to the hospital. They found it, you know."

"But I didn't do anything. And I did what you said just to help you."

"It didn't help. I've just found out Barnaby was up to his eyeballs in debt. Just a few scraps left."

"That's not my fault."

"You aren't his widow. You were just a bit on the side."

"You were separated. I was the one living with him. Remember, he beat us both. Not just you."

"It was all for nothing, and I'm not taking the blame."

"You bitch."

Olivia lunges at Zoey and something's glinting——something in Zoey's hand.

"No, don't!" Zoey screams. I don't understand what's going on, but it has to stop.

"Dogs!" I yell. I open the sliding door just as Zoey thrusts a knife towards Olivia who stumbles and falls backwards. I dive at Zoey and grab her around her legs. I'm kneeling on the cold, hard, tiled floor.

This is a mistake. Zoey's still standing and facing away from me. She twists and thrusts the large kitchen knife downwards.

"Stay!" I tell the dogs. I'm terrified they'll get hurt. Kelly disobeys. She knows I'm in danger. She jumps onto my back while I'm still kneeling—I can't believe it. I've got hold of Zoey's legs but the woman's writhing and plunging the knife at me as my arms tremble with the effort of maintaining my grip. Kelly's fury is incredible. She wants desperately to protect me. My stomach knots and my heart thumps. The dogs shouldn't be with me. It's too dangerous and unpredictable. So, I'm not sure if it's a good or bad thing that Jake appears from somewhere. I should have known he'd want to defend me and his best buddy, Kelly.

Jake stands in front of Zoey and growls, snaps, and snarls, in quick succession, with lips curled and white teeth gleaming. Zoey continues to twist—I could lose my grip. Olivia is no help. She's sprawled on the floor.

In desperation and trepidation, I yell "go!" to the dogs. I don't know what they'll do, but I hoped it might startle Zoey and unbalance her. It doesn't, but Kelly jumps onto her hind legs while she's still on my back and plants her front legs almost around Zoey's neck. At least that's what it looks like from the level of Zoey's knees. Jake jumps up and down barking and growling. I push as hard as I can against Zoey's legs, and we collapse in a heap with Kelly on top. Jake yelps. Kelly growls. Zoey swears. I groan. Olivia's silent.

Zoey is strong and fit. And I'm weakening. But I must get that knife away from her. She's on her hands and knees but she has a firm grip on the knife. Her knuckles are white.

"Get the hell out!" She yells at me. Her spit hits my face.

"Give me the knife. The police know you murdered Barnaby and Thomas. They'll be here soon." I gasp for breath.

"Liar. Olivia did. I said get the hell out." Her voice is close to a growl. She's almost in a downward dog position but struggles to get upright. I heave myself up as quickly as I can to stand in front of her. Her eyes stare at me as she steadies herself. She's swaying. She must be drunk. But then I see the syringe on the floor.

"Olivia tried to kill you?"

Zoey collapses onto her knees and her forehead hits the tiles.

*   *   *

William and I get back into the truck after visiting Edwin in the hospital. He'll be discharged later today. William, Melissa, and I are relieved beyond words. Melissa is at his clinic, helping the locum veterinarian. Edwin will be back at work tomorrow—at both his clinic and the track. His smile said it all.

He explained what happened. Dr. Berzinski approached him as he was coming down the trailer steps, as he told us earlier. There was a strong smell of booze. Dr. Berzinski lunged at him and pushed him sideways. Caught off guard, Edwin fell but didn't think he was badly hurt at the time. He was sore and his head ached, but otherwise he felt fine. So, he went to his clinic as he'd planned. He had to collect some medicines out of the fridge for several horses. He usually has the door open but he knew he'd be a few minutes, so he closed it. The door can be opened from the inside and he's done this before. He reached for one of the bottles he needed and the shelves started to spin around him. Then his knees buckled and the floor seemed to rise underneath him. He doesn't remember anything else until he heard voices. He thought he was dreaming.

So, we've agreed that what Dr. Berzinski did wasn't attempted murder, and he probably told me the truth. But he needs to be held to account, as William put it.

24

Dying For Money

Melissa, Edwin, William, and I sit at the dining room table. William has prepared a delicious meal which had my mouth watering before we reached the dining room. The aromas, including pungent garlic, hung around in the kitchen, and excited my tastebuds.

"Zoey had it all planned from the beginning, but things didn't turn out as she envisioned. Zoey gave the barbiturate injection. How she managed to do that without Barnaby struggling and fighting her off, I don't know. I'm sure Olivia was there at the time, so she probably helped. Barnaby was a heavy drinker and usually had a double whisky first think in the morning before his shower. Zoey knew a barbiturate combined with alcohol could be lethal in the right quantities. But she didn't want to have to dispose of a dead body and thought she'd come up with a brilliant idea to deal with that conundrum."

"Before you go on," Melissa says, "I have to ask why Olivia helped?"

"Zoey knew Olivia hated Barnaby as much as she did. While Zoey's motive was financially driven—she was sure he was worth a lot more than he actually was—Olivia's was pure hatred and possibly fear. Zoey convinced Olivia that stabbing someone who was already dead wasn't a crime—and believed that herself—and told her that they should both stab Barnaby and convinced her the police would never find out who murdered him, and they'd be free."

"So, Zoey knows enough about forensic science," William says, "to recognize that the medical examiner would determine that Barnaby was already dead before he was stabbed."

"But she must have known they'd find barbiturate in his system," Melissa says.

"They didn't think they'd be linked to the barbiturate," I say, "because no one would entertain the idea that they would stab someone they'd previously murdered. It doesn't make sense. But what they didn't realize is it's a criminal offence to interfere with a dead body. And another mistake was that Olivia thought if the injection was linked to them that she couldn't be charged because, even though she'd stolen the drug from the hospital, she didn't administer it. Perhaps she held this over Zoey and that could have led to Zoey's attempts to frame her for Thomas' murder and could have exacerbated the fight I walked into."

"You said she had a syringe?" Melissa asks.

"She managed to inject some barbiturate into Zoey, but not enough to kill her. They're both in hospital recovering from their fight, but they're going to face long sentences, I'm sure."

"No doubt of that," William says.

"Why did they stab him, exactly? I still don't get it," Melissa says.

"Zoey believed the police wouldn't suspect them if they stabbed Barnaby after he was already dead and would assume someone else had administered the barbiturate. And it wasn't difficult for them to knife his body because they both loathed the man. They were confident, of course, that the case wouldn't be solved."

"There are many homicides that remain unsolved," William adds. "They may have thought the police would add it to the list."

"And it meant that they didn't have to dispose of the body."

"Where did the barbiturate come from?" asks Melissa. "Dr. Berzinski?"

"Detective Valeska says it came from the hospital," William says. "Remember that Olivia would have had access to drugs and syringes, perhaps not direct access, but she would have been able to obtain them. Valeska also told me that the partial fingerprint is not clear enough to prove Zoey gave the injection, but that's the best guess."

"Zoey would know how to give an injection to a horse so it wouldn't be much of a leap," Melissa says.

"And another thing," I say. "They were both quick to tell me neither of them missed Barnaby. He was no loss to either of them. My guess is they thought if they stated this up front it would erode any suspicion of their involvement in his death. After all, a murderer isn't likely to admit they loathed the person."

"I suppose so. But what about Thomas?"

"Zoey found out from Thomas, who she got close to, that Barnaby's finances were in bad shape. He'd blown a lot of money on the pharmaceutical venture as well as on the gambling circle. So, Zoey realized she needed to get rid of Thomas if she was to get what she considered to be her rightful inheritance. And she deliberately botched the suicide scene she'd set up for Thomas in the garage attached to Barnaby's house where Olivia was still living. I don't know how she lured Thomas there. The plan was to frame Olivia of course, but she didn't realize Olivia was out and has a strong alibi for the time he died."

"I've been told," William says, "that evidence has been discovered that links Zoey to that crime scene."

"I'm not surprised. And I think it's ironic that Noah, who was the first suspect in Barnaby's murder, is now the person who'll likely inherit what little is left of Barnaby's estate."

"Why did Zoey want to frame Olivia?" asks Edwin.

"Olivia was talking to the police and Zoey desperately need to discredit her. And she wanted Olivia to take the rap for both murders."

"What about Roxi?" Melissa asks. "And Elsa? And Noah? Did they have roles?"

"Noah turned up during the time that Barnaby lay on the floor and just after Zoey and Olivia had stabbed him. He had nothing to do with the murders. I'm convinced of that."

"He's rather a feeble character, in my opinion," says William.

"A wimp, you mean?" I grin.

"I feel like a wimp," he says, "because it must have been Zoey who tied me up. She wanted to stop you. She knew you were getting close."

"She's strong and fit, I can attest to that, if that makes you feel any better." I reach over and touch his arm. He smiles.

"What about Elsa?" Melissa asks.

"When Noah told me—it seems like a long time ago—that Elsa is a pathological liar, I think he's right. But she loves Roxi and tried to help her. I'm uncertain, even now, if she dropped the electrical device onto the track or not. I don't know to what extent she was involved in the Caldermat Gambling Circle, if at all. Both she and Roxi are a conundrum to me, and perhaps to themselves. They need to get their lives in some kind of order. Roxi's living in Elsa's flat at the moment, but she plans to buy a small property on the outskirts of town once she receives payment from the sale of her farm."

"It's a shame she has to sell it."

"She doesn't want to but has no choice. I don't think she's well enough to look after it anyway."

"Who slashed your tires and threw that fire-bomb?" William asks. "I think I can guess."

"This is where things can get confused because there's an over-lap of players in the gambling ring and the murders. Thomas was terrified I was unearthing evidence of the Caldermat Gambling Circle's illegal activities. Remember, Bill Price was stressed to the point that he took his own life. Thomas didn't want to go to jail or lose what he had. He'd already lost a lot. So, he wanted me out of the picture. But, in my view, he was a thug, not a murderer. He beat Jaden up badly, attacked Roxi, and pushed me down the stairs. Not a nice man. Talking of not nice people, what's up with Dr. Berzinski?"

"Ah," says Edwin. "I met with him as you suggested, William. It was at that awful Papa's Kitchen."

"Why does he like that place?" Melissa asks.

"Because no racetrack people go there," I say. "It's the other side of town."

"That's it," Edwin says. "He doesn't want to be seen because he's ashamed, and I believe him. He said he doesn't remember uttering or writing death threats, but he doesn't deny he could have. When he drinks, he gets onery and aggressive. He told me he's just signed up for therapy and he apologized profusely for pushing me off the trailer steps—he has no recollection of that either. He thought someone was trying to frame him for the murders. He's been in a bad place."

"What are you doing about your complaint to the College?" I ask.

"I've already written a letter and notified them I withdraw my complaint, that I was mistaken. And I'm not pressing charges about the death threats. I think he deserves a chance to get his life back together. Being involved with the Caldermat cousins doesn't seem to have worked well for anyone, including him."

"What's happened to Noah?" asks William. "He's a puzzle as well as a wimp, as you put it. In fact, we've come across a lot of complex, disturbed, and I'd add peculiar, people recently."

"But aren't we all peculiar?" asks Edwin.

"Each of us is special," Melissa says, and it's as if her smile lightens the mood in the room.

"Absolutely!" exclaims William. He takes a sip of coffee.

"Noah is his own worst enemy," I say. "I'm meeting him tomorrow. He's leaving for Las Vegas next week. He's hoping to be a successful professional gambler there. It makes no sense to me, but I don't know anything about it, so I shouldn't judge."

"Edwin and I would like to invite you for dinner tomorrow evening," Melissa says.

"As long as it's not at Papa's Kitchen, I'm in," I say.

* * *

Noah sits at a small glass-topped table set out on a make-shift patio on the sidewalk. His shiny ginger hair catches the sun's rays and looks as if it's sparkling. His outfit of a pale mauve golf shirt and slim black pants looks new. He smiles. Even his teeth seem whiter. He stands up and shakes my hand. He appears to have morphed into a different person.

"Thank you," he says.

"For what?"

"You know, for digging up the truth. I was terrified. I went off my head for a while there because I was sure the coppers were going to charge me with murder. They decide who did it and then go about proving it."

"That's not how it works, usually." Unfortunately, I can't honestly say it has never happened.

"I was in the wrong place at the wrong time. I tripped over

Barnaby's body, as you know. I'd not seen a dead body before and it's sure different than in the movies. I've never been so freaked."

"It can be traumatizing, for sure."

"Elsa and I have split up for good, just so you know. I can't cope with that sort of relationship. I know we all lie sometimes, but she's got to get the medal. And she gets so darn depressed and whatever I do doesn't make any difference. It's a downer for me when I can't cheer her up. Honestly, I can't wait to get out of here, away from the insanity."

"So, you're definitely leaving?"

"I've borrowed some money on the strength of the condo sale and I'm going to do what I love—gamble, in Las Vegas, as I told you. I've got a couple of contacts there who will help me find my way. The police have told me I'll need to come back to testify, but that's fine."

"William told me this morning that Zoey and Olivia have both confessed to Barnaby's murder, and Zoey has admitted to killing Thomas."

"That's great. Wow. That's good."

"Best of luck in Las Vegas."

"Thanks. And thanks for helping me out when I was in some kind of funk. I didn't behave well. I lost it."

"I didn't think you were guilty of murder, but the fact that Kelly didn't take to you worried me a bit, I have to confess."

"I don't like dogs, although I got used to her and Jake. I was bitten when I was a kid, so I'm scared of them. She probably picked that up. She's smart, right?"

"Yes, she is."

"Thanks again for everything. Cheers!" We each lift a mug and smile.

I leave him to answer texts and am not sorry to turn my back on him.

25

Milkweed Farm

Kelly and Jake are guarding the Jag. They're sitting on the front seats watching William and I walk into the restaurant. Edwin and Melissa are waiting for us and have chosen a table by the large picture window. We can see the dogs staring at us.

"This is a nice restaurant," I say, as we sit down after embraces and handshakes. "I haven't been here before."

William and I know exactly why we're here, but we don't let on. I'm suppressing an unwelcome chuckle as the menus arrive and drinks are ordered. Edwin and Melissa exchange glances every few seconds. I can't stand the tension.

"What's the great occasion we're here to celebrate?" I ask.

"You've guessed!" Melissa exclaims.

William and I laugh.

"Tell us!" William says.

"We're hoping you'll be happy for us," Melissa says.

313

"I've asked Melissa to marry me," Edwin frowns as if he wonders what our reaction will be.

"Congratulations!" I say.

"Wonderful news," William says. "I'll order some bubbly stuff." The server responds quickly to William's request.

"We have some news too," I say. "Well, it's an offer. You may not want to accept and that's fine. It's just an offer."

"You knew we were getting engaged?" Edwin asks.

"It wasn't hard to figure out. Don't forget I'm an amateur sleuth."

"What do you mean by an offer?" Melissa asks.

"Would you like to live at Milkweed Farm? It's available and it's free for you as an engagement and wedding gift. You don't have to give an answer now. You obviously need to talk it over."

"Oh, no, we don't!" Melissa says. "Do we, Edwin? We'd absolutely love to live there. You see, we were going to ask you if we could rent it."

"That's settled then."

"Milkweed Farm will be in loving hands," Melissa says. Edwin smiles and nods.

"Here's to a long and happy life together," William says, as we clink our glasses.

Tiny bubbles rise to the surface and burst with happiness on our lips.

CPSIA information can be obtained
at www.ICGtesting.com
Printed in the USA
LVHW051115130523
746683LV00006B/9

9 781783 242733